PILGRIM

PILGRIM

DOUG BOWMAN

A TOM DOHERTY ASSOCIATES BOOK
NEW YORK

PILGRIM

This book is printed on acid-free paper.

Design by Heidi Eriksen

A Forge Book
Published by Tom Doherty Associates, LLC
175 Fifth Avenue
New York, NY 10010

www.tor.com

Library of Congress Cataloging-in-Publication Data

Bowman, Doug.
     Pilgrim / Doug Bowman.—1st ed.
        p. cm.
     ISBN 0-312-87864-8 (acid-free paper)
     I. Texas—Fiction. I. Title.

PS3552.O875712 P55 2001
815'.54 21; aa05 02-06—dc01

                                                    2001023179

First Edition: July 2001

Printed in the United States of America

0   9   8   7   6   5   4   3   2   1

A GOOD PAIR OF HANDS

by Doug Bowman

"IT'S A DAY OF MACHINES," SAID A NEIGHBOR OF MINE
"AND NOBODY'S GOT USE FOR A MAN."
"JUST A MINUTE," SAYS I, "LET'S TALK FOR A WHILE
ABOUT A MAN WITH A GOOD PAIR OF HANDS

"HE SCRATCHED A LIVING FROM THIS VERY SOIL
GREW CROPS WHERE WE NOW STAND
BUT HE RAISED NINE SONS AND ONE DAUGHTER
AND HE DID IT WITH A GOOD PAIR OF HANDS

"ONE SON BUILT THAT HOUSE YOU LIVE IN
AND ANOTHER PAVED YOUR STREET
LO, YOU SHOULD WITNESS THE NODS OF REVERENCE EACH SUNDAY
WHEN THE OLD MAN TAKES HIS SEAT

"HIS DAUGHTER SINGS SONGS WHEREVER SHE GOES
MOSTLY FOR ONE-NIGHT STANDS
BUT YOU SHOULD SEE THE WAY SHE EXPRESSES HERSELF
WITH A SMILE, AND A GOOD PAIR OF HANDS

"ONE OF HIS SONS IS AN ARTIST
WHO PAINTS PICTURES OF FARAWAY LANDS
AND ANOTHER IS A VERY FINE SCULPTOR
WITH HIS MUD, AND A GOOD PAIR OF HANDS

"HIS YOUNGEST IS A MASTER OF THE VIOLIN
WHO PLAYS CONTEMPORARY, CLASSICAL AND ALL
AND YOU SHOULD HAVE SEEN THE LOOK ON THE OLD MAN'S FACE
THE NIGHT THE BOY PLAYED CARNEGIE HALL

"ONE SON IS A DOCTOR AND ONE IS A WRITER
AND ONE TEACHES SCHOOL FOR THE BLIND
AND THEY SAY ONE OF HIS SONS CAN TALK TO THE DEAF
NOW, WHAT MACHINE DID YOU HAVE IN MIND?"

PILGRIM

It was nigh onto midnight when the three Pilgrim brothers stepped through the doorway of their southwestern Ohio cabin and hung up their heavy coats. "I'll bet you I'm gonna quit chasing them hogs just as soon as this cold weather's over," the youngest of the boys was saying. "Ain't no way in the world to keep 'em in a fence a quarter mile long, nohow. I'm gonna sell my part of 'em at the first sign of spring, then get me a good saddle horse and head for Texas. I've heard that a man can make a living chasing cows out there, and that he can sit on his butt while he's doing it."

"You shouldn't believe everything you hear, Eli," the oldest of the boys said, as all three pulled up chairs and seated themselves in front of the fireplace beside their mother. "It's been my experience that there's always a catch to anything that sounds all that good."

"So, what if there is a little more to it than I heard?" Eli asked emphatically. "It's still gotta be better'n chasing hogs in the snow three or four nights a week, with the cold wind cutting you in two and blowing your lantern out every time you turn around. I tell you, Lawton, I've made up my mind. I'm heading for Texas as soon as the grass turns green."

Ophelia Pilgrim had been sitting beside the fire listening to the conversation between her sons. She hung the sweater she had been knitting across the back of a nearby chair. "I suppose you're old enough to do whatever you set your mind to, Eli," she said. "Twenty-five percent of them hogs belongs to you, and I believe that'll come to about fifty head. I'll speak to your Uncle Neely tomorrow. If he don't want to buy you out, maybe me and your brothers can scrape up the money."

Lawton spoke quickly. "You don't need to talk to nobody, Ma. We can get the money ourselves." He motioned to his youngest brother. "If Eli wants to walk out on what's gonna be the most prosperous hog farm in Ohio, just let him go. He always did think different from the rest of us, anyhow."

Justin, the brother yet to be heard from, spoke now. "You ought not to be running off nowhere, Eli," he said. "We should have our own bacon- and sausage-making business going in about two years, then we can quit selling live hogs to the other companies and start getting rich ourselves."

Eli shook his head. "I've made my decision, Justin. I'm gonna sell out and go to Texas."

"So be it," the mother said with finality. "I don't want to hear you older boys trying to talk him into changing his mind, either. He's old enough to do his own thinking now, and for all we know, his idea might be better'n ours." She shoveled ashes over the coals in the fireplace, then turned the coal-oil lamp down low. Just before she disappeared down the narrow hallway, she added over her shoulder. "I'm gonna call it a night, and I reckon you boys oughta turn in, too. Them hogs might be out again by daylight."

Three minutes later, the cabin was dark and quiet.

Eli Pilgrim lay awake for a long time making his plans. He appreciated his mother saying he was old enough to do his own thinking. Of course he was. He would turn twenty-one years old on the third day of April, about the same time the grass turned green. Then, leading a pack mule loaded with enough provisions to last a month, he would ride off this hill a full-grown man. And he should have no problem finding his way to Texas. He already had a map, and his father's pocket compass was still lying on the mantelpiece above the fireplace.

He would put the instrument in his pocket so he could refer to it anytime he was uncertain about directions.

And he would not spend one minute worrying about his mother. Though she was fifty-five years old now, her health seemed to be good, and he had never known her to be sick with anything worse than a bad cold. Anyway, his brothers would remain close by even if they should eventually marry, and good old Uncle Neely, the older brother of Eli's dead father, Jake, could always be depended upon in an emergency.

A veteran of the Civil War, Jake Pilgrim had died in a hunting accident in the fall of 1866. "My brother fought that war for nearly four years without gittin' a scratch," Eli had often heard his uncle say, "then accident'ly shot hisself to death tryin' to git a damn Thanksgivin' turkey."

Being only five years old when his father went to war, Eli had not become well acquainted with him until after the conflict was over. Jake Pilgrim had not been home from the war for more than a week when he bought his youngest son a rifle and set about teaching him to stalk game. Father and son hunted together for well over a year, during which time the son became an excellent marksman.

New Year's Eve of 1865 was a day that Eli would remember as long as he lived. That was the morning his father had spotted a big buck lying in its bed but passed up the shot so that his young son might have it. With the cold wind blowing out of the north, they had just walked around to the south side of a frost-covered hill when Pilgrim suddenly put a hand on his son's shoulder and brought him to a halt. He put a forefinger to his lips, then pointed across the hill.

Following his father's point with his eyes, Eli eventually saw the flick of an ear, then was able to make out the head and antlers of a buck deer lying in the tall grass. The animal was looking straight at them. Eli lowered the barrel of his rifle very slowly, then took aim and fired. The big buck dropped its head and kicked a few times, then lay still.

"You hit him right between the eyes, son," his father said

when they had closed the distance. "Right smack in the face!"

"That's the only part of him I could see, Pa," Eli said, then stood by while his father hugged his neck.

Jake Pilgrim slit the animal's throat, then turned the carcass over. "He's a monster, all right," he said. "I've been hunting deer for more'n thirty years, but I never shot one this big. We've got to hang these antlers on the wall."

"Do you know how to mount 'em, Pa?"

"Sort of, but I know your Uncle Neely can do it better. I'll talk to him about it."

Uncle Neely had mounted the antlers on a cedar board, and to this day they hung above the fireplace in the front room of the cabin. Eli himself had eventually begun to ignore them, for thinking about them always gave him a choky feeling. He cherished the days he had spent in the woods with his father, and looking at the antlers brought back too many memories.

Though Jake Pilgrim had treated his wife and all of his sons exceedingly well, he had always seemed to have a special affection for his youngest. And the feeling had been mutual. In fact, even after ten years, a day never passed that Eli did not think of his father. Now, as he lay in bed thinking, he could not help wondering what Jake Pilgrim would think of his youngest son's decision to leave the farm and head west.

Eli's last thought before going to sleep was the same as it had been on countless nights before: if he himself had been on that last turkey hunt, would the situation have turned out differently? Would his father have had the gun pointed in some other direction when it accidentally discharged? Knowing that he would never know the answer, the young man finally fluffed up his pillow and drifted off to sleep.

ON THE first day of April, older brother Lawton handed Eli a stack of double eagles across the kitchen table. "We had to borrow a little of that from Uncle Neely," he said, "but we were bound and determined to treat you right. Your share of the hogs turned out to be forty-eight head, and Ma figures they're worth about three-fifty apiece. Uncle Neely says they wouldn't bring more'n three dollars a head on the open market, but we decided to give you a little above market value." He pointed to the coins. "Two hundred dollars there, and I'd say you're gonna be needing it all in that godforsaken place you're heading off to."

Lawton got to his feet and dropped his empty coffee cup in the dishpan, then walked to the door. He twisted the knob, then turned to face his younger brother again. "By the way," he said, "Uncle Neely says he'll sell you that buckskin of his for twenty dollars, and that seems like an awful good buy to me. If you remember, we kept that little horse down here for about a week one time, and all three of us rode him. Best I can recall, we all bragged on him, too."

Eli nodded. "I remember," he said. "I'll walk over and talk with Uncle Neely this morning, and I'll probably ride back home on the buckskin."

An hour later, the young man knocked at his uncle's door, which was about half a mile from his own. "Lawton says you want to sell that buckskin," he said when Neely Pilgrim answered his knock. "I'm gonna be needing a saddle horse pretty soon, so I guess I'll take him off your hands."

The aging, white-haired man stepped through the doorway. Moving slowly, he walked to the end of the porch and leaned against the railing. "It ain't that I want to sell the horse, son, and I don't reckin I need nobody to take 'im off my hands. Lawton was jist talkin' about you needin' sump'm to ride, so I thought I'd help you out by givin' you a special deal on the buckskin. Lawton says you've already rode the horse, so you know what he is. I reckin I don't have to tell you that twenty dollars is a Santy Claus price, neither. A good animal like him'd cost you sixty or seb'mdy dollars anywhere else."

Eli nodded, and handed over a double eagle. "I sure appreciate the break on the price, Uncle Neely."

The old man pocketed the coin and ignored the remark. He pointed toward the barn. "The horse is in the second stable on the right, and the bridle's hangin' on a peg just outside the door. The saddle and the saddle blanket are both lyin' across a sawhorse in that little room up front. I don't really like the idea of gittin' shed of that saddle, but you need it and the buckskin's used to it. In fact, I believe it might be the only damn one he's ever had on his back."

Eli stood looking at the barn for a few moments, then asked, "You . . . you mean you're giving the saddle to me for free, Uncle Neely?"

"Ain't givin' it to you a-tall," the old man answered, beginning to move toward the door. "I'm givin' the saddle to the buckskin." He stood in the doorway for a moment then added, "There's a saddle scabbard for your rifle hangin' just above the sawhorse, so you may as well take it, too. Now, go git your horse and git your butt on out to Texas. The Lord'll watch over you." He stepped inside the house and closed the door.

Eli saddled the buckskin in short order, then rode through the woods to his own home. Once there, he dismounted and turned the horse into the corral with the four mules. The animals were already acquainted with one another from the buckskin's earlier visit. Now they began to scamper around the lot while making a variety of sounds that were obviously a means of communication. When one of the animals began to rub its muzzle against the saddler's neck affectionately, Eli was pleased to see that it was his own mule, the same one that would be following the buckskin all the way to Texas.

He walked to the cabin and seated himself on the top doorstep. He was still sitting there with his elbows on his knees and his chin resting in his hands when his mother joined him a few minutes later. "I see you made a deal with Neely for that buckskin," she said, pointing to the corral.

Eli shook his head. "Uncle Neely made the deal himself,"

he said. "He just about gave me the horse, and he did give me the saddle and the rifle scabbard."

"Neely's always been like that, son," the lady said, running her hands along the back of her legs to smooth out her skirt as she sat down. "He's got a right smart of stuff over there, and he's always been mighty good about sharing it. Not just with kinfolks, either. I'll bet you he's helped half the people in this county out at one time or another."

Eli nodded. "He's a good man." He sat staring off into the woods thoughtfully for a long time, then suddenly spoke again: "Pa's been dead for more'n ten years, Ma, and it's been about half that long since Aunt Clarissa died. How come you and Uncle Neely don't get married?"

The lady seemed to be no more than mildly surprised by the question. She smiled and patted Eli's arm. "Neither one of us has ever mentioned it," she said. "We don't talk about stuff like that, don't reckon either one of us has ever even thought about it."

"Well, you oughtta both be thinking about it. It just don't seem natural for him to sit over there on that hill year after year with no woman, while you sit over here with no man."

She chuckled softly. "Are you saying you think I should ask Neely to marry me?"

"No," he answered quickly. "I'm saying I think he oughtta ask you. I've got half a mind to ride over there and ask him why he ain't doing it."

She shook her head and patted his arm again. "I think you should just look after your own business, Eli," she said. "When do you plan to leave for Texas?"

"I'm thinking about heading out tomorrow morning," he said. "It's been shirtsleeve weather for the past week, and Lawton says there ain't no rain in sight."

"Lawton's awful good at predicting the weather," she said. "Every time he says we're gonna have a dry spell, that's exactly what we get." She pointed across the hillside. "The graze is coming along all right, but a little rain wouldn't hurt it none. I've always heard that we get two inches of grass for every inch of rainfall during the spring season. I reckon that might be right, 'cause the ground sure turns green in a hurry after it gets a good drenching."

"I've been watching the grass mighty close, Ma. It's pretty good right here, and it oughtta get better as I travel farther south. I'll be taking my time, and even if I do hit a few places where the graze ain't too good, it won't be no big problem. I'm gonna put the packsaddle on old Zebra. Him and the buckskin are both a little bit on the fat side, so it won't hurt either one of 'em to lose a few pounds."

"Sure won't," Ophelia said, getting to her feet. "Especially after hot weather sets in." She stood quietly for a few moments, then added, "I've got work to do in the house. I'll lay out a few changes of clothes and an extra pair of shoes for you, then gather up some cooking and eating utensils that won't weigh old Zebra down too much. He's got a long trip ahead of him, and he don't need to be hauling things around that you can do without. You need to carry enough stuff with you to cook and eat a meal with as little fuss as possible, but that's all. In fact, if you'll go down to the crib and get some of them canvas bags, I'll put everything together for you myself. Just lay the bags on the kitchen table, then go on about your business."

He delivered the bags, then returned to the corral and stood watching the animals for a while. Old Zebra, so-called because of the black stripes around his front legs, would soon be leaving with Eli. At that time his brothers would have no choice but to buy another mule, for the plows and other farm implements were all set up for two-horse teams. The brothers might even have to hire another man before the summer was over. The wheels must keep turning, for bringing in a corn crop large enough to feed two hundred head of swine required enormous amounts of both axle and elbow grease.

The hogs usually ate up a hundred acres of corn between one growing season and the next, and if Lawton and Justin intended to expand the operation, as they had implied at the supper table last night, they might even need twice as much feed. Eli shook his head at the thought. They had plenty of acreage to grow the grain, all right, but neither the manpower nor the implements to get the job done.

Imagining the slow, backbreaking process, Eli shrugged, then shook his head again. He believed that his brothers were strong enough and determined enough to make their bacon- and sausage-making venture a success, but he also thought they might be too old and worn-out to enjoy it once it came about. With that in mind, he walked to the crib and dragged out the packsaddle.

The packsaddle was a Grimsley. Open at the top, it had leather breeching, breast strap, and lash strap, with a broad hair girth. Several metal hooks ran along the top, so that the animal's load could be balanced by hanging individual packs of similar weight on each side. Built with the comfort of the pack animal in mind, with a harness that could be adjusted to fit a horse or mule of almost any size, the Grimsley was widely considered to be the best packsaddle ever manufac- tured by any company. The one Eli was holding at the moment was already adjusted to fit old Zebra, for the mule had been hauling supplies halfway across the county on a regular basis.

Eli moved the packsaddle to the shed so it would be hand- ier in the morning, then turned a water bucket upside down and seated himself. He sat for a long time wondering what the next few years of his life were going to be like. More than one man had told him lately that he should head for Texas. Opportunities were unlimited out there, they said, and a young man with a keen mind and a strong body should have few problems in putting a fortune together.

Eli Pilgrim had a strong body, and his grades had been better than any other schoolboy's in the county. Even now, when his mother or one of his brothers had a column of fig- ures to cipher, the job was very quickly turned over to him. But was he smart enough to make a fortune in Texas? He smiled as he sat mulling the question over. He was as smart as anyone else he knew, he finally decided. And although he had not been cut out to be a hog farmer, he could work as hard as the next man. In fact, he liked hard work, and if that was all it took to get by in Texas, he would do just fine.

Eli was a handsome fellow who had had no shortage of girlfriends during his school days. With dark, curly hair, green eyes, and two rows of perfect teeth, he had a captivating smile that he used often. Standing six foot three in his socks, he was thick-chested and broad-shouldered, with long, muscular arms, wide wrists, and hands the size of small hams.

Although he had been involved in dozens of fistfights with his schoolmates in the early years, he lost none, and his reputation as a good scrapper preceded him into the higher grades. The would-be bullies usually gave him a wide berth, and all of the fights that he did have after he reached his teens had been brought to quick and decisive conclusions. The boys he had fought with had all grown into men now, but the same advice still occasionally passed from one to another: "Unless a fellow's jist lookin' for a good ass-whuppin', he'd be smart to walk around Eli Pilgrim."

Few men who looked young Pilgrim over well enough to truly size him up had ever ignored that advice.

THE SUN was less than an hour high when Eli Pilgrim rode into the yard and dismounted at the cabin steps next morning. He shook hands with his brothers, then kissed his mother good-bye. "I really believe that the bacon and sausage idea is gonna turn this farm into a moneymaker one of these days," he said, addressing all three, "but I've got my heart set on something else. Seems like I just owe it to myself to go see if there's any truth to all the good things I've heard and read about Texas."

His mother squeezed his arm. "You just follow your heart, son; keep your eyes open and look things over good. From what I hear, that country was mostly fought for and settled by men no older'n you, and a lot of 'em a whole lot younger. No reason in the world why you can't do as well out there as the next man. You've been way above average in the thinking department all your life, so I have no doubt that when you see something good, you'll be smart enough to know it."

She untied the pack mule's lead rope from the handrail and handed it to him, then continued, "Mount up and get on outta here. You've got at least ten hours of daylight before you'll need to be stopping for the night. Everything you're gonna be needing is right here on old Zebra's back, so you just take your time and don't work your animals too hard.

Spring's just now getting here, and you ain't in no hurry. Make twenty or twenty-five miles a day, and you'll be out there before you know it."

Eli stepped into the saddle. "Good-bye to all of you, and like I said, I believe you're gonna do well with the business. You can sell more sausage and bacon right here in Hamilton County than you can make. All you're gonna need is contracts to supply a few of the big grocery stores in Cincinnati. That Harper Brothers outfit up in Forestville would probably buy from you too, and it's a lot closer to home." He sat looking down the hill for a few moments, then turned the buckskin in that direction. "I'll be thinking about all three of you every day," he said over his shoulder.

"Try not to forget how to write!" his mother called after him.

He kicked the saddler in the ribs and rode out of sight without looking back.

He boarded the ferry at Caesar's Point four hours later and crossed the Ohio River into Kentucky. He would cross the same river into Indiana the following day, for he had decided to avoid the mountainous country of Kentucky and Tennessee, reaching his destination by way of Indiana, Missouri, and Arkansas. He had studied his map often during the recent past and had his route firmly implanted in his mind.

The only decision he had not been able to come to was exactly where he wanted to go once he reached Texas. His mother had said that he was plenty smart enough to recognize something promising, so he would take her words as gospel. He had as much money as he was likely to need in the near future, so he would simply keep moving until he came upon something that tickled his fancy.

He had not gone through everything that the mule carried on the packsaddle, but his mother had said that the packs contained everything he would need on his journey. He had simply taken her word for it, for he knew that she was an exceptional woman who usually thought of everything. She had even made up the bedroll that was now tied behind his saddle: a thick quilt doubled and sewed to a seven-foot-long strip of waterproof canvas. With his wool blankets for covering, he would sleep warm at night even if the ground was cold and damp.

Knowing that traveling across the country alone in this day and time could be a dangerous undertaking, young Pilgrim was leaving little to chance. Aside from the twelve-shot Henry rifle that rode in his saddle scabbard, tucked in his saddlebag was a copy of the Colt .45 caliber 1873 model army revolver, the celebrated "Peacemaker." He had ample ammunition for both weapons and was an excellent marksman with either.

And though he had never deliberately pointed a gun in the direction of another human, he knew that he would not hesitate if the preservation of his own well-being demanded the use of firepower. He had even practiced shooting at man-sized targets with both the Henry and the Peacemaker. He could consistently hit a small fence post at three hundred yards with the rifle, and knock gourds off the top of the same post with the Colt at forty paces. Gourds that were much smaller than a man's head. Indeed, in the event that he ever had to defend himself with either long or short gun, he had no doubt that he would hit his target.

He stopped at a roadside spring at noon, allowing his animals to graze while he ate a few chunks of ham and several biscuits his mother had rolled up in an old newspaper. He knew that there was a coffeepot and plenty of grounds in his pack, but he did not want the bother of building a fire. The springwater was cold, and it was sweet.

He was back on the road in less than an hour, and he had traveled no more than a mile when he met two middle-aged men on horseback. As they drew near, they pulled up and turned their animals sideways, almost blocking the road. "Hold on there, fellow," the largest of the two men said, as

Eli attempted to guide his own animal around them, "I've got a question to ask you."

Eli brought the buckskin to a halt. "Ask away," he said.

The big man spat a stream of tobacco juice. "Didja see anything of a skinny man and a redheaded woman back up the road, there? I reckin they'd be ridin' double on a big roan."

Eli shook his head. "No," he said. "I haven't met anybody on horseback all day." He kneed the buckskin around the riders.

"Wait jist a damn minute," the big man said. "I happen to know they're travelin' north on this road. You expect me to b'lieve you ain't seen 'em a-tall?"

Eli pulled up and turned his animal broadside. He sat looking from one of the men to the other for a few moments, then spoke to the big man again. "I don't give a damn what you believe, mister. I said no, and I meant no."

The man sat trying to stare Eli down for a few moments. Then, when it became obvious that he could not intimidate the muscular youngster, he turned his horse north without another word and was followed closely by his smaller companion.

Eli sat watching them till they rode out of sight, then he turned his own animal south. He pushed the encounter with the ugly man out of his mind quickly, then kicked the buckskin to a trot.

He traveled steadily throughout the afternoon, then left the road immediately after crossing a small creek. Though he knew that there was at least two hours of daylight left, he also knew that a downpour was probably coming, for he could already see the dark clouds a few miles ahead.

The first order of business must be the erection of his sleeping tent, so he tied his animals thirty yards off the road and, selecting an almost-level spot of ground that sloped slightly toward the creek, set up the canvas shelter in short order. He unburdened his animals and placed his guns, bedroll, saddle, and packsaddle inside the tent, then led the horse and the mule to good grass and picketed them on individual forty-foot ropes.

When he returned to his campsite he had barely enough time to dig a small trench around the tent with his hatchet, before the rain came. Just as he crawled inside, the first raindrops began to bounce off the canvas noisily. "Big drops, heap of it," he said aloud, echoing the old Indian saying that he had been hearing for most of his life.

And this night there was indeed a heap of it. Even after full darkness came on two hours later, the rain continued to come down hard. Sitting high and dry on his bedroll, and pleased with the result of the runoff he had dug around his tent, Eli struck a match and began to fiddle around in his pack for something to eat. He found a pone of corn bread right away, then found half of a smoked ham in a different pack. He sliced off a large chunk of the meat, then washed a big supper down with water from his canteen.

The meal would have to last him a while, he was thinking, for he had no intention of trying to find something to build a fire with in the morning. He would hit the saddle shortly after daybreak and put some miles behind him while he was waiting for the sun to dry out the deadwood scattered about. After eating a pound of ham and half as much of the corn bread, he pulled off his boots, folded one of his blankets to use for a pillow, then stretched out on his bedroll. He was asleep quickly.

When he was awakened by the need to relieve himself, he knew immediately that the rain had moved farther north to water other fields and pastures. He struck a match and looked at his watch to see that it was two o'clock in the morning. When he pulled on his boots and crawled from the tent, the stars now shone brightly, creating enough light for him to see two covered wagons parked between his tent and the road.

He attributed the fact that he did not already know the

wagons were there to the continuous drone of the heavy raindrops falling on his tent. Horses and wagons made noise, and
there was simply no way that they could have gotten so close
to him without his realizing it if the rain had not drowned out
the sound of their movements. He stood gazing at the vehicles
till he was through pissing, then returned to his bedroll and
slept till after daylight.

The sun was already climbing above the tree line when
he crawled from the tent and stood up on the muddy ground.
He saw immediately that the wagon folks had had no problem
starting a fire. The steady stream of smoke from a cook fire
billowed from somewhere beyond the wagons, and though he
could understand none of what was being said, he could hear
people talking. Knowing that they had no doubt been carrying
dry kindling in one of the wagons, he smiled, then picked up
his two bridles and headed for the grassy meadow.

The four draft horses that had pulled the wagons in during
the night were grazing a short distance beyond his buckskin
and his pack mule. He stood admiring the big beasts for a few
moments, then watered his own animals and led them to his
campsite. He saddled the buckskin, then tied his bedroll behind the cantle. He had just laid the packsaddle across the
mule's back when he realized that he had company.

Stoop-shouldered and graying at the temples, the man appeared to be about forty years old, and stood at least as tall
as Eli himself. "Thought you might could use a little help
with this packsaddle," he said. "They're a whole lot easier to
balance out with somebody on each side."

Eli nodded and flashed his easy smile. "Plenty of truth in
that, sir, and I appreciate the offer." He brought his four packs
from inside the tent and set two of them in front of the mule.
"Those two go on that side, and I'll hang the others over here.
That's the way I had 'em yesterday, and they seemed to balance out fine."

The man went to work without another word, and the job
was finished quickly. "Another reason I walked over here was

to invite you to eat breakfast with us," he said. "You not having no wagon, I knew you wouldn't have no dry kindling, and we've got a lot more food and coffee than we're gonna be needing. You just stop off at our fire before you hit the road, and we'll get acquainted while we eat some hot vittles." He walked away without looking back.

A few minutes later, Eli led his animals to the wagons and tied them both to one of the wheels. The tall man was on his feet quickly with his right hand outstretched. "By the way, my name's Harvey Homestead."

Eli grasped the man's hand. "I'm Eli Pilgrim."

Homestead nodded, then motioned to the three people sitting beside the fire. "That's my brother Ed, and the ladies are our wives, Ruth and Sarah." Pointing to a wooden box, he added, "Get you a plate, cup, and a spoon outta that box over there and hand it to one of the women. You'll be eating a good breakfast pretty doggone quick."

Eli did as he had been told and was soon enjoying a hot meal of bacon, fried potatoes, hot biscuits, and strong coffee. "I sure do appreciate all of this," he said, addressing no one in particular. "I had already decided to skip breakfast this morning and wait till later in the day to look for some dry wood."

The man named Ed nodded, then said, "That sun looks like it's gonna keep shining all day, so you oughtta be able to find something dry enough to burn before suppertime."

"Yes, sir," Eli said around a mouthful of food, "that's what I was thinking."

They sat beside the fire eating in silence for a while, then Harvey spoke again. "Which way you headed, Eli?"

"West," Pilgrim answered. "Got my mind set on living in Texas."

"Texas?" Harvey asked with a wide grin. "Texas? Heck, that's where we're coming from; on our way back to Jackson County, Ohio, right now. Things didn't turn out too well for us in Texas, but that's just because Pa got so sick." He pointed to the smaller of the canvas-covered vehicles. "He's lying flat on his back over there in that wagon right now, and he knows as well as we do that he ain't gonna get no better. It's his lungs.

"What he's got is a bad case of consumption, and he finally talked us into taking him back to the old home place to die. He's expecting us to dig a grave out behind the barn, then shoot him and get him outta his misery." He dashed his coffee grounds over his shoulder, then refilled his cup from the smoky pot. "I don't know who'll fulfill the last part of his request, but I reckon one of us will."

"Why, you'll do it yourself," an old woman said as she stepped from the rear of the nearest wagon. "You're the oldest son he's got, so the job naturally falls to you."

Harvey sat staring into his cup for a moment, then nodded and spoke softly. "Yes, ma'am," he said, "I reckon so." Then, speaking to Eli, he motioned to the old woman. "That's our ma, and she pretty well decides what happens among us now that Pa ain't able."

The lady leaned against the wagon for a moment, then greeted Eli with a wave of her bony arm. When she began to hobble toward the fire haltingly, he decided that she was most likely twice as old as either of her sons. She accepted a cup of coffee from one of the younger women, then spoke again. "Smells mighty good," she said, then seated herself on a nearby log and began to sip the liquid noisily.

"Like I was about to say," Harvey continued, "the only reason we ain't still in Texas is because Pa didn't want to die out there. Fact is, we're liable to go back out there once we get him in the ground."

"You'll certainly be going without me!" the old woman shouted from her seat on the log. "I ain't never leaving Ohio again!"

Harvey was quiet for several moments, then began to talk about Texas again. He said that for the past two years the Homesteads had been living near the town of Cuero, where they had earned their living growing hay and grain on a rented farm. "We done right well till Pa started getting so bad off," he added. "Ain't no reason in the world why you couldn't do awful good around there, too. There's always a demand for stout, young fellows like you." He bit a corner off a square plug of chewing tobacco, then spat a stream of brown juice between his feet.

"Cuero's located on the Guadalupe River in DeWitt County, about eighty miles southeast of San Antonio. If it turns out that you do decide to try your luck around there, I'd suggest that you look up a man named Oliver Benson, the man who bought all the grain and hay we could grow on our four hundred acres. His Oxbow outfit is the biggest ranch in the area, and I'd bet a dollar he could use a man of your caliber. Sure wouldn't cost you nothing to ask him.

"Now, Cuero's a long way from here and it would probably take you at least a coupla months to get there, but I can see that you've got good stock, so you shouldn't have no problems. You got a good map?"

Eli nodded. "Yes, sir. Got a compass, too."

Harvey nodded, then got to his feet and dropped his empty cup into the wooden box. "Well, I think you'd be smart to use 'em both getting on down to South Texas, and Cuero's the best place I know of for a young man like you to light. The little town's about as busy as a beehive, and I don't remember ever hearing nobody say they had trouble finding work around there." He motioned to his horses in the meadow. "Time for us to catch up our stock and get moving east, and I know you're anxious to be on your way." He offered a handshake. "Whether you take my advice about Cuero or not, it's been nice meeting you, and I wish you all the luck in the world." He pumped Eli's hand a few times, then picked up two bridles and headed for the grazing horses. Moments later, Ed Homestead hung a bridle across each of his own shoulders and followed his brother to the meadow.

Eli dropped his eating utensils into the box, then spoke to

the same lady who had served his breakfast. "I can't thank you enough for the food, ma'am. Tell Mr. Harvey that I'll most likely take his advice about going to Cuero." He untied his animals, then stepped into the saddle and took up the slack in the mule's lead rope. "In fact, I guess you could say that I'm on my way there right now." He kicked the buckskin in the ribs and moved out onto the road.

"You'll do well in Cuero, young man!" the lady called after him. "You take care, now!"

As Eli rode out of sight he was wondering if Harvey Homestead was really going to kill his own father. By the time he reached the top of the hill he had decided that the answer was yes. Once the old man was back on the family farm, he would be shot in the head and laid to rest behind the barn.

P<small>ILGRIM RODE</small> steadily and uneventfully for the next three weeks, and today he was following a wagon road in south-central Missouri, a few miles north of the Arkansas border. He had eaten his noon meal on the west bank of a shallow stream, then returned to the road immediately thereafter. He expected to cross the state line into Arkansas any time now. The weather had been exceptionally good, and there was plenty of green grass for his animals almost any place he chose to camp. He had no complaints, and certainly no reason to regret his decision to leave home.

He did need a few supplies, however. This morning he had stopped at a small roadside grocery store intent upon buying some tinned meat, tinned fish, cheddar cheese, and crackers, only to learn that the man's shelves were bare. "If you're heading south, there's a bigger store right after you cross the state line," the storekeeper said. "Old man Lovell's got a whole lot more stock than I do, and I'd say that he'll have just about anything you want. At least I ain't never been able to think of nothing he didn't have. He's got things piled on top of things, stuff that he don't even know he's got. Better talk kinda careful to him, though. He does a right smart of drinking, and if you happen to catch him drunk, he's liable to cuss you out and order you off the premises before you even find out if he's got what you need."

"You mean he cusses out his own customers?" Eli had asked. "How does he get away with that?"

"I reckon they must like it," the man answered. "Every time I stop by I see the same old people in there. Anyway, Lovell don't care whether they like it or not. I guess he's got all the money he thinks he's gonna need, so he ain't concerned about nothing but his next drink of whiskey."

Eli stood thoughtful for a moment, then pointed over his shoulder. "You say his store is on this same road?"

The storekeeper nodded. "Yep. Just keep riding south and you'll run right into it. It's on the right-hand side of the road, just after you cross the state line." The conversation had ended there, and Eli had taken to the road again.

At midafternoon, after riding past a roadside sign welcoming him to the state of Arkansas, Eli spotted the store a hundred yards ahead. Moments later, he guided the buckskin off the road and dismounted in front of the dilapidated building. "Pat Lovell's Grocery," the lettering at the top of the establishment read. Since a buggy team and a saddle horse were already standing at the lone hitching rail, Pilgrim tied his own animals to a post at the corner of the porch, then stepped inside.

Two middle-aged women were standing at the counter as if waiting to be served, and a man who appeared to be a few years older stood at the head of the middle aisle. "Are you Mr. Lovell?" Eli asked.

The man shook his head, then pointed toward the back door. "Lovell's out back," he answered. Then, lowering his voice, he added, "I got the idea that he went to answer nature's call."

Suddenly a man appearing to be in his seventies stepped through the back door and slammed it noisily. Eli had no doubt that he was now looking at Mr. Pat Lovell. "Son of a bitch!" the storekeeper said loudly, then stopped to finish buttoning his fly. "Damn yellow jacket flew up outta that damned toilet hole and stung me right on the head of my dick!"

Though the women at the counter had no doubt heard
Lovell's outburst of profanity, neither appeared to be annoyed
or even surprised by it. Maybe they knew the man well, Pilgrim
was thinking, and were used to hearing such talk from him.

With the top button on his fly now secured, Lovell turned
his attention to the man at the middle aisle. "What do you
want?" he asked.

"Nothing right now," the man answered. "I'm just looking."

"Nothing?" Lovell asked, raising his voice to a higher
pitch. "Nothing? What the hell did you come in here for, if
you don't want nothing?"

The man did not answer. He stood staring at the floor for
a moment, then left the building quickly.

The storekeeper glanced at Eli without speaking, then
stepped behind the counter and spoke to the women. "What'll
you have, ladies?" he asked softly.

One of the women handed him a list. "I've got it all
written down," she said. "If there's anything on there that
you don't have, just cross it off."

Lovell accepted the list, then picked up an empty cardboard box and began to move up and down the overstocked
aisles. About ten minutes later he set the box on the counter.
"Nothing on this list that I didn't have, Ida," he said, still
speaking softly. "The bill comes to three dollars and a dime.
You want to pay cash, or sign old Jesse's name to the ticket."

"I'll be paying cash," the lady said, then counted out the
money.

"Want me to put that stuff in your buggy for you?" Lovell
asked.

"I can handle it very well," the lady answered, then
picked up the box and carried it through the doorway.

Lovell watched the women leave the building, then turned
his attention to Eli. "Something I can help you with, young
man?" he asked in a civil tone.

Pilgrim nodded. "I need a few things for my pack," he answered. He pointed to the shelf behind him. "I see you've got canned tomatoes over there, and I'd like about three cans of 'em. Then if you happen to have it all, I'll take three cans of beef, three tins of fish, a pound of cheese, and a bag of soda crackers."

Lovell nodded, then picked up a paper bag. "Don't never allow myself to run out of none of them things," he said. "You need a can opener to go with 'em?"

Eli shook his head. "I've already got one," he said. "If I break it, I've always got a sharp knife."

"Knife usually works better anyway," the storekeper said. "That's what I use most of the time." He began to whistle softly, then walked down one side of the aisle and back up the other. A few moments later, he set Pilgrim's order on the counter. "Figgered up the price in my noggin," he said, "but I'll go ahead and put it on paper just to make sure." He picked up the stub of a pencil and wet it with his tongue, then began to scribble on a lined tablet. "Dollar thirty, all told," he said after a time. "Sound reasonable to you?"

Eli nodded. "Sounds just right," he said. He laid the money on the counter, then changed the subject. "I'm headed south, and I'd like to sleep on a soft bed for a change. How far is it to the next town?"

Lovell chuckled. "You ain't gonna sleep on no soft bed tonight, not unless you got a thicker bedroll than most men carry. Little town called Leeds about thirty miles south of here. It's got a livery stable and a hotel both, but you ain't got more'n three hours of daylight left. I'd say that you've got at least one more night of sleeping on the ground."

Eli smiled and picked up his sack of groceries. "Sounds like you've got it figured right," he said, then headed for the door.

"You'll run into the White River about five miles down the road!" Lovell called after him. "My advice would be to get on the west bank before you make camp. If you sleep on this side of it and it happens to rain upstream tonight, you might not be able to cross that son of a bitch for a week!"

Eli turned to face the man, then nodded and walked through the doorway. Moments later he added his groceries to the pack mule's burden, then mounted and headed south.

The sun was at least an hour high when he forded the White River and pulled off the road. The water had been almost belly-deep on the buckskin in places, and Eli knew that the storekeeper's caution about high water had probably saved some poor soul from a long wait at one time or another. The advice had hardly been necessary in Pilgrim's case, however. He had known that weather was completely unpredictable for most of his life, and his father had discussed such foolish things as sleeping on the wrong side of a river with him many years ago.

Thankful that the water had not been deep enough to wet any of his belongings, he had allowed his animals to drink their fill, then rode a hundred yards off the road and stopped at a campsite that, judging from the many piles of ashes and chunks of charred wood, several other campers had selected in the past. He could also see that green grass was plentiful no more than twenty yards to the north.

He dismounted and dropped his saddle and his packsaddle to the ground, then, with the picket ropes across his shoulder, led his animals to the small, grassy meadow and staked them out fifty feet apart.

Back at his campsite he had a blaze going quickly, for all it took was a few handfuls of dead grass to light some of the dry, charred pieces of wood left by other campers. As soon as he was satisfied with the fire, he filled his coffeepot with water from the river, then dumped in a handful of grounds. While waiting for the coffee to boil, he opened his pack and began to spread out the things he had bought at Lovell's store. He opened a can of beef, a flat tin of sardines, and a can of tomatoes, then tore open the crackers and sliced off several chunks of cheddar cheese with his pocketknife. As soon as his coffee was ready, he would dig into a meal like traveling men seldom enjoyed.

The first thing he began to eat was the tomatoes, which tasted almost garden fresh. With one hand full of crackers and a spoon in the other, he devoured half of the contents of the can. While sipping at the juice, he remembered his father telling him that a few times while he was in the army, tomatoes were all he had to eat at night. Jake Pilgrim had said that most of the troops in both the Union and the Confederate Armies were farm boys who had never even seen food preserved in a can until they went to war, at which time the canned tomatoes quickly became a nutritious and satisfying supplement to their weevil-infested hardtack and salt pork.

Even after the long, drawn-out conflict was over, travelers could sometimes trace the paths of the armies by the heaps of rusty tin cans marking their camps. And the juicy delicacy was hardly limited to the military these days. Indeed, the advent of canning, coupled with the upheaval of the Civil War, had enshrined the tomato as one of America's most popular foods. Eli himself preferred them over anything else that grew in the garden. Now, he took a final sip of the juice, then set the can aside and turned to the meat and cheese.

The sun had fallen behind the treetops when he finished eating his supper. By now, he had decided that he would not sleep where he was sitting, for anyone passing on the road now or after the moon came out would have an unobstructed view of his campsite. He kicked dirt over the remaining coals of his fire, then carried his belongings about forty yards up the hill and deposited them behind an old, decaying brush pile that someone had stacked and then decided not to burn. He moved his animals to new grass just before dark, then spread his bedroll and stretched out for the night. With both his long and his short guns within easy reach, he was asleep in a matter of minutes.

PILGRIM RODE into the town of Leeds two hours past noon the following day. Laid out from east to west across a steep hillside, the community appeared to be inhabited by less than a hundred people, and the main road served as its only street. After halting at the edge of town for a few moments, Eli moved on, for he could see everything he needed at a glance. A dilapidated, two-story hotel with an adjacent restaurant was situated on the south side of the street, and a building two doors down had a tall sign stating that whiskey, wine, and beer could be found inside. The livery stable and corral were plainly visible at the west end of town.

He dismounted in front of the hotel and tied his animals at the hitching rail. Then, with his rifle in the crook of his arm and his saddlebags lying across his shoulder, he stepped inside. The building had an even cruder appearance inside than outside, and as he walked across the squeaky floor he quickly began to doubt the quality of the bed he had come in to rent. It was obvious that no one had ever even attempted to paint the lobby, and a large piece of the overhead ceiling hung loose at one end, looking as if it might fall to the floor at any moment.

A Christmas tree that had shed its brown needles months ago stood in the corner near the front door, and a potted plant that appeared to have been dead for several years was set on the rough plank counter. An old man with a peg leg and a full shock of white hair stood leaning against the same counter. He spat a mouthful of tobacco juice into a tin can, then nodded and spoke to Pilgrim. "Come in, young feller," he said with a snaggletoothed grin. "I reckon we could say that the place is all yore'n for th' time bein', leastwise you're th' first customer that's showed up today." He pushed the brown quid out of his mouth with his tongue and let it fall into the can, then added, "I reckon ya are a customer, ain'tcha?"

Eli answered with a question of his own: "Have you got a room with a good bed?"

The man answered quickly. "Now, I'm right glad to hear ya askin' about a good bed, young feller, 'cause you're in luck. I've got two rooms with new mattresses that wuz jist delivered yesterday. One upstairs and one downstairs. Which one ya want?"

"How much money are you gonna charge me for a night's stay?" Eli asked.

The old man stood thoughtful for a moment, then took out his plug of chewing tobacco and bit off another chunk. "Wouldja feel right payin' a dollar?" he asked finally.

"No," Pilgrim answered quickly. "I'd feel right paying about half that much."

The man bounced his fist off the counter lightly. "Dammit, I told th' ol' lady that nobody weren't gonna pay no dollar a night jist 'cause a bed had a new mattress on it, but she kep' tellin' me they would." He spat into the can again, then faced Eli with one raised eyebrow. "How wouldja feel about sixty cents?"

"Better," Pilgrim answered, then laid the money on the counter.

The man scooped the coins up quickly, then stepped behind the counter and produced a key. "This fits the padlock on room number four. The door swings to the inside, so you can keep it barred as long as you're in th' room. I'd advise ya to lock it ever' time ya leave it, though; ya cain't trust nobody these days."

Eli nodded, then walked down the hall and twisted the key in the padlock. He stepped inside the room and laid his rifle and his saddlebags on a small table beside the window, then turned his attention to the bed. When he bounced his fist on the mattress he became convinced that the old man had told the truth about it being new, and he suspected that he himself might even be the first man to ever sleep on it. When he turned back the covers to find two clean sheets, he decided that the sixty cents he had paid for the room was a fair price.

A wash pan and a pitcher of water rested on a table across the room. A thick towel hung on a nearby wooden peg, and a small mirror had been glued to the wall above the table. Eli took off his shirt and dug out his shaving gear, then soaped his face and began to scrape off his thick beard. He would not change his clothing, for he had bathed in a creek and put on a clean shirt no more than eight hours earlier.

Nor did he intend to spend much time in this town. He would stable his animals for the night and treat himself to a good supper and a cold beer, then after a good night's sleep have a hot breakfast and continue on his journey. Hundreds of miles and dozens of creeks and rivers lay between Leeds, Arkansas, and Cuero, Texas, and it had already turned into summertime. A man had to travel slowly and keep a sharp eye on his animals during such hot and humid weather, for they could very easily overheat and leave him afoot. Indeed, Eli expected to be on the road for at least another month yet.

When he had finished shaving, he pushed his saddlebags and his rifle under the bed. He brushed the dust off his hat with his shirtsleeve, then stepped out into the hall and locked the door. Moments later, he untied his animals at the hitching rail, then led them toward the livery stable. Several men who were loitering on the sidewalk nodded or spoke to him as he walked down the street, and he returned all of their greetings with a wave of his hand.

A middle-aged, stoop-shouldered man stood waiting in the wide doorway as Eli halted in front of the livery stable. "I know ya ain't from nowhere aroun' here," the hostler said, reaching for the animals' reins. He chuckled loudly, adding, "I don't reckon no man livin' in this county's quite as big and good-lookin' as you are. Ya been on th' road for a good while, have you?"

Pilgrim nodded, then released the reins. "Yes, sir," he answered.

"Thought so," the man said, chuckling again. "I saw ya tie up at th' hotel, an' I said ta myself right then, I said, 'That young feller looks like he's been travelin' for quite a spell, an' I'd bet a purty 'at he's gonna brang his animals on down here ta th' stable as soon as he gits done rentin' hisself a room.' I jist kep' standin' here watchin', an' bygosh 'at's whatcha done."

Pilgrim stood quietly for a moment, then pointed over his shoulder with his thumb. "How's the food in that hotel restaurant?"

A feeble smile appeared on one side of the hostler's mouth. "I've been eatin' in it off an' on for several years now," he said, "an' I ain't never been served nothin' 'at I'd call bad." He laughed loudly now, adding, "Anyhow, it don't make no hell of a lot of differ'nce how good or how bad it is, it's all we've got. I mean, it's th' only restaurant within twenty miles of this town."

Eli chuckled along with the old-timer. "Well, I suppose I'll give it a try," he said. "I'll leave the saddler and the mule with you, and pick them up about sunup." He spun on his heel and headed for the hotel.

"I'll grain 'em an' hay 'em tonight an' in th' mornin, too!" the hostler called after him. "They'll be all rested up an' ready for th' road at sunup!"

Moments later, Eli used the door that opened directly off the street to enter the hotel restaurant. He was both pleased and surprised to see that the establishment was much cleaner and better kept than the hotel itself, and it was only after he seated himself on a stool that he learned the name of the hotel in which he had just rented a room. "Welcome to the Lybrand Hotel Restaurant," a sign behind the counter read. A sheet of blackboard containing a chalk-written bill of fare had also been hung on the wall. A short, fat man stepped from the kitchen offering a big smile. "Good afternoon," he said in a deep voice, then pointed over his shoulder with his thumb. "See anything on the menu you want, or should I be thinking about putting something else together?"

"No need to fix anything else," Pilgrim said, motioning to the bill of fare. "The first thing on that list looks mighty good to me. If you still have some of it left, just heat it up and bring it on."

"The pork stew?" the cook asked. "Don't have to heat it up, 'cause it's been on the stove simmering all afternoon." He smiled sheepishly, adding, "Nobody complained about it, but to tell you the truth, the meat in it wasn't quite done enough to suit me at dinnertime. It oughtta be nice and tender now, though."

"Sounds good," Eli said. "I guess you could say that pork stew's mostly what I was raised on."

"Me, too," the cook said, then disappeared into the kitchen.

While waiting for his food to be delivered, Eli sat on the stool looking the restaurant over. Though it had most likely been built at the same time as the hotel, it had obviously been treated much better. All four walls and the ceiling were painted a glossy white, and judging from their appearance, they received at least an occasional scrubbing. There were eight stools at the counter, and enough tables and chairs scattered throughout the room to accommodate forty or more people. At the moment, Pilgrim was the only customer in the building.

The cook was not long in returning to the counter. He set a steaming, oversized bowl in front of Eli, saying, "Stew don't taste right with biscuits, so I heated up some of the corn bread I had left over from dinner. You want coffee, too?"

Eli nodded. "Please," he said.

The man walked back into the kitchen and returned in less than a minute. "You staying at the hotel?" he asked, as he set a platter of corn bread and a cupful of hot coffee beside Eli's bowl.

Pilgrim swallowed a bite of the stew, then nodded. "I rented a room for one night," he answered. "I'll be on the road again at sunup."

The man shook his head. "I can't say that I envy you having to travel in this kind of weather. I never have seen it so hot around here this early in the year before." He stood quietly for a few moments, then motioned toward the kitchen. "I've got a lot to do back there before I'll be ready for the supper crowd, so I'd better get at it. The price of your food and coffee will be fifteen cents, and you can just leave the money on the counter when you finish eating." He spun on his heel and disappeared quickly.

When Eli paid for his meal ten minutes later he laid an extra nickel on the counter, as the stew, the bread, and the coffee had all been exceptionally good. When he stepped from the building onto the boardwalk he turned west, for he had already decided to visit the establishment next door that a wooden sign with faded white lettering identified as the "Frontier Saloon." He had been thinking all day about hunting up a cold beer, and the four saddled horses standing at the hitching rail suggested that he was not the only thirsty fellow in town.

He elbowed his way through the bat-wing doors and stood for a few moments waiting for his eyes to adjust, then walked to the near side of the bar. He seated himself on a stool about midway down, and a tall, fat bartender wearing a white apron was there quickly. Dark-haired, with a ruddy complexion, and appearing to be about forty years old, the man twisted the ends of his waxed mustache with his thumbs and forefingers, then spoke in a high-pitched voice that sounded almost feminine. "Howdy, young fellow," he said through smiling lips, "and welcome to the Frontier. What're you gonna have?"

Pilgrim nodded and offered a smile of his own. "I've been thinking about a cold beer for quite a while, now," he said. "Have you got one?"

"Yep," the big man answered, then moved to fill the order. Moments later, he slid the foamy mug of brew down the bar in front of Pilgrim, then held out a cupped hand for payment. "That'll be a nickel," he said.

"Take a dime," Eli said, laying the shiny coin in the outstretched hand. "I think it'll take at least two of 'em to quench my thirst."

The bartender dropped the money in a metal box beneath the counter, then walked back to his own stool and continued his conversation with the three drinkers seated on the opposite side of the bar. Though Pilgrim could understand none of the things they were saying, he could very clearly hear the loud burst of laughter that followed when the youngest of the three men stared across the room at him for a few moments, then mumbled a few words to the others behind his hand. Though Eli had no doubt that he himself had been the butt of some humorous remark, he chose to ignore the incident. He continued to sip slowly till he had drained his mug, then held it aloft to gain the bartender's attention. The big man drew a second beer for him quickly, then returned to his own stool.

While Pilgrim sipped at his beer and drew circles in a wet spot on the counter with a forefinger, the muted conversation continued on the opposite side of the bar. Though Eli kept his eyes to himself for the most part, he did look the drinkers over well enough to determine that two of them were obviously in their forties. The young man who was doing most of the talking appeared to be about half as old. When Pilgrim glanced at the trio for the third time, it was the young man who shouted across the room. "What the hell you staring at over here, fellow? You see something you don't like?"

Pilgrim sat for a few moments gazing at the counter, ignoring the question.

"Dammit, fellow, I'm talking to you!" the man shouted, his voice even louder now. "You hard of hearing or something?"

Eli stared at the bar for a moment longer, then leaned back on his stool and looked directly into the man's eyes. "No!" he answered just as loudly. "I don't have any problem at all hearing things that I want to hear!"

The young man, a six-footer who appeared to weigh at least two hundred pounds, set his drink on the counter noisily, then slid off his stool, his face flushed with anger. "Well, bygod I think you'd better hear this!" he said. "I'm pretty well known for kicking men's asses when they start sitting around staring at me!"

Pilgrim sat biting his lower lip for a moment, then set his mug down on the counter quietly. "What do they all do while you're busy kicking their asses?" he asked.

The young man cursed loudly and exploded into action, and even though one of the older men took hold of his arm in an effort to restrain him, he broke free and moved around the end of the bar almost at a run. Eli was off his stool quickly, stepping out into the aisle to meet his antagonist.

Even as he reached the spot where Pilgrim stood, the young man was already swinging a roundhouse right. No stranger to fisticuffs, Eli blocked the punch easily and countered with a hard right to the man's jaw that sent him to the floor instantly. The man was now lying flat on his back at Pilgrim's feet, and he did not move again. The fight was over before it had really begun.

Both of the older men were there quickly, though neither of them showed any interest in taking up the argument. After kneeling beside the fallen man and assuring themselves that he would probably be all right, both men stood up and leaned against the bar. The man who had tried to restrain the young man spoke to Eli: "I can't think of nothing else you could've done," he said. "Trent gets a wild hair in his ass sometimes, and won't pay no attention to nobody." He chuckled softly, then added, "To tell you the truth, the fight ended about like I thought it would.

"I reckon I'd done looked you over a little better'n Trent did, and that's why I was trying to hold him back. He's my brother's boy, but he won't even listen to his daddy, much less me." He pointed to the prone figure. "He'll be all right in a few minutes, though, and I can tell you right now that he ain't gonna feel hard at you for knocking him out. He'll be more likely to congratulate you for being able to punch him so hard."

"That's nice," Pilgrim said, "but I don't intend to be here. If it turns out that he does feel that way, just tell him that I appreciate the compliment." He walked through the front door and headed for his hotel room with long strides.

At daybreak next morning, Eli sat on the side of his bed rubbing the sleep from his eyes. He had turned in before sunset the night before, and even without consulting his watch he knew that he had slept around the clock. Refreshed and well rested after the long night's sleep, he washed his upper body and dried it with the fluffy towel, then dressed and pulled on his boots. Ten minutes later, he picked up his saddlebags and his rifle and walked down the hall, noticing when he passed through the lobby that there was no clerk behind the counter.

When he stepped through the doorway connecting the hotel to the restaurant, he stopped and stood leaning against the wall, for he could see at a glance that every seat in the establishment was taken. A waiter approached him shortly. "All of our diners are mighty good about volunteering to double up, sir," he said, then pointed to a table near the back wall. "As you can see, that table has only one occupant, and he told me to tell you that you are more than welcome to eat there with him."

When he followed the waiter's point with his eyes, Eli had no problem at all recognizing the young man he had punched in the Frontier Saloon the afternoon before. The man was on his feet now, smiling and motioning Pilgrim over. At least a little bit reluctant, Eli stood thinking for a few moments, then shrugged and walked to the table. "Good morning, mister," the young man said, extending his right hand. "Bygod I don't hesitate to call any man with a punch like you've got mister, either. I've been laid out before, but you're the only fellow who's ever done it with just one pop. My name's Trent Newberry."

Pilgrim grasped the hand. "Eli Pilgrim," he said.

Newberry pushed out the only other chair at the table. "Sit down, Mr. Pilgrim," he said, "and just any damn thing you take a notion to eat is on me."

Eli seated himself and laid his rifle and his saddlebags beside his chair, then picked up the bill of fare. "I appreciate you sharing your table with me," he said, "but I'll buy my own food."

"No, no," Newberry said, raising his voice a little. "I'm the fellow you knocked on his ass yesterday, so the least you can do is give me the satisfaction of anteing up for your breakfast." He rubbed his left cheek with the palm of his hand, adding, "It'll give me something else to think about while all this damn swelling goes down."

Eli chuckled. "Have it your way," he said. "I've always made it a point not to argue with a man when he's trying to save me money."

Newberry took the menu from Pilgrim's hand and handed it to the waiter, who had just arrived at the table. "Bring my friend here a double order of ham and eggs," he said. "He could probably eat a good-sized stack of those flapjacks, too." He looked across the table at Pilgrim with raised eyebrows. "That sound all right to you, Eli?"

Pilgrim nodded. "It sounds perfectly all right," he said.

The waiter tucked the menu under his arm. "Very well, sir," he said, then headed for the kitchen.

The two men sat at the table talking about many things during the next several minutes, but the altercation of the afternoon before was never mentioned again. Finally, Newberry looked at his watch, then slid his chair back and got to his feet. "I've got a meeting set up with a fellow five minutes from now," he said, "and it's something that I just can't put off. I'll stop by the counter and pay for your breakfast on my way out of the building. When I point you out to the cashier, just wave your hand so she'll know whose breakfast I'm paying for. That way, you won't even have to stop by there when you get ready to leave. Good-bye to you, Mr. Pilgrim, and I won't be forgetting the lesson you taught me."

"Thank you for the breakfast, Trent," Eli said, "and you take care of yourself. They've got a big crowd in here this morning, and there ain't no telling when the waiter'll be back with my food. It'll probably take me at least half an hour to eat that much grub even after I get it in front of me."

Though Eli was soon distracted by the waiter's arrival with his breakfast, he nonetheless kept a close eye on the counter, where Trent Newberry stood talking with an elderly woman. When Newberry finally pointed him out to the cashier, Pilgrim nodded, then poked his hand high into the air and waved to the lady. That done, he dug into a meal that he spent longer than half an hour eating. Finally, after taking his last sip of coffee, he picked up his rifle and his saddlebags and headed for the front of the building.

He was just about to push the front door open when the cashier stopped him. "Sir!" she called, her voice slightly above the volume of a normal conversation.

Eli stopped in his tracks and turned halfway around.

"Aren't you forgetting something, sir?" the lady asked.

Not sure he had heard her correctly, he shrugged and headed in her direction.

"Did you forget to pay your bill?" she asked when he reached the counter.

Eli stood biting his lower lip. "Trent Newberry didn't pay for my breakfast?"

"Of course not," the lady answered. "He said you were paying for his sirloin steak and eggs, and I remember you approving it by waving him on through, too."

"Waved him on through?" he asked. He began to snicker as the realization of what had happened dawned on him, then turned his head as the snicker escalated into loud laughter. After a few moments, he was facing the lady again. "Waved him on through?" he repeated, continuing to chuckle as he reached into his pocket for his poke. "Yes, ma'am, I'm afraid that's exactly what I was doing. How much is the damage?"

"A dollar eighty," she answered. "You had the best breakfast the restaurant has to offer, and the price of those sirloin steaks like Trent Newberry eats has just gone out of sight lately."

"Yes, ma'am," Eli said, counting out the money. He tipped his hat to the lady, then retrieved his rifle and his saddlebags from the counter and disappeared through the doorway. Hoping he might come upon Trent Newberry somewhere during the two-block walk to the livery stable, he headed west. It was not because he held any ill will against the man, he merely wanted to compliment him on his sense of humor. "Waved him on through, my ass," he said softly, then kicked at a small stone as he stepped into the street.

Just as had been the case the day before, the liveryman was waiting for Eli in the open doorway. "Good mornin', big man," he said. "I saw ya when ya first stepped outta th' restaurant, an' I figgered ya'd be on down here in a coupla minutes. Want me ta gitcha buckskin an' ya mule out here?"

"Yes, sir," Pilgrim answered, seating himself on the office doorstep to wait.

The hostler took a coil of rope from a wooden peg on the wall, then headed down the wide hallway. He was back much sooner than Eli had expected. "Easiest animals ta ketch 'at I've had in here in a good long while," he said. "Don't neither one ubb'm eeb'm make no effort to dodge th' rope."

Pilgrim chuckled loudly. "I suppose that's a good thing in my case," he said. "If they ran from the rope, I might not ever catch 'em."

"Ya sayin' ya ain't no good with a rope, are you?"

"Aw, I guess I'm a little better than I made it sound," Eli answered. He got to his feet and reached for the animals' reins, adding, "If you'll get my packsaddle, the two of us can buckle it down on the mule in short order. I always make it a point to saddle the buckskin myself."

The hostler nodded and handed over the reins. He retrieved Eli's packs and his packsaddle from the office, and working as a team, the men had the pack mule ready for the road in less than five minutes. Then the liveryman pointed to half a dozen saddles resting on wooden racks that resembled sawhorses. "Reckin ya won't have no problem pickin' ya own saddle outta 'at bunch," he said.

"No, sir," Eli said, heading for the racks. He saddled the buckskin quickly, then led both of his animals forward a few steps. The hostler was still sitting on the office steps, watching. "How much money will it take to make us both happy?" Pilgrim asked.

The old man got to his feet. "Well, I grained an' watered both ubb'm twice, so it all comes ta a dollar twenty: forty cents apiece for th' feed, an' twenty cents apiece for stayin' overnight. Now, 'at's what it'll take ta make me happy, how 'bout you?"

Eli flashed his broad smile. "I'm happier than I've been in months," he said. He paid the man, then mounted and headed west. Ten minutes later, he had ridden on across the side of the hill and out of sight.

He traveled at a steady pace for the next four days, then a ferryman floated him and his animals across the Arkansas River at midmorning for a charge of fifty cents. After looking the murky, fast-moving water of the wide stream over, Pilgrim quickly began to consider the fare to be the biggest bargain he had encountered since leaving home.

After being deposited on the south side of the river, he looked at his watch to see that it was ten-thirty. He decided on the spot that he would not stop for a nooning but would continue on till about two o'clock in the afternoon, then make an early camp for the night. He was hungry for a pot of beans, and he would need plenty of time to cook them before dark.

He crossed several creeks and passed a few roadside springs during the remainder of the morning and early after-noon, but it was almost three o'clock when he came to a campsite that he liked. He pulled off the road and watered his animals at a boxed-in spring, then tied them to a low-hanging tree limb and poured shelled corn in their nose bags. They would eat where they were standing, then he would unburden them and stake them out on good grass about sunset.

He found deadwood for his fire easily enough and kindled a flame between large, flat rocks that had been lined up just right by earlier campers. He laid one of his blankets on the ground beside the fire, then walked the forty feet to his pack mule and returned with two of his packs. He had also taken his Peacemaker out of his saddlebag, and now he laid the weapon down and pulled the edge of the blanket over it.

He filled his coffeepot and his cooking pot with water from the spring, then brought them to the fire. He dropped in a handful of grounds and set the coffee on the flame to boil, then began to concentrate on the preparation of his supper. He poured half of the water out of the cooking pot, then dumped in a few handfuls of lima beans. He would let them soak in the cold water for an hour, then set the pot on the fire. He knew that they actually needed longer than an hour of soaking time, but an hour was all the time he had. He intended to eat his supper and move his belongings to a well-hidden sleeping place before darkness closed in.

Still lying on his blanket half an hour later, he was leaning on one elbow and sipping a steaming cup of coffee when he spotted two riders coming down the road from the west. They turned off the road and watered their horses, and since the spring was no more than thirty yards from his own position, Eli could read them clearly enough.

The fact that the two men were brothers was obvious, for not only did they sit their saddles alike, they were about the same size, had the same facial features, the same sandy hair, and the same two weeks' growth of rusty-looking beard. They were done watering their animals now but continued to sit their saddles staring toward Eli's fire. As if to give himself some added peace of mind, Pilgrim patted the Peacemaker under the fold of his blanket, for he had not liked the looks of this situation right from the start.

The two men sat talking back and forth in muted tones for a few moments, then nodded to each other and kneed their animals toward Eli's fire. They came to a halt about thirty feet away. "Looks like ya jist a-layin' on ya ass an' watchin' th' worl' go by," the man appearing to be the older of the two said. He pointed to the blanket, then jerked his head toward Eli's animals. "I guess ya got a lot o' eats an' stuff like 'at in them packs right there," he said in a raspy nasal twang. "Whatcha got in them two 'at's still hangin' over there on th' mule?"

Pilgrim was slow to answer. "Why should that concern you?" he asked after a while.

After a quick glance at his brother, the talker drew a Colt revolver from his hip, pointing it straight at Eli's nose. "I see ya ain't wearin' no short gun," he said. "Ya got anythang else that shoots besides 'at rifle over there on ya saddle?"

"No," Pilgrim answered quickly. "I've never had a reason to carry a short gun around."

The talker spoke to his brother. "Git t'at rifle off'n his saddle, Ben. Brang it here to me, then take a look in them two packs he left on 'at mule."

The man named Ben nodded, then dismounted and walked to Pilgrim's buckskin. He unsheathed the rifle from the saddle scabbard and delivered it to his brother, then hurried over to the mule. Even before he had had time to go through the packs, he was talking again. "He's got all sorts o' good stuff in these thangs, Chip!" he said loudly. "Got nearly a full sack o' shelled corn, too."

The man named Chip jacked a shell into the chamber of

the Henry, clearly surprised when another live shell fell out of the barrel and dropped to the ground. "Well, bygod," he said. "You had 'er full up an' ready to go, didn't ya, feller?" He pointed the rifle at Eli, then spoke again. "You sure you ain't got no other weapon 'sides this'n?"

"I'm sure," Pilgrim answered.

The man drew one leg over his horse's neck, then slid out of his saddle. "You'll jist keep right on a-settin' where you're at if'n ya know what's good for ya," he said. "I'm gonna walk over there an' help him figger out what's on 'at mule, but I'll be keepin' a sharp eye on ya."

As the brothers stood beside the mule talking a few moments later, it quickly became obvious to Eli that the minds of both men were completely preoccupied with the contents of the packs the animal carried on its back. Though he found it difficult to believe that men bent on robbery and possibly even murder could be so careless, he nonetheless began to ease his Peacemaker out from underneath the blanket, for he believed that the weapon might be his only chance of staying alive.

He cocked the Colt and held it alongside his leg till he decided the time was right, then he shot the man named Chip in his right temple. When the brother named Ben whirled and began to claw at the weapon on his own hip, Eli shot him in the throat. Each man dropped the pack he was holding, then fell to the ground in a heap. Pilgrim was there quickly and could see at a glance that both men were now staring at the world through sightless eyes.

Eli stood looking around him in every direction. Though he must think fast, he knew that he also must keep a cool head, for the last thing he needed was somebody asking questions about the dead men. With his Colt tucked behind his waistband, he dragged the bodies up the hill one at a time, where he deposited them in a thick patch of weeds behind a brush pile. He turned their horses loose, then piled both men's saddles and bridles in the tall weeds beside their bodies.

When he was done, he stood looking the area over for a few moments, then decided that a passerby would never know the men had been here. Even a man who camped here for the night would not know it unless he climbed up the hill and looked into the patch of weeds, a happenstance that was highly improbable. No, sir, he did not expect the bodies to be found until after they had created a foul odor, but he himself expected to be long gone before then.

He took his animals' now-empty nose bags off and returned them to the proper pack, then walked back to his blanket. He emptied the coffeepot and the bean pot into the fire, then put the still-warm vessels in the pack that was lying closest to his feet. Now, happy that he had not yet unburdened his animals when the robbers showed up, he rolled up the blanket and tied it behind his saddle, then hung all four of his packs back on the packsaddle. Mounting the buckskin and taking up the slack in the mule's lead rope, he watered the animals at the spring once again, then took to the road.

He kicked the buckskin to a fast trot and held the pace for almost two hours, for he wanted to put as many miles as possible between himself and the senseless thing that had happened at the campground. Even after he pulled his animals down to a fast walk he continued on, for he intended to keep traveling till the moon came out, which he believed would be sometime around midnight. The glow would furnish him all the light he would need in order to set up camp and find good grass for his livestock. Even then, he expected to be back on the road at daybreak, for he doubted that any of his answers would sound very believable if somebody should start questioning him about the two dead men.

THE TOWN was founded in 1872 and named for a nearby creek that was notorious for trapping cattle in bogs. Seeing that the hides were almost always recovered by white skinners, the Indians were quick to name the treacherous stream "rawhides." Translating into Spanish as *cuero,* the word was adopted by the community's founders, and all agreed that their new town should bear the same name as the creek.

Located on the Guadalupe River in the center of DeWitt County, Cuero early on became a roundup point for a leg of the Chisholm Trail. And although the rich topsoil of the area was capable of producing a wide assortment of crops even without the use of commercial fertilizers, most of the settlers turned to the raising of cattle, for with its perennial grasses and its never-ending water supply, DeWitt County was a virtual cattleman's paradise.

The community had begun to prosper right from the day of its inception, and though most of its inhabitants were of a law-abiding nature, many were not. Whores, gamblers, and con men of every stripe set up shop immediately after the sun went down each evening, and seemed to be at least tolerated by local law enforcement. Notorious gunfighter Basil Allgood had even taken up residence there, and many others of the same ilk walked the streets day and night. The town early on acquired the reputation of being a hell-raising outpost where women and children were forbidden after dark, and even the saloon women refused to set foot on the boardwalks at night unless accompanied by a well-armed member of the opposite sex.

Riding in from the north, Eli Pilgrim reached Cuero at midafternoon on a hot day in June. After glancing at a marker on the corner identifying the street he had ridden in on as Esplanade, he brought his animals to a halt and sat looking things over. The layout of the town impressed him immediately, for every building he could see looked as if it had been erected in exactly the right place. Appearing to be three or four blocks long, Esplanade Street was at least a dozen wagons wide, and Eli smiled faintly as he considered the long odds against the town ever experiencing a traffic jam. He returned the greeting of a man riding past him in the opposite direction, then kneed the buckskin on down the street.

The Elkhorn Saloon stood on the northeast corner at the intersection of Esplanade and Main, and every hitching rail in the vicinity was occupied by as many saddled horses as it could accommodate. Eli even suspected that most of the animals standing on the opposite corner belonged to saloon patrons, for, after all, this was a Saturday afternoon, and he could already see that he had ridden into a very busy town.

Knowing that the best place to pick up local information in any town was inside one of its popular saloons, and that he would surely visit the oversized watering hole later in the afternoon, he rode on past the Elkhorn. At the moment, he was more interested in finding lodging for his animals, and a hotel room for himself. And since he expected to be in town for a while, he would be a little bit more picky about the hotel room than usual.

He continued to ride south till the town played out and Esplanade Street became the narrow main road again. Once there, he could see the trees and other growth that lined the banks of the Guadalupe River, and he wanted a closer look. He kicked his saddler to a trot and rode on. Since the water appeared to be much more accessible from the west bank, he rode across the river on a bridge made of heavy timbers, then left the road.

Pilgrim was a man who enjoyed fishing and was already looking for a good place to cast a line. He dismounted and dropped a heavy rock in the river, immediately deciding that the water was at least ten feet deep. Deep enough for hundreds of big catfish to be lying back under its cut banks, waiting to ambush the first thing to swim by that appeared to be the right size.

He could see that plenty of people other than himself had had the same idea, for the first fifty yards or so of the west bank were completely barren of small vegetation, and the ashes left over from dozens of campfires littered the entire area. A rarity on the bank of any large stream, there was a clear spring with a white sandy bottom located under the canopy of a large oak, and the tin cup hanging on a nail driven into the tree was a signal that the water was good to drink. He filled the cup and drank his fill, then watered his animals in the runoff that ran down to the river. Then, having already decided that he would be dropping a fishing line into the Guadalupe before long, he remounted and headed back to town. He still had to locate a livery stable and a hotel.

A man on the street directed him to the livery stable at the end of East Main Street and informed him that there were several hotels in that vicinity. "Three or four of 'em right there close together," he said. "Just turn right off of Esplanade onto Main, and you'll pass 'em all before you get to the livery. I've heard a few men brag on the services at the Clancy Inn, but I've also been told that they charge an arm and a leg. There's a place right across the street from it that ain't quite so fancy, called the the Drover's Rest. A man can probably get anything he needs there for about half the money."

Eli thanked the man for the information, then rode on. Once he turned onto Main he could already see the livery stable's sign at the end of the street. Riding past both of the hotels that the man had mentioned, he decided that the Clancy appeared to be a little too rich for his blood. Knowing that he would soon be discussing a room with someone at the Drover's Rest, he rode on down the street.

A large, red-haired man who appeared to be about thirty-five years old was standing in the livery stable's open doorway. "You got room for two more?" Pilgrim asked.

The man was a talker. "Sure do," he said quickly. "You got here at the right time of day, too, 'cause I don't remember when the last time was that I didn't fill up on a weekend." Stepping forward and reaching for the animals' reins, he continued to talk. "Yessir, by the time the sun goes down on a Saturday evening I'm usually turning people away, and I don't expect today to be no different." He loosened the cinch on the buckskin, adding, "A friend of mine owns a stable on the west side of town, though, so I always send him any business I can't handle."

"I'll bet he appreciates that," Eli said, handing over the reins. "He probably considers himself lucky to have a friend like you."

"I hope he does," the man said, laying Pilgrim's saddle across a wooden rack. "We've been knowing each other for more'n twenty years, and that's exactly how I feel about him. Everybody else who knows Roscoe feels that way, too. I'd say the only reason he ain't got more business than he can handle, is 'cause his place is located too far from the center of town." He chuckled, adding, "Most of these jokers who ride into Cuero on the weekend ain't gonna walk one step farther than they have to."

Eli nodded, then changed the subject. "I don't know how long I'll be around," he said. "I've been on the move since the first of April, so I intend to rest up for a while. I met a man on the road back in Arkansas who spoke mighty highly of this town, and he seemed to think I ought to stop off and see what I think of it."

"I reckon it's as good as any other place I can think of,"

the hostler said. He stood quietly for a moment, then asked, "That man you talked with on the road, do you happen to remember his name?"

"Sure do," Pilgrim answered. "His name is Harvey Homestead."

The big man slapped his leg. "Well, I'll be doggone," he said. "I know him and his brother Ed, both. Fact is, I greased their wagons a few days before they left for Ohio, then sold 'em a can of grease to carry with 'em. Harvey said they were gonna carry their pa back home to Ohio to die. Was the old man still alive when you met 'em in Arkansas?"

"Yes," Eli answered. "Harvey made it a point to tell me so."

"That's good to hear," the hostler said. "I'll bet that old fart'll still be alive twenty years from now."

"You never can tell," Eli said. He saw no reason to mention the fact that the man's family had decided to put him out of his misery once they reached the old home place.

Leaning his rifle against the wall, Pilgrim took a change of clean clothing out of his pack, then spoke again. "A fellow on the street told me that the Drover's Rest is a good place to stay, so I guess that's where I'll spend the night. Might stay there a little longer, if the rent's reasonable."

"It is," the liveryman said. "Six bits'll get you the best room in the house, and I reckon about anything else you might need is there for the asking." He extended his right hand, adding, "By the way, my name's Hank Fry."

Eli grasped the callused, ham-sized hand. "I'm Eli Pilgrim."

Fry pointed to the office. "That door stays locked all the time, and your packs'll be in there. If you need anything out of 'em later on, I reckon you'll just have to hunt me up. I usually walk up to the Drover's Saloon for a drink about dark. If you happen to be in there about that time, maybe we can wet our whistles together."

"Maybe," Eli said. "I'll most likely be there, and I'll

make it a point to look for you." He released the hostler's
hand, then turned and headed up the street.

The Drover's Rest was an unpainted, two-story building
in the middle of the block, and the single-story affair adjoining
it on the east side sported a tall sign identifying it as the
Drover's Saloon. Eli glanced over the watering hole's bat-
wing doors as he walked by, then stepped into the hotel lobby.
A blond-haired youth who appeared to be in his late teens sat
behind the counter. "Welcome to the Drover's Rest," he said,
laying the book he had been reading aside and getting to his
feet. "Got a few rooms left on each floor, so you can take
your pick."

Pilgrim walked across the room and laid his saddlebags
and his rifle on the counter. "I'd like to rent the coolest room
in the house," he said, chuckling loudly.

The young man's smile revealed a row of crooked teeth.
"I guess you meant that as a joke, but I believe the downstairs
rooms are a little cooler, especially the ones on the corners.
They've got windows on the side and the back wall too, so
you'll get a good draft going when you raise 'em both. Won't
be no mosquitoes sucking on you neither; we just put new
nets on the windows about a month ago."

Pilgrim nodded and continued to smile. "That's good to
hear," he said. "I suppose just being protected from the bugs
is worth the price of a room." He spun the hotel register
around, then picked the short stub of a pencil up off the
counter. "How much do you charge for the rooms?"

"Sixty-five cents a night," the clerk answered, "but three
dollars and a half'll pay you up for a week if you want to
stay that long."

Pilgrim signed the register, then counted out sixty-five
cents. "I'll just pay for one night," he said, "but I'll certainly
take you up on that weekly rate if I decide to stay in town
for a while."

"Very good," the young man said, handing over a key.
"You'll be in number twelve, on the northeast corner, and no

matter whether your stay is long or short, I hope it's a pleasant one."

Moments later, Eli let himself into the room and barred the door. He felt the cool draft immediately after raising the opposing windows and knew that he would spend the night in comfort. He sat down on the side of the bed and pulled off his boots, then undressed and dug his shaving gear out of his saddlebag. He shaved off the thicket of black beard hiding most of his face, then used the washcloth and soap provided by the hotel to bathe his body. After changing into clean clothing, he brushed the dust off his hat with his dirty shirt. Ten minutes later, he walked through the hotel lobby and stepped out onto the boardwalk.

He was hungry, and he could see two restaurants even from where he stood. What appeared to be the newer of the two was located directly across the street from the hotel. Taking care to avoid wagon traffic headed in both directions, he crossed the street at a trot. A man who was just leaving the establishment held the door open for him, and, nodding his appreciation, Pilgrim walked through. Once inside, he seated himself on a stool at the counter, where a bearded man wearing a white apron looked at him questioningly. "Can I help you?" he asked.

"I believe so," Pilgrim answered. "I'll have whatever you consider your best beefsteak."

The man nodded, then spun on his heel and disappeared into the kitchen. A few moments later, he returned with a cup of coffee in his hand. "Most fellows like to sip on this stuff while they're waiting," he said. "It's gonna be about twenty minutes on your steak." He set the steaming cup at Eli's elbow, then headed for the kitchen again.

Pilgrim was soon served a thick T-bone steak, along with a large helping of fried potatoes, a bowl of lima beans, and two thick slices of bread that tasted like it had been baked this very afternoon. He enjoyed the meal immensely, and when he got to his feet to pay for it, he said so to the man who had cooked and served it.

The man smiled, then drummed his fingers on the counter a few times. "I fix 'em like that six days a week," he said. "I don't reckon there was anything special about it, but I appreciate the compliment." He reached under the counter for the money box, then added, "That'll be twenty-five cents for the food, and the coffee's free."

Eli laid a quarter in the man's hand, then headed for the door. "I'll be back when I get hungry again," he said over his shoulder.

"You do that," the man said. "I'm open from six o'clock in the morning till eight o'clock at night."

It was only after Eli was back on the street that the name of the restaurant in which he had eaten registered in him. "The Cattleman's Steakhouse," the sign at the top of the building read, "Frank Upjohn, prop." Pilgrim smiled, then walked on down the street. It had undoubtedly been Mister Frank Upjohn who had just cooked and served him a meal that he would not soon forget.

He crossed the street to the Drover's Saloon, then elbowed his way through the bat-wing doors. Once inside, he moved to his left and stood leaning against the wall till his eyes adjusted to the dim lighting, then walked on to the bar. Seeing that he himself was the only customer in the building, he stood between two stools with his elbows on the bar for a moment, then spoke to the bartender, a skinny man who appeared to be about fifty years old. "How's business?" he asked, smiling broadly.

Apparently seeing no humor in Eli's question, the man answered curtly. "It'll be a little better after you buy something," he said, a granite expression on his leathery face.

Realizing that the man had probably heard the same thing a dozen times today, Eli spoke again: "I don't usually say such silly things on purpose," he said. "Will you please overlook the question and draw me a beer?"

The man nodded, and a hint of a smile appeared on his face. "Be glad to," he said. Moments later, he set a mug of foamy brew on the bar, saying, "Five cents."

Pilgrim laid the coin on the counter, then watched the bartender scoop it up and head for the opposite end of the bar. He had just taken a sip of his beer when he recognized a voice behind him. "I see you've already got a head start on me," Hank Fry said.

Eli turned halfway around on his stool. "I'm not far ahead of you," he said. "I haven't been here more'n five minutes. Are you done for the day?"

"I closed up a little earlier than usual," Fry said, sliding onto a stool. "Ain't been a soul in that stable since you left there."

"Maybe you'll make up for it tomorrow," Pilgrim said.

"Tomorrow or some other day," Fry said. "My business comes in spurts, and it's been spurting mighty heavy here lately. To tell you the truth, I'm glad to get away from it for a few hours. I'd close the doors for a week or so every once in a while if I could get away with it."

Pilgrim nodded, then changed the subject. "Order up, Hank. Anything you want is on me."

Fry shook his head, then spoke to the bartender, saying, "Give me a bottle of that same brand of whiskey I had the other day, Willy. It goes down a little easier than the rotgut you used to sell me." He laid money on the bar. "Give me a coupla glasses and a pitcher of water, then me and my friend'll be moving to a table over there along the wall."

The bartender nodded, then reached under the bar. "This stuff came all the way from Bourbon County, Kentucky," he said as he set the bottle in front of the liveryman. "It'll taste good tonight, and it'll go easy on your head tomorrow."

Fry took the bottle and the glasses across the room to a table, and Pilgrim followed with the pitcher of water. The liveryman did the pouring, and both men were soon sipping drinks. "How long have you been living in Cuero, Hank?"

Pilgrim asked, wiping his mouth with the heel of his hand.

"Most of my life," the liveryman answered. "I was born about twenty miles east of here. In fact, I had already come into the world when DeWitt County was organized in 1842, and I lived in Cuero a good long while before the Drover's Hotel and Saloon were built."

Eli nodded and took another sip from his glass. "Who built 'em, Hank? I mean, who owns 'em?"

Fry chuckled, then poured more whiskey in his glass. "A man named Bill Leighton built 'em," he said, "but he left town about a year later. Some folks think he went back to Florida, but I don't know nobody who knows for sure. As to who owns 'em now, that seems to be a big mystery." Fry continued to talk for the next several minutes, during which time he answered many questions that Eli had not even thought of asking.

The liveryman said that, although a man named Bo Beardsley professed to be the owner of both establishments, few men in the area thought that he was the last man to count the money. Most believed that the profits from both the hotel and the saloon ended up in the pockets of Basil Allgood, a man of questionable character who had moved to Cuero from Houston three years before.

Loudmouthed and overbearing, Allgood was a thirty-year-old six-footer who weighed two hundred pounds. Dark-haired and exceedingly handsome, he walked around with his nose in the air and a permanent smirk, giving one and all the impression that he considered himself too important to associate with the common herd. And though he was truly liked by none, he was feared by most, for men who had seen him in action claimed that he was unbeatable with a six-gun.

Stories of gunfights that Allgood had survived in Houston abounded, and he had even killed four men since moving to Cuero. Three of those men had fallen to his Colt in this very saloon, the liveryman said, while the fourth, an eighteen-year-old boy of Mexican descent, had accepted a challenge to a shootout in the middle of the street. Clearly overmatched, the young man had died without ever clearing his holster.

At least half a dozen witnesses testified that Allgood's draw was little more than a blur; that none of them had actually seen the gun in his fist till it was already spitting flame. Almost two years had passed since the shootout in the street, and Basil Allgood had not drawn his Colt in public since. There had been no reason to, for there was not a man in DeWitt County who would raise a hand against him. "Ain't nobody around here gonna take on a man like Allgood," Fry said, ending his long narration.

"You say he's overbearing, Hank," Eli said finally. "Does he just pick on men that he knows won't stand up to him?"

"Well, not exactly," Fry answered, taking a long swig from his glass. "He's a good scrapper with his hands, too, and from what I hear, he'll get on anybody's ass who gives him any shit. Ain't nobody around here ever gets in his way, though, so I reckon he's settled down a little during the past year or so. He sure don't walk the streets like he used to, and I ain't even seen him in this saloon since way last winter."

"Sounds to me like I don't ever want to see him," Eli said, chuckling.

They sat talking for another hour, with Pilgrim describing what his life had been like back in Ohio, and his recent journey to Texas. Finally, he upended his glass and got to his feet, for he could see by looking through the window that it was already getting dark outside. "I hate to leave good company," he said, "but like I told you earlier, I've been on the road a long time. I've got a soft bed rented at the hotel, so I'm gonna stretch out on it and rest my bones."

Fry got to his feet and offered a handshake. "It's been nice talking with you," he said. "I keep the coffeepot on down at the stable most of the time, so if you're out and about with nothing better to do in the morning, stop by for a cup."

"I'll do that," Eli said, pumping the liveryman's hand. "I don't expect to need my horses, but I'll make it a point to stop by your place anyway." He released the callused hand, adding, "You have a good night, now." He walked through the side door and into the hotel lobby, then down the hall to his room. He went to bed without even lighting the lamp.

IN A further effort to acquaint himself with the town, Pilgrim walked the streets of Cuero for most of the following day. And though he bought nothing, he passed in and out of several of the stores. He ate breakfast, dinner, and supper in three different restaurants, and shortly after sunset ordered up a pitcher of beer at the Elkhorn Saloon. Moments later, he was sitting at a table by the window, sipping the cold brew.

As he had promised Hank Fry the night before, he had shown up at the livery stable early this morning, joining the hostler in several cups of coffee and another conversation. When informed that Pilgrim was interested in finding work on a ranch, Fry had repeated Harvey Homestead's advice: "The Oxbow's the biggest outfit around here," the liveryman said, "and I'd say they might need a man of your caliber occasionally. Old Oliver Benson has got more money than he knows what to do with, and he got it all raising cattle on that very spread.

"He settled here not long after statehood, and started running longhorns on every acre of land he could get his hands on. He must have known something the rest of the men around here didn't, 'cause even during the years when there was no demand at all for beef, he kept right on raising cows. Back then you could get a section of land for a song, 'cause there was so much of it that nobody thought it would ever be worth anything. Benson just kept right on accumulating acreage any way he could, and by the time the war was over he was laying claim to over fifty-one thousand acres.

"When the railroad and the cattle buyers came to Kansas in '67, he was ready for 'em, 'cause cows were thicker'n jackrabbits on his place by then. A man don't have to be real smart to figure out that he can raise a hell of a lot of longhorns on eighty sections of land, Mr. Pilgrim, and that's exactly what he'd been doing." Fry refilled their coffee cups, then continued: "Benson bought a bunch of Hereford bulls and started breeding the longhorn strain outta his whole herd a few years back, and I ain't seen a single one of his cows lately that showed any sign of longhorn blood. He sends at least three herds north to the rails every year; he sells 'em all as purebred Herefords, too."

Pilgrim finished off his coffee and set the empty cup on the table. "Sounds to me like Mr. Benson's in business, all right," he said. "Maybe I'll ride out tomorrow and talk with him about a job."

Fry pursed his lips and shook his head. "No, no," he said, "that wouldn't do you a bit of good. The old man don't even know the names of all the people who work for him nowadays, much less what their jobs are. If you want to work at the Oxbow, you're gonna have to talk to Big Step Benson; he's the man with the say-so."

"Big Step Benson? He's the foreman?"

Fry shook his head again. "He's the ranch manager. He's got a foreman or two who work under him, but I don't think it would do you any good to talk to one of them either. Everybody says that no man goes to work on the Oxbow Ranch till he's been approved by Big Step." He sipped the last of his coffee and set the cup on the table, adding, "Now, it makes sense to me that one of them other bosses could probably fire a fellow who wasn't taking care of his job, but I've always been told that Big Step's the only one who can put a man on the payroll."

"Big Step Benson," Eli repeated. "Is he part of Oliver's family?"

Fry nodded. "He's the middle son. The Bensons had three of them boys, but two of 'em are dead now. The oldest was killed by a mule about ten years ago, and the youngest was gunned down by a drunk in Dodge City back in '74. They didn't have any daughters, so Big Step's the only one of their offspring left. Folks around here say he's the cream of the crop, too."

"That's nice to hear," Pilgrim said. He was quiet for a few moments, then asked, "How old is he, and what does he look like?"

"I reckon he's somewhere around forty," Fry answered, then chuckled loudly. "As to what he looks like, I can promise you right now that you're gonna know him when you see him. He's damn near seven feet tall, and he's got legs even longer than you'd expect to see on a man that size. His given name is Robert, but nobody ever calls him anything but Big Step. I've heard that he picked up the nickname before he was even done growing, and it damn sure fits him. One step for him is about like two for an ordinary man."

Pilgrim nodded. "Are Oliver Benson and his wife both in good health?"

"Mrs. Benson died right after the war was over," Fry answered, "and it's hard to tell about Oliver. He's close to seventy-five years old now, so you don't expect much out of him."

"No," Eli said. He got to his feet and took a step toward the doorway. "I'll be going now, but I'll be back early in the morning for my buckskin. It's like Harvey Homestead told me back in Arkansas: I don't have anything to lose, so I might as well ride out to the Oxbow and put in my application for a job." He walked through the doorway and on up the street to a restaurant. It was long past his normal breakfast time.

Now, sitting in the Elkhorn Saloon, Eli had just poured the last of the beer from his pitcher when the bartender walked around his table and drew the shade on the window. "It's done got dark outside," he said. "With you sitting here under the light, people could be standing around outside staring at you and you'd never know it."

Eli offered a broad smile. "I believe you're right," he said, "but I sure don't know why anybody would want to stare at me."

The bartender was a short man, with a thick chest, muscular arms, and brown hair. He appeared to be about thirty years old. He placed his hands on the edge of Pilgrim's table, then leaned forward and smiled broadly. "My name's Bob Strangelove," he said. "What's yours?"

Pilgrim offered a handshake. "The name's Eli Pilgrim," he said.

The bartender pumped the hand a few times, then released it, saying, "Didn't it cross your mind that there might be somebody out there who just don't like your looks, Eli?"

Pilgrim returned the smile, then shrugged. "No," he said. "I guess it didn't."

Strangelove straightened up to his full height of about five foot six, then spoke again. "Well, I know you ain't been around here very long, so let me tell you a few things about this town. If you paid any attention to the men on the street out there, you noticed that just about all of 'em were packing iron."

Eli nodded.

"Well, there's a reason for that," the man continued, "and it's because they all know that somebody might pull a gun on 'em at any minute, then invent an excuse for it later on. There must be at least a dozen gunmen in this town who'd shoot a man down just for the hell of it, and Marshal Teeter or Sheriff Beasley neither one wouldn't try to do a damn thing about it. Both of 'em have always bought any old cock-and-bull story them damn gunslingers told 'em, or at least they've always acted like they did.

"The truth of the matter is that both of our local lawmen

would tremble in their boots at the thought of having to arrest a member of the town's sporting crowd. A damn shootout would definitely be involved, and I believe that Teeter or Beasley either one would resign their jobs before they'd take on a gunman with know-how." He stood staring at the window shade for a moment, then added, "Besides, I believe them sons of bitches are in on a lot of this crooked shit that goes on around here. I told both of 'em that to their faces during the last election, too." He returned to his work as two men walked through the bat-wing doors and seated themselves at the bar.

Eli sat sipping the last of his beer and thinking about the things Strangelove had said. He was a talker, all right, and had seemed to be totally unconcerned about whether or not the words he had used were repeated. After all, the man knew nothing whatsoever about Pilgrim, or whether Eli himself was a cohort of some of the men involved in the "crooked shit" he had mentioned.

After thinking on the situation a little longer, Eli decided that Strangelove probably did not give a damn; that he himself might be one of the men who packed iron every time he ventured out on the street. Watching his motions as he worked behind the bar, Pilgrim came to the conclusion that the short man might very well be handy with a six-gun. Every motion of his muscular arms was quick and fluid, and his hands were plenty big enough to fit the grips of a Peacemaker. Eli smiled slightly, then nodded at his thoughts. The man probably had a gunbelt within easy reach under the bar, he was thinking, and would strap it on his hip the moment he closed the saloon for the night.

Pilgrim upended his beer, then got to his feet. He set his empty pitcher and his glass on the bar one minute later, then spoke to the bartender. "I enjoyed meeting and talking with you, but I'm tired. I've been walking all day, so I've decided to head for the Drover's Rest and a soft bed."

Strangelove turned halfway around to face him, then nodded. "They'll treat you right down there at the Drover's," he said. "You just be careful, and remember all them things I told you."

"I certainly will, Bob," Eli said, then headed for the doorway.

Ten minutes later, he was lying in his bed thinking of the conversations he had had during the day with both the liveryman and the bartender. Hank Fry had been the most informative, but it was the bartender that Eli was thinking of at the moment. He had by now decided that, although Bob Strangelove had not said so, he himself was probably the owner of the Elkhorn Saloon.

And the man was most likely a dreaded gunhand; otherwise, where would he get the nerve to call both the county sheriff and the town marshal crooks, while talking to a man that he knew absolutely nothing about. A hint of a smile played around the corner of Eli's mouth as he fluffed up his pillow. He nodded again: Bob Strangelove was a gutsy talker all right, and most likely handy enough with a six-gun to back up his words. Pilgrim turned onto his preferred sleeping side and was still smiling when he dozed off.

He ate breakfast in a small restaurant at sunup next morning, then walked down to the livery stable. Hank Fry was standing in the doorway sipping from a tin cup. "You got time to join me in another cup of coffee?" he asked. "Or are you ready for your saddler?"

"I've already had three cups of coffee this morning, Hank. I reckon I'll just take the buckskin and be on my way."

The liveryman dashed his leftover grounds into the powdery dirt at his feet, then hung the empty coffee cup on a nail. Taking a coil of rope from a wooden peg, he pointed toward the office. "Just have a seat on the steps over there," he said. "This might take me five or ten minutes." Then he was gone down the hall toward the corral.

Eli seated himself on the top step to wait, his saddlebags across his shoulder, and his Henry rifle across his knees. He had no more than made himself comfortable when Fry led the buckskin down the hall and came to a halt just inside the doorway. "I may not be very good at gauging time," Pilgrim said to the liveryman, "but I don't believe it took you half as long as you thought it would."

Fry chuckled. "Your horse walked right up to the gate like he was ready to be on the road again, and I got the rope around his neck with the first chunk. Considering how bad a roper I am, that's rare." He dropped the reins to the ground, laid the blanket across the horse's back, then threw on the saddle and cinched it down. "Most every man I know who's as big as you are, rides a bigger animal than this buckskin," he said. "Did this little fellow bring you all the way from Ohio without any problems?"

"I believe so," Eli answered. "I intended to stop off somewhere and trade him for a stronger animal if he ever showed any sign of fatigue, but he was still wanting to run when he got to Cuero." He shoved his rifle into the boot, then picked up the horse's reins and mounted, adding, "I've got your directions to the Oxbow, so I'm gonna head on out there before the day gets any hotter."

"Good idea," Fry said, giving the buckskin a final pat on the neck. "I believe it's gonna be another scorcher, too."

Eli nodded, then guided the horse through the wide doorway. Once on the street, he kicked the animal to a fast trot and held the pace till after he crossed the river bridge, where he pulled up and sat his saddle looking at the campground and fishing hole he had visited two days ago. The liveryman had said that the Guadalupe itself was the Oxbow's east boundary, and this morning there were at least twenty head of Herefords milling around on the west bank. Pilgrim saw no bulls, and the cows' white faces and similar size made them all look alike. From his position on the main road he could not make out any kind of brand, but he had no doubt that they all had an oxbow burned into their hides. He kicked the buckskin in the ribs and continued on down the road.

According to Fry, he would have to travel five or six miles yet before he reached the turnoff leading to Oxbow headquarters. "There's a sign there," the liveryman had said. "You can't miss it."

It was almost ten o'clock, and the buckskin was already beginning to lather, when Eli reached the turnoff. A green sign with white lettering advised one and all that Oxbow Ranch headquarters were located five miles to the north. A large white arrow pointed the way. Shortly after Pilgrim had made the turn he pulled his saddler to a halt, for he could see an oversized wagon coming in his direction. Drawn by four large horses with only one man sitting on the seat, the wagon was no doubt an Oxbow freighter, Eli was thinking. He guided his animal off the road and sat his saddle, yielding the narrow right of way to the approaching vehicle.

Pilgrim sat wiping the sweatband of his hat with his shirtsleeve as the freighter drew alongside. The driver, a blond-haired man about Eli's own age, brought the large animals to a halt. "Howdy," he said, offering a broad smile. "You headed out to the Oxbow?"

Eli nodded. "Yes," he answered. "Thought I'd go out and put in an application for a job."

The young man stared straight ahead for a moment, then pulled a plug of tobacco from his vest pocket and bit off a chew. He replaced the plug and worked his lower jaw up and down a few times, then spat a yellow stream of juice on the front wheel. "I'm sure they've already got a stack of them things a foot high," he said, "but I guess one more won't hurt nothing. Anyway, I hope you have better luck than I did. Took me over a year to get on. When you get out there, just pass everybody else up and go right to Big Step. I doubt that he'll hire you, but he ain't never too busy to talk to a man." He slapped the left-hand wheelhorse on the rump with the reins, and the big vehicle rolled away quickly.

Eli guided the buckskin back onto the road and allowed the animal to select its own fast-walking gait. He was thinking about the teamster he had just talked with. Though the man had not introduced himself, Pilgrim thought that he had a pleasant nature, and felt that the two of them would likely become friends if he himself found employment at the Oxbow.

There had been a Henry rifle exactly like his own lying on the floorboard of the wagon, and Eli had immediately noticed the holstered Colt Peacemaker attached to the wide leather belt encircling the young man's waist. Maybe Bob Strangelove had known what he was talking about: maybe most of the men in the area did walk or ride around armed to the teeth.

Eli still carried his own gunbelt in his saddlebag and had never in his life strapped it on in public. Though he felt that his marksmanship was at least as good as that of the next man, he also knew that walking about with a gun on his hip could lead to trouble. Due to the fact that there had simply never been any reason for it, he had never even attempted to jerk a gun from its holster with excessive speed. Consequently, he knew that he might find himself in a situation that he could not handle if a gunslinger like the one Strangelove had mentioned ever decided to pick a fight with him.

He could not imagine himself actually being faced with that problem, however, for he believed that such confrontations could easily be avoided by using a little forethought. It had always been his nature to go his own way and keep his nose out of the next man's business, and he had no intention of changing the habit. While it was true that he had been involved in hand-to-hand combat many times over the years, at no time had it ever gone beyond the fistfighting stage. A fistfight was one thing, but a gunfight was quite another. Both combatants almost always lived over a fistfight, with the loser often shaking the winner's hand and walking away smiling. Such was rarely the case when gunpowder came into play, however. A man usually didn't lose but one gunfight. Convinced that his decision to keep his own gun out of sight had been the correct one, Pilgrim kicked the buckskin to a fast trot. Oxbow headquarters were no more than three miles ahead.

Half an hour later, after having ridden past what he believed to be several hundred head of Hereford cattle, he topped a rise and pulled up at a sign welcoming him to the Oxbow Ranch. He sat his saddle for a few moments while his eyes took in the picture: a hundred yards down a well-kept driveway that had been fenced in with peeled poles stood the ranch house and the outbuildings, all of which looked to be brand-new. Painted white with green trim and shutters, the main house was a two-story affair with both upper and lower front porches. It appeared to be large enough to have at least fifteen rooms, and Eli doubted that any of them would ever be cold in the wintertime. Even from where he sat he could see four chimneys.

He rode on at a slow walk, paying close attention to the barn off to his right. The two-story building appeared to have more than a dozen stalls, with a wide hallway and open doors at either end. The shingle roof looked as if it had been nailed on this very day, and the large corral would no doubt stand for the next forty years. Several horses stood with their necks stretched over the top pole of the corral, staring at him.

The bunkhouse, a narrow brown building with two hitching rails, was off to his left, across the road and about forty yards from the corral. A boardwalk with a tin roof led from the bunkhouse to the cookshack, a clapboard building of medium size that stood north and west of the ranch hands' sleeping quarters. Eli suspected that the ranch cook lived in the building, and that he might have insisted on the twenty yards separating his sleeping quarters from the nightly bunkhouse noises. A rope attached to a large bell that was no doubt rung at mealtime hung from an arch in front of the doorway. Seeing no one at the corral, the bunkhouse, or the cookshack, he rode on at a slow walk.

The driveway ended at the ranch house yard, where Pilgrim pulled up at the hitching rail. A water well surrounded by a wooden curb stood between two large oaks, and at the moment, a middle-aged man of Mexican descent was drawing one bucket of water after another and pouring it into a V-shaped plank trough that reached all the way to the corral. The force of gravity carried the water down the slope very quickly, where it ran into a wooden tank large enough to accommodate several horses at a time. Eli continued to sit his saddle quietly, smiling broadly as he watched the man water a corral full of animals without ever leaving the well.

Finally, after giving the windlass one last series of cranks, the man poured the water in the trough and set the empty bucket on the curb. Only then did he realize that he had company. "Well, hello," he said. He closed the distance between the well and the hitching rail quickly, then added with no trace of a foreign accent, "I musta been thinking I had the world all to myself, didn't have the slightest idea nobody else was on the premises. Get down and tie up, then tell me if there's something I can do for you."

Offering his habitual toothy smile, Pilgrim slid from the saddle and tied his animal to the hitching rail. "I've just been sitting here admiring the way you water your stock without having to haul or tote the water," he said. "I don't recall ever seeing it done that way before."

The man chuckled. "Ain't nothing new about it," he said. "Everybody I know in these parts does it the same way."

Eli nodded. "Now that I've seen it, it makes all the sense in the world," he said. He added a chuckle of his own. "Could be that folks back where I came from just ain't all that smart."

"Aw, you're joshing me," the man said softly. He stood quietly for a moment, then spoke louder as he offered a handshake. "My name is Joe Garcia," he said. "I reckon I'm pretty much in charge here at the moment, and I don't recall ever seeing you before. Are you here on business?"

Pilgrim pumped the man's callused hand a few times, then released it. "My name is Eli Pilgrim," he said, "and I'm sure hoping to do some business. I'm a long, long way from home,

Mr. Garcia, and I'm out of work. I rode out here to apply for a job."

Garcia shook his head a few times. "I told you I was in charge," he said, "but I ain't quite that much in charge. I can't put nobody on the payroll. Big Step's the only man who can do that." He pointed to the house. "His office is just inside that door at the east end of the porch, and I saw him go in there about twenty minutes ago. All you gotta do is walk up there and knock."

"Thank you," Pilgrim said, stepping around the end of the hitching rail. "I'll do that."

His rap on the door a few moments later brought an immediate response. "Come on in!" a deep voice called from inside the room. Eli twisted the knob, and his entrance brought him face to face with the man called Big Step. Sitting behind an oaken desk piled high with paperwork, the man got to his feet instantly when he saw that his visitor was someone other than one of the ranch hands. "Come on in and make yourself at home," he said, pointing to a cane-bottom chair on the near side of the desk. "How do you do?"

"Thank you," Pilgrim said through his biggest smile of the day, "and I'm doing very well." Knowing that he was now looking at the tallest man he had ever seen, Eli gauged the ranch manager's height to be at least six eight, maybe even six ten. He also noticed that the man wore his belt very high on his waist, bringing to mind Hank Fry's words about him being all arms and legs. It was obvious without even seeing him walk that "Big Step" would be a very descriptive nickname.

The man was hatless at the moment, revealing a thick shock of brown hair. His eyes were also brown, as was his well-trimmed beard, and his complexion was the color of old leather. Though an exceptionally tall man, he did not have a skinny look, and Pilgrim gauged his weight to be at least two-fifty. Eli extended his right hand. "My name is Eli Pilgrim," he said.

"I'm Robert Benson," the man said, "but most folks just call me Big Step." He shook Eli's hand, then pointed to the chair again. "Have a seat there," he said, then moved behind the desk. He pulled up a padded stool for himself and sat down. "Now, Mr. Pilgrim," he said softly, "what can I do for you?"

"I'm a long way from home and I'm out of work," Eli answered. "I've been told that you hire a man occasionally."

Benson pursed his lips and audibly bounced his tongue off the roof of his mouth a few times, then began to shake his head slowly. "Occasionally is about the size of it, Mr. Pilgrim. The only men I've hired all year were drovers to take two herds of Herefords to Kansas. They just hired on for the drive, though, and they'll all be hitting the road again as soon as they get paid for that job." He was quiet for a few moments, then added, "Not many of our regular hands ever quit us out here, Eli. The truth is, we pay a little more money than most of the ranches in these parts, and I don't think I ever heard anybody complain about the grub."

Pilgrim chuckled, then offered the most disarming smile he could muster. "Sounds to me like a mighty good place to work, Mr. Benson. I don't suppose you could call me a ranch hand, but I grew up on a farm, and I certainly don't mind getting a little sweat on my brow."

Benson sat staring at his desk for a few moments, then pulled out a drawer. "I've got three different piles of applications in here already," he said. "I stack 'em up and mark 'em according to what I think of the applicant." He took a pad and a pencil from the drawer, then added, "Guess I'll be starting a new pile with you, though, 'cause you damn sure look like a man who could carry his end of the log."

Pilgrim continued to smile and said nothing.

Benson wet the lead tip of the pencil with his tongue, then put it to the pad. "Where are you staying right now, Mr. Pilgrim?" he asked.

"I rented a room at the Drover's Rest when I first got to

town. I haven't checked out yet, so I guess that's where I'm staying at the moment."

Benson wrote the information on the pad, then said, "You mentioned earlier that you were a long way from home. Where is home?"

"Southwestern Ohio," Eli answered, "about ten miles from Forestville. I left there during the first week of April."

Benson raised his eyebrows. "Hamilton County?" he asked loudly.

"Yes, sir. Hamilton County."

"Well, I'll be damned," Benson said, then dropped the pencil on the desk. "We lived just a little bit east of there ourselves, right on the southwestern tip of Brown County. We made the trip out here in covered wagons the year I turned thirteen." He leaned back on his stool and folded his arms. "Hamilton County," he repeated. "Well, I'll be damned." He was quiet for a few moments, then got to his feet and walked around the room. When he returned to his seat, he said, "It could be that I might have something for you about two weeks from now. I've got a line rider who's gonna be quitting on the Fourth of July. I reckon you could take over his job without having any experience. Nothing to it really, all you gotta do is try to keep Oxbow stock on Oxbow property."

Eli nodded. "Yes, sir," he said. "I believe I could catch on to that pretty quick."

"Like I was saying, there ain't really nothing to it," Benson said. "There'll be a man up there with you the first day or two, anyway. He'll make sure you get started off on the right foot." He placed his elbows on the desk and cradled his chin with his folded hands. "Now the line riding don't pay but thirty dollars a month, but you can save all of it, 'cause there ain't nothing up there to spend it on. The pay here at the Oxbow is actually thirty-eight fifty a month, so that's what you'll be making once you move into the bunkhouse with the regular hands."

"Thirty-eight fifty?" Eli asked. "That's good money."

Benson nodded. "It's quite a bit above the average pay scale for ranches, but I believe that's the main reason we've always been able to attract and hang on to good men. Like I said before, it's pretty rare for a man to walk away from a job at the Oxbow."

Deciding to quit talking while he was ahead, Eli pushed back his chair and got to his feet. "I guess I won't take up any more of your time, Mr. Benson. You just tell me when you want me to show up, and that's when I'll be here."

By now, Benson was already standing. "Try to be here about daybreak on July the fifth. Just tie up at the hitching rail in front of the cookshack. The light'll be burning in there a long time before then. I'll be down there myself to make sure you get started off right." He drummed his fingers on the edge of his desk a few times, then said, "Speaking of the cookshack, I think that's where you and I oughtta be headed right now. It's getting close to dinnertime." He led the way through the doorway with Pilgrim close on his heels.

A few minutes later, Eli saw what Benson had meant when he said nobody griped about Oxbow grub: beef, ham, potatoes, beans, and green leafy vegetables from the garden were all there for the choosing, along with corn bread, hot biscuits, and strong coffee. A large yellow pound cake rested on a platter in the middle of the table. After Benson mentioned the fact that Pilgrim was a soon-to-be member of the Oxbow crew, Eli shook hands with the cook, a small man with no hair who introduced himself as Baldy King. Appearing to be in his fifties, King poured coffee for both men, then ushered them onto a bench beside one of the long tables. "Both of you have a seat right there," he said. "If you eat fast, you can fill up before the rest of the bunch gets here."

"I believe I can handle that," Benson grunted, then began to fill his plate.

"Me, too," Pilgrim said, then followed his new boss's example.

As the cook had suggested, they ate their meal quickly,

and twenty minutes later, both men stood at the hitching rail beside Eli's buckskin. "That little horse you've got there is just about the right size for a cow pony," Benson said. "He'll catch on to what he's got to do in no time."

"I hope so," Eli said. "He's a whole lot stronger'n he looks, and he don't burn out right away, either."

Benson patted the buckskin on the neck. "The horse'll do just fine," he said, "and so will you." He offered a parting handshake. "I'll be expecting you on the fifth of July." He released Pilgrim's hand, then turned and began to walk toward the house.

"Mr. Benson!" Eli called after him.

Benson stopped in his tracks and turned around to face the newly hired young man.

"Over there at Cuero where the Guadalupe runs under the big bridge," Pilgrim said, "don't that property on the west bank belong to Oxbow?"

"Sure does," Benson answered, chuckling. "Wanna buy it?"

"Ain't got that kind of money," Eli answered. "I was just wondering if you'd mind if I pitch my tent and camp there while I'm waiting for the job to open up. Two weeks is a long time to stay cooped up in a hotel room, and besides, moving out of there would save me a little money."

Benson nodded. "Move outta there," he said. "Camp anywhere you want to on the west bank of the river. The only reason I didn't offer you a bed in the bunkhouse is 'cause I'd be setting a precedent, and I don't think I oughtta do that." He headed for his office and did not look back.

Moments later, Pilgrim mounted the buckskin and kicked the animal to a canter. He could save the price of a night's rent if he got to the Drover's Rest before checkout time.

At midafternoon, Eli informed the hotel clerk that he had made other arrangements for lodging, then rode on to the livery stable to retrieve the remainder of his belongings. When he told Hank Fry that he would be going on the Oxbow Ranch's payroll in two weeks, the liveryman chuckled happily. "I've been thinking about that all day," he said, pumping Eli's right hand several times. "I'm surprised to hear that they hired you right off, but I'm sure glad they did." He released the hand, and his face took on a serious look. "I was expecting 'em to give you the runaround, but I guess Big Step really does know a good man when he sees one."

"I don't know about that," Pilgrim said, "but I was sure glad to get the promise of a job. Big Step didn't say so, but it sounded to me like the main reason he hired me was because I was born and raised in southwestern Ohio. That's where the Benson family originally came from, you know."

Fry shook his head. "No," he answered, "I didn't know. Oliver Benson was here long before the rest of us showed up, and if he ever told anybody where he came from I sure never heard anything about it. I doubt that anybody ever asked him."

Eli dropped the buckskin's reins to the ground. "I'll be going to work out there on the fifth day of July," he said. "Till then, I'm gonna be living in my tent on the west bank of the river. I'll set it up under that big oak if it turns out that I've got the campground to myself. There's a clean, sandy-bottom spring right there close, you know."

Fry nodded. "I know," he said, "and I have no doubt that you'll sleep a lot cooler over there. Of course, the damn mosquitoes are gonna eat you up if you don't keep the flap closed on your tent, and that ain't easy to do in hot weather like this."

"I know," Eli agreed. "I've been through that before."

Fry smiled broadly, then spoke again: "Stop by one of the saloons and pick yourself up a quart of liquor. After you suck on that bottle a little while you won't give a shit how many of the thirsty little bloodsuckers show up." He was quiet for a moment, then added, "I'll pick up a bottle myself and visit you sometime around dark if you want me to. It sure wouldn't be the first time I ever sat around a campfire mixing my whiskey with muddy water from the Guadalupe."

"That sounds good to me, Hank," Pilgrim said. "I'll cook up a pot of something this afternoon, so we won't be drinking liquor on empty stomachs." He pointed down the hall, then changed the subject. "If you'll go catch up my mule, I'll get outta here right now."

A few minutes later, the two men smoothed out the pack-saddle and buckled it down on the pack animal's back. That done, Eli stepped into a stirrup and threw a leg over the saddle. He took up the slack in his mule's lead rope, then pointed his saddler's nose toward town, saying, "I'll be looking for you on the river sometime after sunset. You should be able to spot my tent before you ever leave the road." He kneed the nervous buckskin through the doorway, then guided the prancing animal up the street.

A few minutes later, he tied up in front of a grocery store on South Esplanade, about fifty yards before the street veered west toward the river bridge. When he stepped inside the building he was immediately impressed with the wide assortment of goods on display. Even from his position just inside the front door he could see that one aisle after another was stocked with everything from horse collars to tinned meat, and several large loaves of wheat bread and a few boxes of cookies rested on a table directly in front of him.

Noticing that Eli was paying close attention to the goods on the table, a middle-aged man walked from behind the counter. "My sister does the baking," he said. "She baked everything you see there last night, and my brother-in-law brought it all over here this morning." He nodded a few times, then added, "Yes, sir, that stuff is about as fresh as fresh ever gets."

Eli nodded, then pointed. "I'll take one loaf of bread, and two boxes of the oatmeal cookies," he said. "I think my horse and my mule like the cookies even more than I do."

"I'm sure they do," the storekeeper said. "I believe they like anything with sugar in it." He put the bread and the cookies in a small cardboard box, then asked, "Do you need anything else today?"

"You got summer sausage?" Pilgrim asked, "the kind with a lotta hot pepper ground up in it?"

"I certainly do," the man said. "A fellow delivered it to me from San Antonio last week, and to tell you the truth, it's hot as hell. The little sticks are priced at fifteen cents, and the bigger ones cost a quarter."

"A little stick'll be enough," Eli said. "I just want to chop it up in a pot of beans."

"It'll certainly season 'em all right," the man said. He led the way down the middle aisle, adding, "The wife and I put half a stick of it in a pot of Mexican beans just two nights ago. Talk about good eating." He selected a small roll of the dark brown meat from a shelf at the rear of the room, then dropped it into the box. "Anything else?" he asked.

Pilgrim nodded. "Yes, sir," he said. "I'll have six tins of fish, a pound of cheese, a dozen eggs, a bag of oatmeal, and a pound of coffee. I reckon I'm short one tin plate, a tin cup, and a middle-sized spoon, too. You got all that?"

"Absolutely," the storekeeper answered. He shuffled off to the opposite side of the room, then reappeared behind the counter a short while later. "I've got everything you ordered right here in this box," he said. "The bill comes to two dollars and thirty-three cents."

"Sounds reasonable to me," Eli said, counting out the money. He motioned to the dozens of overstocked shelves, adding, "I don't believe I ever saw a store that kept this much merchandise on hand before. You've got an awful lot of stuff in here."

The man chuckled softly, saying, "You're right about that, but the truth of the matter is that the people in this town don't leave us merchants no other choice. If they show up once or twice and we ain't got what they want, we've seen the last of 'em."

Eli chuckled. "Thank you," he said, "you explained that very well." He nodded a farewell to the storekeeper, then turned and walked through the doorway. At the hitching rail, he untied his animals and set the cardboard box in front of his saddle, then mounted the buckskin and led the mule out of the yard. Five minutes later, he crossed the bridge and rode down to the riverbank. As he had hoped, there were no other campers in sight.

He dismounted in the shade of the big oak, then set the box on the ground. He unburdened his animals and watered them from the spring's runoff, then led them farther up the riverbank and picketed them on forty-foot ropes, careful to stake them out in an area where he could see them at all times. Then, having already noticed that there was nothing anywhere near the spring that would burn, he began to walk around in search of kindling. After meandering for a hundred yards or more, he had gathered up an armload of deadwood that he believed would fuel his cookfire for several meals. He needed a fire for no other reason than to prepare his food, so a few sticks at a time would be all that was needed.

Returning to the spring, he chopped a small pile of shav-

ings off a dead limb with his hatchet, then kindled a fire between two flat rocks that had been placed there for that
purpose. He filled his pot half-full of water and poured in a
few handfuls of lima beans, then added the highly seasoned
sausage, which he had cut into bite-sized chunks with his
pocketknife. He added another stick of wood, then pushed the
pot over the flame. Supper would be ready about sundown.

When the thought of a cup of coffee entered into his mind,
he wiped the sweat from his brow and shook his head. He
would wait till the day cooled off before he put on the coffeepot, and he might not even do it then. The last thing he
wanted at the moment was something hot to drink, and since
Hank Fry had said that he was going to be drinking whiskey,
he most likely would not want coffee either. Eli put the
grounds back in his pack. He would simply ask the liveryman
if he wanted coffee, if not, the idea would keep till breakfast
time.

Making sure that he stayed beneath the canopy of the oak,
he spent the next several minutes smoothing out the levelest
place he could find to pitch his tent. While it was true that
the roosting birds would cover it with their droppings, there
was no help for it, for unless it remained in the shade all day,
sleeping inside it in this kind of weather would be next to
impossible.

After setting up the tent and digging a shallow trench
around it in case it rained, he moved his belongings inside.
He spread his bedroll between his saddle and his packsaddle,
then laid his Colt and his rifle on the bed and covered them
with a blanket. He left the cardboard box outside, making sure
he would remember to offer his visitor some fresh wheat
bread, a hunk of cheddar cheese, and some oatmeal cookies.

Leaving his pot to simmer on a bed of hot coals, he began
to dig around in his pack. He was hoping to have fish for
dinner tomorrow, and he had no doubt that the Guadalupe
would be productive if he was lucky enough to drop a fishing
line in the right place. Using a bent twenty-penny nail for a

weight, he tied a fifteen-foot length of stout twine to a fish-hook, then baited the hook with a ball of cheese. After repeating the process with two additional lines, he dropped all three into the river, tying each of them to a root or a bush growing along the bank. Once the lines had begun to lie on top of the water limply, assuring him that the weighted hooks had sunk to the bottom, he nodded, then walked back to his cookfire. He might even have fish for breakfast in the morning, he was thinking. All fishes were night feeders, and he expected to hear some splashing sounds before the night was over.

At sunset, he lighted his lantern and set it on a smooth rock beside the spring. He and his visitor would eat their supper there, then blow out the light, for he had no intention of sitting in its glow any longer than was necessary. He would also kick dirt over the remaining coals of the campfire, for the beans had been done for almost an hour now. He set the cardboard box on the rock beside the lantern, then dipped a cup of water out of the spring and sat down to await the liveryman's arrival.

He waited for half an hour. He first heard the sound of a horse's hooves striking the bridge, then was able to make out the shadowy figure of a rider in the fading twilight. He moved out of the lantern's glow quickly, stepping beneath the pitch-dark canopy of the tree to wait for the horseman to identify himself. Once the rider had crossed the bridge, he left the road on the north side and turned his animal's head toward the spring. Though Pilgrim had little doubt that he was looking at Hank Fry, he held his tongue.

The rider covered about half the distance between the road and the spring, then pulled up. "Hello, the light!" a familiar voice called loudly.

"Come on in, Hank!" Pilgrim answered. "Supper's still warm enough to eat." He walked back to the spring and stood waiting to welcome his newfound friend.

Fry rode in on a big gray gelding. "Hold this for me,"

he said, handing Eli a bottle of whiskey in a brown paper bag. He dismounted and loosened the cinch on his saddle, then led the gray to the far side of the tree and tied the reins to a low-hanging limb. Then he returned to the spring. "Got side-tracked more'n once trying to get through town," he said. "It just seemed like everybody I know was on the street and wanting to talk today." He sat down on the ground cross-legged, then added, "I reckon I oughtta call it time well-spent, though, 'cause I ran into a fellow in the liquor store who's been owing me ten dollars for nearly a year. He paid me half of it, too."

"Sounds like you caught him at the right time," Eli said. "I've always heard that a man who don't pay his bills on time or offer a mighty good excuse, is usually a deadbeat."

"Why, hell, yes, the man's a deadbeat," Fry said quickly. "He's been avoiding me like the plague since September, and every time I've accidentally run into him he's looked me right in the eye and claimed to be broke. The only reason he paid me five bucks tonight is 'cause I just happened to walk up to the bar while the bartender was giving him change for a twenty."

Pilgrim chuckled. "Like I was saying, you caught him at the right time." He laid the whiskey bottle on the ground and picked up the lantern, then pointed to what was left of the cookfire. "We need to fill our plates and get some hot food down before we start on that whiskey," he said. "I'll kick some dirt over that fire, then we can move away from the light to eat. I didn't make any coffee, so you'll have to wash your food down with springwater."

"Sounds fine to me," Fry said. "The only reason I didn't have supper before I got here was 'cause you'd already prom-ised to cook something. I don't guess I'll be able to eat it before I start drinking, though, 'cause I hit that bottle twice on my way over here." He got to his feet and followed Pil-grim to the fire.

They were soon sitting beside the spring, with their plates

on their knees. "Bygod, this is some mighty fine eating," Fry said after a few mouthfuls. "Where in the hell did you get this good wheat bread?"

Eli pointed over his shoulder with his thumb, answering, "Right up there on South Esplanade, no more'n a hundred yards from here."

Fry raised his eyebrows. "Shutland's Grocery?" he asked. "I've been knowing that old fart for several years. His name's Hank, too."

"Thanks," Eli said. "I'll call him by his name if I'm ever in there again, maybe that'll make him give me a discount."

"Keep on dreaming," Fry said with a chuckle. He cut off another chunk of bread with his pocketknife, then dropped a pile of the cheese that Eli had sliced up earlier on his plate. He put a slice of it in his mouth and began to chew. "Good cheese, too," he added. "Old Shutland keeps a whole lotta stuff in that store, but I never woulda thought he'd have any yellow cheddar on hand. No fresh-baked wheat bread either, for that matter."

"According to him, his sister baked it last night," Eli said. "There's a bunch of her oatmeal cookies in that box behind you, too. Just help yourself if you want some."

Fry shook his head emphatically. "No cookies for me," he said. "Don't ever offer me anything sweet when I'm drinking liquor. My sweet tooth leaves me about the time I hear the pop of a cork."

They finished their supper in silence for the most part, then Eli walked to the river's edge and washed their eating utensils. He put the lid on the blackened pot and pushed it aside, for it still contained enough beans and sausage for another meal. Then he blew out the lantern and seated himself a little farther up the slope. "Sitting around at night with a light burning gives me an uneasy feeling," he said. "I mean, you can't see a damn thing yourself, but anybody who takes a notion to is looking right at you."

"You're right," Fry said, scooting himself along the

ground till he was sitting beside Pilgrim. "Ain't no telling how many men have been killed while they were sitting in the glow of a lantern or a campfire. I don't really do any camping nowadays, but back when I did, I always made it a point to cook my food and put out my fire long before dark. You never know when some son of a bitch is gonna take a pot shot at you; kill you first, then see if you've got something he wants later."

"I think about stuff like that every time I set up camp nowadays," Eli said. "I'm a lot more cautious than I used to be."

"Keep it up," Fry said. "Make it a habit to stay out of the light till it becomes second nature to you." He stepped to the spring and dipped their cups half-full of water, then finished filling them with whiskey. He handed one to Eli, saying, "Take a few slugs of that; it'll knock the kinks outta your body and help you get a good night's sleep."

Pilgrim stirred its contents with a forefinger, then brought the cup to his lips. "I'm overdue for some good sleep," he said. "I don't know why, but here lately my eyes just pop open after four or five hours. Lying around on a bedroll waiting for daylight to break ain't easy, but what the hell else can you do at two o'clock in the morning?"

Fry was quiet for a few moments, then said, "What I do when it happens to me is just lie there figuring out what all I'm gonna do that day. Even if you ain't sleeping you're still resting, and you're gonna feel a whole lot better when you finally do get up."

They had been sitting in the darkness drinking and talking for two hours when Fry got to his feet and announced his decision to be on his way. "I reckon we've already discussed about everything either one of us knows," he said, "so I'm gonna call it a night. You be careful, now, and stop by the stable tomorrow if you feel like it." He walked to his horse and mounted, then rode away without another word.

Once the sound of the horse's hooves striking the wooden

bridge had faded, Pilgrim stepped away from the spring and relieved himself, then opened the flap on his tent and crawled inside. The night air was now cool enough to be comfortable, and the whiskey he had drunk had made his eyelids feel heavy. He pulled off his boots and stretched out on his bedroll, his Colt and his Henry close to hand. Using a folded blanket for a pillow, he turned from one side to the other a few times, then slept the night away.

The sun was already up when he crawled from the tent next morning, and even as he stood beside the big oak reliev-ing himself he knew that he had caught a fish while he slept: the bush that he had tied one of his lines to was swaying from one side to the other now, and bent much closer to the water. Eli lost no time in getting to the bush, where he pulled on the line till he felt resistance. Convinced that he had several pounds of good eating on the other end, he brought the line in hand over hand until he was looking a big channel catfish right in the eye.

The moment its head broke the water, Pilgrim had his fingers in its gills. He broke the line loose from the bush, then carried his catch up the slope. Deciding that it weighed five or six pounds, he laid it on a fallen log a short distance from the spring, then reached for his pocketknife. If he filleted and cooked it right now, he would be able to eat on it for the remainder of the day with no concern about spoilage. He dis-patched the fish with his knife, then walked back down to the riverbank and checked the other two lines. Nothing. The bait on neither of the hooks had been disturbed.

He ate catfish fillets and fried potatoes for breakfast an hour later, then repeated the process at dinnertime. He visited Hank Fry at the livery stable during the afternoon, then me-andered about the town for the remainder of the day. Half an hour before dark he returned to his camp and picketed his animals, then ate the last of his catch. Knowing that the last thing he wanted to see in the near future was another catfish, he returned the fishhooks and the fishing lines to his pack, then went to bed early. He slept soundly.

PILGRIM HAD been on the river for more than a week now and had spent almost all of that time at or near the west-bank campground. He had ridden his buckskin only once during the past several days, then only because he knew the animal needed the exercise. Nor would he saddle the horse tonight, for he knew that he needed to work some of the stiffness out of his own body. He had decided to walk to town and drink a few beers. About an hour before sunset, he moved his animals to new grass, then stepped out on the road and crossed the bridge at a fast clip.

By the time he reached the corner of Esplanade and Main, he had decided to do his drinking at the Elkhorn Saloon, for he saw no reason to walk another two blocks just for the sake of doing business at the Drover's Rest. As he elbowed his way through the doors of the popular watering hole, he was immediately recognized by Bob Strangelove, who stood behind the bar wearing a red-and-white checkered apron. "Come on in, Eli!" he called, almost shouting to be heard above the din of several men standing around the piano and singing "Home Sweet Home." He pointed to the stool directly across from him, then pecked on the bar with a forefinger. "Have a seat right here, your beer's gonna be on the house!" He broke into a broad smile as Pilgrim neared the bar, adding, "Now, I didn't mean that your beer is gonna be on the house all night long."

"Of course not," Eli said, returning the smile. He eased himself onto the stool, then pointed to several upside-down pitchers on a shelf behind the bartender. "Fill one of them up with beer," he said, "then give me a cold glass to drink it from. Is a whole pitcherful gonna be on the house?"

Strangelove bit his lower lip for a moment, then chuckled. "Hell, I guess it is," he said finally. "A pitcherful of beer is still a beer, ain't it?"

Eli nodded. "Of course," he said, his smile remaining constant.

Strangelove drew the foamy brew and set it on the bar, then selected a mug from a large ice chest off to his right. "Here you are, sir," he said. "This first pitcher's on me, but of course the next one's on you."

"Of course," Eli repeated, drawing the frosty mug to his lips.

When Strangelove moved down the bar to serve other drinkers, Eli spun around on his stool so that he faced the opposite direction. Sipping at his beer occasionally, he was looking the place over more closely than he had done the last time he was here. The men who had been standing around singing had by now returned to their table, and the noise level in the room had dropped considerably. A scrawny, red-haired man was sitting at the piano, striking the keys and looking around the room every so often, no doubt hoping someone would ask him to play. A wooden box sporting a hasp and a small padlock rested on top of the instrument, and the slit that had been cut into its lid suggested that anyone who requested a particular tune should be in a gratuitous frame of mind.

It was barely dark outside and there were already at least thirty men in the saloon, Eli was thinking. This was a Saturday night, and the saloon would probably be filled to its capacity in another hour or so. With liquid spirits flowing freely, and with each man having a favorite song, the piano player's kitty would no doubt begin to fill up rapidly. Pilgrim slid off his stool and walked to the edge of the dance floor to put in his own request. He stepped up on the riser, then leaned over the piano and spoke to the redhead. "Can you play a song called 'Greensleeves'?" he asked.

The man nodded, then offered a smile through broken, yellow teeth. "Any particular key you want it played in?" he asked.

Though the redhead's question contained no hint of sarcasm, Eli took it to imply that the song would pose no problem whatsoever for such a master musician as himself. As Pilgrim dropped a quarter in the box rather than the dime that he had originally intended, he realized that the few words spoken by the musician had served their purpose. The man was no spring chicken and had obviously been working at his trade long enough to learn how to get the most money out of it. "You choose the key," Eli answered, stepping down from the riser. "I don't know one note from another." The strains of the beautiful melody were already falling on his ears by the time he reached his barstool.

He sat sipping beer for the next hour, occasionally turning on his stool so that he had a better view of the three saloon women who were now busy dancing with one man after another. Between dances, the girls sat on a padded bench near the piano player's riser, so that every man in the house had ample chance to look them over. If a man wanted to dance, he simply walked over to the bench and paid a dime for the privilege. All of the girls were pretty, but a young brunette that appeared to weigh about a hundred pounds was enough to catch and hold the eye of any man. Pilgrim sat gazing at her till a bearded man paid his due and whisked her across the dance floor, then he turned his stool back around to face the bar.

He had just handed his empty beer pitcher to Strangelove and ordered a refill when a tall, blond-haired man with a six-gun on his hip and appearing to be in his mid-twenties sat down on the next stool. The man set his near-empty beer mug on the bar noisily. "I've been watching you sitting over here by yourself for about an hour," he said, "and I finally decided that you might like to have a little company." He extended his right hand, adding, "My name's Johnny Hook."

Pilgrim grasped the uncallused hand and pumped it several times. "I'm Eli Pilgrim."

When the new pitcher of beer was delivered, Eli laid a double eagle on the bar. Strangelove dropped the twenty-dollar coin in a metal box and counted out Pilgrim's change, then headed for the opposite end of the bar. Eli looked the money over, then shoved it into his pocket. As he poured his own beer, he noticed that Hook's mug was empty. He slid the pitcher toward the man's elbow. "It looks like you could use a refill," he said. "This stuff's pretty cold when it first comes outta the pipe. Just help yourself."

"Thanks," Hook said, reaching for the pitcher. "The next time I see you in here I might be able to return the favor, but right now I ain't got nothing but a bad headache."

"I've always heard that a cold beer'll either give you a headache or cure the one you've already got," Pilgrim said, lifting his own mug to his lips.

Hook nodded, then wiped the foam from his mouth with the back of his hand. "That's what I'm hoping for," he said. "I drank a whole lot of corn liquor last night, and I imagine that's where the headache came from." He took another sip and wiped his mouth again. "I don't remember ever seeing you around here before, you just passing through?"

"I was when I got here," Eli said, "but now I expect to be around for quite a while. I'll be going to work out at the Oxbow Ranch a few days from now."

Hook pursed his lips and blew enough air through his teeth to create a whistle that was barely audible. "You must know how to do something that they consider mighty valuable, then," he said. "I mean, a fellow coming into town and hiring on at the Oxbow right away is something that's unheard of. I've been trying to get on out there myself for more'n four years, but I'll bet you a million dollars that Big Step Benson don't even remember my name." He took a sip of his beer, then continued, "I think somebody's been telling him a lotta stuff about me that ain't so. Now, it is true that I got drunk and beat up the cook when I was working on Joe Sealy's spread, but I walked right up to the old man next morning and apologized for it. Hell, that oughtta count for something."

"I suppose so," Eli agreed. "Maybe the cook appreciated it, at least."

They sat at the bar drinking and talking till the pitcher was empty a second time, then Pilgrim slid off his stool. "I'm gonna call it a night, Johnny," he said. "I've enjoyed the conversation, and I hope you find a job soon."

Hook was also on his feet. "Are you already staying out at the Oxbow?" he asked.

Eli shook his head. "No such luck," he said. "Big Step said he couldn't offer me a bunk till after I go on the ranch payroll. I've got my tent set up in that campground on the west bank of the river. Stop by and visit with me tomorrow or the next day if you feel like it."

"I might do that," Hook said. Then he moved closer, speaking much softer now. "I couldn't help noticing that you had money when the bartender gave you change for that double eagle, so I was hoping you'd lend me three dollars till I see you again. A dollar of it'll buy my drinks for the rest of the night, and I'll use the other two bucks to take on that little brunette over yonder."

Eli began to shake his head emphatically. "My pa always told me not to lend money to strangers, and my ma told me not to lend money to anybody. I've never been a lender or a borrower, so I'm not in a lending mood tonight." He fished around in his pocket for a moment, then laid a dollar on the bar. "This is not a loan, Johnny, just consider it a gift." He smiled broadly, then chuckled, adding, "I don't mind buying a man a few beers, but there ain't no way in the hell that I'm gonna pay for his pussy, too."

Hook offered an understanding smile, then raked the

money off the bar and dropped it into his pocket. "I appreciate this a lot," he said. "I'll probably be seeing you over at the campground before you know it."

"You do that," Pilgrim said, then headed for the bat-wing doors. Once on the street, he headed for the river at a fast walk. He could see his way clearly enough, for the moon was now in its first-quarter phase. He met only one person on his way to the river: an elderly man wearing overalls and a wide-brimmed straw hat. The stoop-shouldered old-timer halted a few feet away and waited for Eli to close the distance. "You got a quarter you can spare, son?" he asked. "I'm about as shaky as a man ever gits, and I shore do need a drank." Without a word, Eli laid a quarter in the man's hand, then walked on.

Once at the campground, he crawled into his tent and pulled off his boots, then stretched out on his bedroll fully clothed. Using a folded blanket for a pillow, he lay for a while thinking about his mother and his brothers back in Ohio, then turned his thoughts to the Oxbow Ranch. Now that he was just a few days away from being an Oxbow employee, he was wondering what his new job was going to be like, and if he would still be working there a year from now. Big Step had said that very few of the hands ever left the ranch voluntarily, and Hank Fry had told Eli that it was a rare thing for Benson to send a man packing. After deciding that he would most likely be working on the ranch for several years to come, Pilgrim turned on his side and curled up his long legs, then drifted into a deep sleep.

Two hours later, he was wide awake. Having no idea what had awakened him, he lay still, his eyes and ears attuned to the slightest sound or movement. Had he heard something? Had something touched him? Careful not to move any other part of his body, he began to roll his eyes from side to side in order to see as much of his surroundings as possible. Though the light of the quarter moon did not actually shine through the thick canvas, it did create a very faint glow inside the tent.

Knowing that his eyes would eventually adjust to the dim lighting, Pilgrim continued to lie still. He had already decided that someone besides himself was on the scene, for he could see that the tent flap was now hanging at an unusual angle. Was someone inside the tent with him right now? After making an all-out effort to strain his eyes, he believed he could make out the figure of a man crouched in the corner on the left-hand side of the doorway, his hand resting on Pilgrim's saddle.

Eli continued to stare at the figure till he was convinced that he had read the situation correctly. And though his own Peacemaker was no more than an arm's length away, he believed that reaching for it might very well cost him his life. After all, the man he was looking at was also looking at him, and would no doubt start shooting if any sudden movement occurred. Since Pilgrim knew that the man could not see his face well enough to know whether his eyes were open or closed, he decided that playing the waiting game was the smart thing to do. He continued to lie still, his eyes never wavering from the shadowy figure in the corner.

When the intruder rose to his haunches and began to creep toward the bedroll a few moments later, Eli's mind began to race wildly. His body stiffened, rigid and ready to spring instantly. He had already decided that the man was going to try to kill him, and that he planned to do it with a knife. After all, any man who intended to use a gun would have no reason to sit around in the corner of the tent watching and waiting; he would have opened the flap and lined up his target as quickly as possible, then fired.

Suddenly Pilgrim saw the knife. As the man raised his right arm high above his shoulder, the fact that he held something in his hand became obvious. With the quickness of a cat, Eli grabbed the arm with his own left hand, and then the struggle for possession of the knife began. Although Pilgrim sensed very quickly that he himself was the stronger of the two men, he had no intention of making a game out of it. Using all of the strength he could muster, he managed to slowly muscle the man's knife arm away from his own face with his left hand, then hit him on the cheek with his right fist.

The sharp blow had its desired effect. As Eli felt the intruder's resistance begin to wane, he pried the man's knife hand open with such force that he heard at least one of the fingers break. Then, Pilgrim himself was in sole possession of the weapon. In one fluid motion, he dumped the man on his back and began to stab him about the upper portion of his body repeatedly. He drove the long-bladed knife home over and over again, ceasing only after there were no more signs of life.

Eli dropped the knife and picked up his Colt, then crawled out of the tent. He shoved the gun behind his waistband, then hobbled barefoot across the rocky terrain till he reached his lantern. After touching the wick with a burning match, he lowered the globe and drew his Colt, then headed back to the tent. He wanted a better look at the man who had just tried to kill him.

With the lantern in one hand and his Peacemaker in the other, he knelt beside the open flap and peeked inside. He could see that the intruder had not moved again, and he had little doubt that the man was dead. He crawled into the tent and stood up to his full height, then held the lantern above his head so that he was looking into the glassy eyes of the corpse. "Well, I'll be damned!" he said loudly. "Johnny Hook!"

10

FIVE MINUTES later, Pilgrim mounted the buckskin bareback and took the road to town. Hank Fry's livery stable was his immediate destination, for the liveryman had informed him earlier that he would be sleeping at the stable for the remainder of the week. "I've got an awful lot to do right now," Fry had said, "and the only way I'll be able to get an early start on it is to sleep with it. That way, I'll have it all staring me right in the face when I open my eyes every morning."

Eli put the buckskin to a canter and headed north on Esplanade. As he had expected, he saw no one on the street till he turned east on Main. There, standing under the dark shadow of a wooden awning, Pilgrim could make out what appeared to be the figures of two men and a woman. He rode on by.

"Hey, fellow, slow down there!" one of the men called after him. "I want to talk with you a minute."

Eli neither slowed down nor looked back. He held his pace and continued on down the street, for the last thing he wanted to do at the moment was talk to a stranger. He had looked at his watch while he had the lantern in the tent and knew that it was almost three o'clock in the morning. Any man who was out on the street hailing passing riders at that time of night was most likely up to no good.

He pulled up as he neared the dark stable, then approached

it at a walk. Since there was no light shining from any of the small windows, he had no idea where Fry was sleeping, but decided to try the front of the building first. He dismounted and tied the buckskin at the nearest hitching rail, then stepped over to the wall and rapped his knuckles against the pane of what he knew to be the office window. "I ain't asleep!" Hank Fry's voice bellowed from inside. "I don't mind getting out of bed either, but I hope to hell you're somebody wanting to pay me some money you owe! Just hold your horses!"

As the area where Eli was standing suddenly became bathed in the glow of light from the shadeless window, he stepped into the shadows at the front of the building. When the big door finally opened, Fry stood there with a lighted lantern in his hand. "Well, hello there, Eli," he said in a much softer tone of voice. "What in the hell brings you out at this time of the night?"

Pilgrim pointed to the office. "Can we go in there?" he asked.

"Sure," Fry said, leading the way. He took a seat on the cot he had been sleeping on, then pointed to a cane-bottom chair. "Have a seat there and tell me all about it," he said, a big smile on his face.

"I met a man up at the Elkhorn last night and bought him a few beers, Hank," Eli began. "When I decided to leave the saloon early, I even gave him a dollar to drink on for the rest of the night. Then the son of a bitch thanked me a few hours later by attacking me in my tent and trying to kill me. I managed to take his knife away from him and turn the tables. I killed him, and he's lying over there in my tent right now."

Fry raised his voice again. "You did the only thing you could do," he said. "The no-good bastard meant to kill you and rob you. Shit like that happens around here all the time. You've got to admit that I've cautioned you about it more'n once."

"Sure you have," Eli said, "and I didn't forget it. I'm the one who's still alive, ain't I?"

Fry ignored the question and asked one of his own. "You say you met this fellow up at the Elkhorn, did he happen to tell you what name he answers to?"

"Claimed his name was Johnny Hook."

Fry slapped both of his knees with his hands. "Why, hell, yes, his name was Johnny Hook," he said. "He wasn't the only bastard around here who would have knifed you in your sleep for a few bucks, but he was damn sure one of 'em."

Fry went on to explain that some folks around town called Johnny Hook "The Creeper" behind his back, for he had been accused of and even stood trial for a similar crime three years before: a sheepman had been murdered and robbed a few miles north of Cuero, and several times when he was drunk Hook had boasted about pulling off the caper to so many people that it eventually brought about an indictment by a grand jury.

A middle-aged man of Basque descent, the hardworking shepherd had been stabbed to death in his bedroll with a wide-bladed knife, and it was believed that the killer had made off with what amounted to half a year's pay for the man. The trial lasted two days but was finally dismissed for lack of evidence. By then all of the witnesses had recanted their stories out of fear of retaliation by Hook's friends.

Fry ended the narration by adding, "That son of a bitch intended to leave you lying the same way he left that sheep-herder, Eli."

"Sounds like it," Pilgrim agreed.

Fry had answered the door barefoot and in his underwear. Now he put on his pants and pulled on a shirt, then reached for his boots. "That area where you set up your tent is not in the town limits," he said, "so it's out of Marshal Teeter's jurisdiction. Do you know where Sheriff Beasley lives?"

Pilgrim shook his head. "No."

Fry continued to sit on his cot till he had pulled on his boots, then got to his feet. "The sheriff has to be told about this as soon as possible, so I'll ride out to his place and take care of it." He pointed to the small wood stove in the corner. "Get a fire going in that thing and make a pot of coffee while I'm gone. Beasley don't live far from here, so I shouldn't be gone more'n half an hour."

Pilgrim nodded and moved toward the stove, while Fry disappeared through the doorway. A few minutes later, Eli heard the liveryman ride away at a gallop.

Starting the fire was a simple task, for the kindling in the woodbox was all dry pine. After filling the coffeepot from the water bucket and using a soupspoon to measure in the grounds, Pilgrim pulled the pot over the stove's firebox and sat back down in the chair to wait for a cup of coffee. He needed it more right now than at any other time he could remember.

When the coffee came to a boil fifteen minutes later, he laced a cupful of the hot liquid with sugar, then returned to his chair. As he sat sipping from the tin cup he was wondering about Sheriff Beasley. He had no idea what kind of treatment to expect from the lawman, for he had never even seen him. Not even at a distance. The only person he had ever heard speak of Beasley was Bob Strangelove, and the outspoken saloon owner had made it plain enough that he neither liked nor trusted the man. Believing Strangelove to be a straight shooter, Eli suspected that there was at least one well-founded reason behind the man's lack of respect for the county's top elected official.

He had just poured his third cup of coffee when he heard the sound of running horses. He stepped through the open doorway just in time to see three riders dismount at the closest hitching rail. He immediately recognized Fry in the glow of light shining through the window, but the other two men were strangers to him. He stepped out to meet them, and as he got closer, he had no problem spotting the large badge pinned to Beasley's shirt. The man beside him appeared to be twenty years younger, and although Pilgrim could see no badge, he thought the man was probably the sheriff's deputy.

Beasley motioned to Pilgrim, then spoke to Fry. "Is that him?" he asked.

In answer to the lawman's question, the liveryman crooked his finger at Eli. "Step out here and meet the sheriff and his deputy, Mr. Pilgrim."

Moments later, Eli was shaking hands with Sheriff Rone Beasley, a graying six-footer who appeared to be about forty-five years old. The lawman pumped Pilgrim's hand a few times, then nodded toward the younger man. "This is my son Roy, who's also my deputy." The deputy shook Eli's hand with a firm grip.

"Now," the sheriff said to Pilgrim. "Hank tells me that you killed Johnny Hook tonight. Where's the body?"

"Lying in my tent," Eli answered. "The tent's in that campground on the west bank of the river."

"The one just north of the bridge?"

"Yes, sir."

"You got a coal-oil lantern over there?"

"Yes, sir."

"Well, I'd best be getting over there to look things over, and I'd appreciate it if you'd come along with me." He motioned to Fry. "Fact is, I don't think it would hurt nothing if you went along too, Hank. You know, so you can be a witness to everything."

"I wouldn't miss it for the world," the liveryman said. "Hook's comeuppance was long overdue."

The sheriff curled his upper lip and gave Fry a surly glance, then led the way to the hitching rail. The quartet rode through town at a slow trot, arriving at the campground ten minutes later. Pilgrim dismounted and lit the lantern, then handed it to the lawman and raised the tent flap. "Hook's lying right beside my bedroll, Sheriff. He sneaked into the tent and tried to kill me while I was sleeping, but he must have made at least a little bit of noise. Anyway, something woke me up in time to take the knife away and turn it on him."

Fry and Pilgrim continued to stand outside while the sheriff, with the lantern in his hand and followed by his son, crawled into the tent. The two men remained inside for several minutes speaking back and forth in muted tones, then crawled back outside. "Ain't never seen that much blood in one place in my life except at hog-killing time," the sheriff said to Pilgrim. "How many times did you stick him, anyhow?"

"I didn't count 'em, Sheriff," Eli answered. "I knew that he'd crawled into my tent intending to kill me in my sleep, so once I got my hands on his knife, I just kept hitting him with it till he stopped moving."

The sheriff set the lantern on the ground. "You damn sure kept hitting him, all right," he said. "Even with that poor lighting I counted more'n a dozen wounds, and one of 'em clipped his jugular vein just as clean as a whistle. For a man who claims to have been wielding a knife in total darkness, I'd say that you're a mighty good marksman, fellow."

Hank Fry spoke quickly. "What's that supposed to mean, Sheriff? Are you saying you don't believe it happened the way Mr. Pilgrim says it did?"

"What I'm saying is that, except for the blood, everything looks awful neat in that tent. I mean there ain't nothing in there that looks out of place or knocked over, nothing a-tall to indicate that a man might have been struggling for his life. Now, you tell me, Hank. Wouldn't a man kick over a few things and raise a little hell while somebody was cutting his gizzard out with a damn butcher knife?"

"I know Eli Pilgrim, Sheriff," was Fry's answer. "If he says Hook tried to kill him in his sleep, you can bet your bottom dollar that's exactly what happened."

"Maybe yes, maybe no," Beasley said. He took a plug of tobacco out of his pocket and bit off a chew. "I say this thing calls for a lot more investigation than we can carry out by lantern light. I'll be able to see better on up in the day, so I want everything in that tent left exactly like it is right now; don't want nobody else even going in there."

The liveryman picked up the lantern, saying, "You said yourself that you wanted me to witness everything, Sheriff, so that's exactly what I'm gonna do." He was inside the tent before Beasley could think of an answer. Two minutes later, he crawled back through the opening with Pilgrim's guns in his hands. "You just might need these things as soon as the word gets around," he said, handing the weapons to Eli. "Hook had a few friends and a bunch of relatives that were all cut from the same cloth he was."

Sheriff Beasley pointed to the guns. "Now, I don't know—"

"The man needs his guns, Sheriff," Fry interrupted. "You don't aim to deny him the means of self-defense, do you?"

The lawman stood scratching his chin for a moment, then spat a stream of tobacco juice on a rock. "I reckon not," he said finally. "But I don't want nothing else in that tent touched till after I finish my investigation."

Pilgrim buckled on his gun belt, then motioned toward the tent and spoke to Beasley. "I think I oughtta try to wash some of that blood off my pack and my saddle before it sets up too hard, Sheriff. It may be too late already."

Beasley shook his head. "Nothing doing, and I don't intend to talk about it no more. As for you, Mr. Pilgrim, I want you to leave this campground immediately and stay away from it till I say it's all right. Don't go running off so I have a hard time finding you, neither. You could do me and yourself both a favor by sticking close to the livery stable for the next few hours."

Eli stood quietly for a few moments, then pointed upriver. "Well, unless you intend to impound my pack mule, I think I'll take him up to Hank's stable, too." He headed for the grassy meadow to retrieve the animal.

"Go ahead!" the lawman called after him. "The mule ain't done nothing!"

The sheriff and his deputy stayed at the campground, while Pilgrim and the liveryman vacated the premises as ordered. Even as Fry and Pilgrim rode across the bridge, they could see father and son crawling into the tent with the lantern again. "I don't like the idea of them two hanging around over here by themselves," Fry said. "I mean, their so-called investigation could turn out just any old way they want it to."

"I know," Pilgrim said. "I don't like it either, but I sure don't know anything I can do about it."

They ate breakfast at the only restaurant in town that stayed open all night, then rode on to the livery stable. Eli turned his saddler and his mule into the corral, then joined the liveryman in the office. Seating himself on the edge of his cot, Fry let out an audible sigh. "I don't trust Sheriff Beasley any farther than I could throw the son of a bitch," he said.

"You're not the only man I've heard say that," Eli said, "but he's the law."

"Yep, he's the law."

Sitting in the cane-bottom chair shortly after daybreak, Eli insisted that Fry go on about his business, for he knew that the liveryman was behind with his work. "Go ahead and try to get something done, Hank," he said. "I'll be all right. I've got some thinking to do, anyhow."

Fry stood looking through the window. "Well, I guess I could put them new rims on old Seth Wilkerson's wheels this morning," he said. "His wagon's been parked out there for more'n a week now, and he's asked me about it twice already. I'm running out of excuses."

Pilgrim was busy kindling a fire. "Get on with your work," he said. "I'll have a pot of coffee on the stove in case you want a sip later on."

Fry nodded, then headed for the doorway. "Make yourself at home," he said over his shoulder.

Pilgrim slammed the door to the stove's firebox noisily. "If I get restless, I'll just look around back yonder till I find something to do," he said.

When the coffeepot came to a boil a few minutes later, Eli poured himself a cupful and dragged his chair over to the window, where he sat watching the traffic move along the busy street. Wagons and men on horseback were traveling in both directions, and although the day was young, people were already beginning to move up and down the sidewalks. More than a few of the walkers were women.

An hour later, Eli walked to the corral and stood watching the animals for a while. As he realized that his own saddler was the smallest horse in the enclosure, a smile appeared at one corner of his mouth. The little buckskin was most likely the toughest piece of horseflesh in the lot, he was thinking. He nodded at the thought, then began to look around for something to do. When he opened the door to the corn crib, he found a pile of harnesses that Fry had no doubt set aside for repair. He selected a bridle and a ball of leather string, then sat down in the doorway and went to work. Though the bridle had seen better days, it would soon be as good as new.

He was still repairing harnesses several hours later when he heard Hank Fry call his name. He laid the leather aside, then walked to the front of the building quickly. Beasley and his son stood just inside the doorway, along with two middle-aged men Eli had never seen before. Standing a few feet away, Fry had been ranting and raving at the sheriff loudly, but suddenly grew quiet as Pilgrim came into view.

The lawmen did not hesitate. Both father and son drew and cocked their weapons, then stepped forward. "You're under arrest, Eli Pilgrim!" the sheriff said loudly. "Put your hands behind you and turn around with your back to me!"

Unable to believe what he was hearing, Eli stood motionless for a moment, then slowly complied with the order. "What's the charge, Sheriff?" he asked.

"Murder and robbery," the sheriff answered. Then he spoke to his son: "Put the handcuffs on him, Roy."

When Pilgrim's hands had been cuffed behind his back, Beasley stepped forward and began to search his prisoner. He extracted a leather money pouch from Eli's pocket, then went about counting its contents. "A hundred and twenty dollars," he said finally, waving the purse around for the others to see. "Now it's a known fact that Johnny Hook had a hundred and twenty bucks on him when he went over to that campground, so I'd say that makes this man look mighty bad.

"And that's just part of it," the lawman continued. "Me and my son Roy have been from one end of this town to the other this morning, and we've talked to an awful lotta people. I've got four witnesses who'll swear that Johnny Hook had a hundred and twenty dollars in his pocket when he went over to that campground, and they all say that he left the Elkhorn Saloon about midnight with this man right here." He held the purse up again. "Now, I searched Johnny Hook's body before the undertaker took it away, and the man didn't have a dime on him. It's pretty obvious to me that his hundred and twenty bucks is right here in this pouch." He spun his prisoner around, poking him in the back with the barrel of his six-gun. "Now, let's get going, Pilgrim. Just keep right on walking till you cross Esplanade Street; the county jail's about halfway up the hill on West Main."

Eli obeyed the order without comment. The liveryman stood about twenty feet away looking as if he was going to cry. "Your guns are right here in the office and your animals are in the corral, Eli!" he said loudly. "I'll bring everything you left on the river over here, too. It'll all be right here when you need it."

As Pilgrim was leaving the barn, he came to a halt beside the liveryman and spoke softly, his words barely above a whisper. "I'll appreciate it if you'll see that Big Step Benson hears about this shit, Hank."

Fry answered just as softly. "I'll take the word to him myself," he said. "He'll know about it before the sun goes down."

Beasley prodded Pilgrim with his gun barrel. "Keep moving, there," he said. "You've done been told where to go. Keep off the sidewalk, now; I want you to walk right up the middle of the street."

With drawn guns, the sheriff and his deputy made a big show out of parading Pilgrim along the street. Several men and a few women stood on the boardwalks watching, and Eli supposed that word of his impending arrest had spread around the town long before the fact. When an old woman balled her fist and shouted that he was headed for a date with the hangman, he had little doubt that she knew he was charged with murder. Narrowing his vision to the street in front of him, he quickened his pace.

A few minutes later, he was ushered into the sheriff's office and introduced to his jailer, a tall, blond-haired man who appeared to weigh at least three hundred pounds. "This is Tiny Udall," the sheriff said, "and he'll be taking care of you till the circuit judge hears your case."

The deputy snickered, then added sarcastically, "He'll sure enough take care of you if you start giving him any shit."

The jailer unlocked the handcuffs and handed them to the sheriff, then took Pilgrim by the arm and led him across the room. "Take everything out of your pockets and lay it on the desk," he said.

As Eli complied with the order, the sheriff stepped forward and added the prisoner's money pouch to the pile. "He's got a hundred and twenty smackers in this purse, Tiny," he said. "The exact same amount that Johnny Hook had on him when the two of them left the Elkhorn Saloon together."

"We didn't leave the saloon together!" Pilgrim protested loudly.

The sheriff chuckled softly. "Well, now," he said, "that ain't exactly the way I heard it. Digger Hook and all three of the Horn brothers say otherwise. They say you and Johnny Hook walked through them bat-wing doors side by side, laughing and carrying on like old buddies. Now, that's eye-witnesses talking, Mr. Pilgrim, and their testimony ain't likely to help you none in a court of law."

"Damn liars!" Eli said loudly. "All of 'em!"

"We'll see," the sheriff said. "Things always get settled

in the courtroom." He disappeared through the doorway and was quickly followed by his deputy.

The jailer took his prisoner by the arm and led him to an iron cage. "This front cell is the best one I've got," he said. "You can see and hear everything that's going on up here, so you won't feel near as lonesome as you would way back yonder." He motioned for Eli to step inside, then locked the door behind him. "You'll be fed twice a day, Mr. Pilgrim, and the restaurant across the street caters the meals. You'll get a late breakfast at nine o'clock in the morning, and an early supper about four in the afternoon." He chuckled, then pointed to a stove in the corner of the office. "I fire that thing up and put on the coffeepot two or three times a day, and every prisoner who don't cuss me to my face gets offered a cup of coffee and a spoonful of sugar." He twirled a large ring of keys around on his forefinger a few times, then walked away. "Supper'll be along about two hours from now," he said as if talking to the wall.

Standing at his cell door, Eli watched the large man cross the room and take a seat in the oversized chair behind the desk. He pulled out a drawer and dropped the ring of keys inside, then lit up a cigar and blew a cloud of smoke toward the ceiling. He leaned back in the chair as far as he could, then yelled to his prisoner: "Are you claiming you didn't kill Johnny Hook, Pilgrim, or are you saying you done it in self-defense?"

"I'm saying Johnny Hook crawled into my tent last night and tried to kill me with a damn butcher knife," Eli answered. "I managed to turn the tables on him."

The jailer blew another cloud of smoke, then spoke again. "Well, even if you are lucky enough to beat the case in court, I still wouldn't want to be in your shoes. Ain't no doubt in my mind that you're gonna have to fight Digger Hook. He's about three or four years older than Johnny was, and he's been fighting his little brother's battles for years. I believe he'll come hunting you right away if the judge don't hang you or send you to prison. In fact, I'd bet my next paycheck on it.

"Even if you do manage to take him, the Horn brothers're gonna pick it up right where he left off. They're first cousins to the Hooks, and I'd say that any one of 'em is more dangerous than Digger. Clem, Clayton, and Booger are their names. Ain't none of 'em more'n twenty-five years old, and all three of 'em are mighty good gun hands.

"Better gun hands than either one of the Hooks, is what everybody says." He took a final drag from his cigar, then snuffed it out in a tin can. "Now, I don't mean to scare you by talking about all this stuff, but I thought somebody oughtta be telling you how things really are around this town." He got to his feet, then walked to the window and pulled the shade. "I don't have any idea how good you are with a six-gun, but if you don't know how to use one, you damn sure better learn in a hurry. I think you'll believe what I told you before this thing's over with, too."

"I believe you now," Eli said.

"Glad to hear that," the jailer said. "Ain't no reason for us to talk about it no more, then." He retrieved his hat from a peg on the wall, then pushed the front door open and stepped out onto the boardwalk.

11

At TEN o'clock the following morning, Big Step Benson jumped down from his buggy in front of the Dewitt County jail. He tied his horse at the hitching rail, then stepped up on the boardwalk. He stood for a moment adjusting the gun belt around his waist, then tested the door to find it locked. He was about to turn away when he spied Udall crossing the street hurriedly. "Good morning, Mr. Benson," the jailer said as he reached the tall rancher. "I've been over at the restaurant eating a big slice of Mrs. Green's apple pie." He unlocked the door and pushed it open, motioning for the rancher to enter. "Is there something I can do for you?"

"I think so," Benson said. He stepped inside the building, then turned to face Udall. "I want to hear the charge against Eli Pilgrim, then I want to talk with him."

"I think the sheriff is gonna charge him with murder," the jailer said. "Most likely murder in the first degree."

Benson spoke quickly, "Gonna charge him? Gonna charge him, you say? Are you telling me that Sheriff Beasley ain't got a warrant charging the man with a specific crime?"

"Oh, he's got a warrant, all right," the jailer answered. "I don't know exactly what it says, but he's got a warrant. Judge Tarrington gave it to him early this morning."

Big Step nodded, then motioned toward Pilgrim's cell. "I'd like to talk with the prisoner, now," he said.

"Don't see nothing wrong with that," the jailer said. He pointed to Benson's hip. "Of course, the rules say that you've gotta leave that six-gun up here."

Without a word, Benson handed over his Peacemaker. Udall took a moment to deposit the weapon in one of his desk drawers, then led the way down the hall. He unlocked Eli's cell and allowed Benson to step inside, then slammed the heavy door behind him. "Just sing out when you're ready to leave," he said. He twisted the big key in the lock noisily, then walked to the front of the building and seated himself behind his desk.

Big Step shook Eli's hand, then took a seat on the cot, motioning for Pilgrim to do likewise. "Sit down here and tell me the whole story," he said. "How in the hell did you manage to get yourself charged with first degree murder?"

"It wasn't first degree murder or any other kind of murder," Eli said, seating himself. "I acted in self-defense, Mr. Benson. Johnny Hook sneaked into my tent and tried to kill me while I was sleeping, and I took his knife away from him." Pilgrim related the entire story to the rancher during the next several minutes, including the fact that he had left the Elkhorn Saloon by himself, not in the company of Johnny Hook as Sheriff Beasley was claiming. "Hook said he was broke, and even asked me to lend him three dollars," Eli said as he ended his narration. "I gave him a dollar to drink on for the rest of the night, and I even told him it was a gift, not a loan. Johnny Hook or nobody else left that saloon with me. When I left there, he was ordering up another beer."

"So he comes over to your tent a few hours later and tries to kill you, huh?"

"That's exactly what he did," Eli answered. "He'd already seen that I had at least a few dollars on me, so I guess he decided to kill me, then rob me. Hank Fry says he stood trial for the same damn thing a few years ago."

Benson nodded, then sat scratching his bearded chin for a while. "Hank told me that Hook had a six-gun on him," he said finally. "Why do you think he didn't use it on you?"

Pilgrim shook his head. "The only reason I can figure, is because guns make noise," he said.

Benson chuckled, then got to his feet. "I think you've got it figured right, too," he said. He stood peeking through the bars for a moment, then spoke again. "I'm gonna see what I can do about getting you out of here, Eli. No telling where the sheriff is, but I don't feel like arguing with him nohow. I'll just go down and have a talk with Judge Tarrington. It could be that he'll let me sign your bail and take you on out to the ranch with me."

Pilgrim smiled for the first time that day. "I'd sure be grateful, Mr. Benson."

"Big Step," Benson corrected. "People just call me Big Step."

Eli nodded. "Big Step," he said.

Benson called to the jailer, and two minutes later he was out of the building.

Pilgrim stood staring between the bars for a few moments, then reseated himself on the cot. Though he had been down in the dumps ever since his arrest, the visit from the ranch manager had lifted his spirits somewhat. Could Big Step Benson really get him out of this cage? he asked himself. After thinking on the matter for a few moments, he decided that the answer was probably yes. After all, the Oxbow Ranch was known all over Texas and beyond, and it made sense that the boss of such a big operation would have a certain amount of influence locally.

After convincing himself that Benson was going to be able to put him back on the ground, he sat with his head in his hands trying to plan what he was going to do when he got out of jail. Yesterday and again this morning, the jailer had said that Eli would be smart to learn how to use a six-gun. "I already know how to use a six-gun," Pilgrim assured him.

Udall folded his arms across his ample midsection, then

smiled. "Can you use it well enough to outdraw Digger Hook and the Horn brothers?"

Eli shook his head. "Probably not," he said.

"Well, Mr. Benson acted like he was gonna get you outta jail, and like I told you yesterday, you damn sure better learn to put some speed on that six-gun. The Horn brothers and Digger Hook are all fast, and I'll guarantee you that they're gonna come hunting you." He headed back to his desk, adding over his shoulder, "I'm just telling you all this for your own good, you know. It's up to you whether you take my advice or not."

Pilgrim had decided to take the jailer's advice, all right, for the man had had nothing to gain by lying about Digger Hook and the Horn brothers. He had said that all four of them were good gunmen, and Eli was taking his words as gospel. He had also decided that he himself would be a fast gunman in the near future. He would soon be working on the Oxbow Ranch and would spend every minute of his free time practicing the fast draw.

There was no telling when he would get a chance to tell his story to a jury, but he had known of such cases dragging on for months or even years. If he got out of jail today he would get his animals and the rest of his belongings from the livery stable, then follow Big Step to the ranch. Then, once he had been given a work assignment, he would spend every minute of his free time practicing with his Peacemaker. Never in his life had he feared another human being, and he was not ready to start now. He would walk the streets of Cuero any old time he took a notion, for he intended to be the fastest gun in the county.

He was still sitting with his head in his hands an hour later, when he heard the jailer's keys rattling. "All right, Pilgrim," Udall said loudly, "time to go! Judge Tarrington says to cut you loose!"

Eli got to his feet instantly, then grabbed his hat and rushed through the open doorway. Big Step Benson was standing at the jailer's desk. "Judge Tarrington set your bail at five hundred dollars," the rancher said. "He didn't set a date for the trial, but he said he'd let us know when he did. I signed your bond, so you're free to go anywhere you want to." He smiled, then added, "I'd suggest that you hurry on out to the Oxbow. It's not nearly as easy for a man to get in trouble out there."

Pilgrim nodded. "My animals and the rest of my stuff are down at the livery stable. It'll take me about half an hour to round it all up, then I'll be on my way to the Oxbow. Uh . . . thank you for getting me out of that cage, Big Step. I believe I'd have gone crazy in there in a few days."

Benson shook his head and continued to smile. "I doubt that," he said. "They say people can adjust to anything, and in more ways than one, I'm living proof of that." He motioned to the jailer, who was now seated behind his desk, then spoke to Eli again: "Pick up your personal belongings from Tiny, then we'll ride on down to the stable. I'll wait for you to put your things together, then we'll head for the ranch. You can tie your animals to the tailgate, then ride in the buggy with me."

The jailer opened a drawer and laid out the odds and ends that Pilgrim had taken out of his pockets the day before, including his long-bladed pocketknife. Eli looked the items over, then raised his eyebrows and glanced at Udall. "It's all here but the leather pouch," he said. "I'll be needing my money, for sure."

The jailer shook his head, then lowered his eyes. "Sheriff Beasley told me to hang on to that, Mr. Pilgrim. He says it'll probably turn out to be the main piece of evidence at the trial. He says the prosecutor's gonna need to show the jury that hundred and twenty dollars in order to convince 'em that you killed Hook for his money."

Benson stepped forward and banged his fist against the desk. "Cough up this man's goddamn money, Tiny!" he said loudly. "If I have to make another trip down to Judge Tarrington's office, I'll certainly do it, and I'll say every damn thing I can think of to make you and the sheriff both look bad." Suddenly appearing to calm down a little, he shrugged, then pointed to Eli with his thumb. "Give the man his purse, then we'll both be on our way." He chuckled loudly, then added, "Tell the sheriff that if he still thinks the prosecutor needs to show the jury what a hundred and twenty dollars looks like on trial day, I'll be more than happy to lend him the money."

Udall stared at his desk for a few moments, then shrugged and pulled out a lower desk drawer. "I'm gonna go along with this, Mr. Benson," he said, his voice suddenly taking on a higher pitch, "but I'll certainly need you to sign something."

"Why should he have to sign anything?" Eli asked quickly. "I'm the man you took it from, and I'm willing to sign something saying you gave it back."

Udall shrugged and turned his palms upward, then slid a blank sheet of paper across the desk. He handed Pilgrim a fountain pen. "Just sign that bottom line," he said. "I'll fill the rest of it in later."

Standing as straight as a fence post with his arms folded across his chest, a smile played around one corner of Pilgrim's mouth. He shook his head curtly. "I've got plenty of time," he said, "and I don't mind waiting while you fill it out."

Udall sat motionless for a moment, then dated the paper and began to write. He slid the document back across the desk about two minutes later and handed the pen to Eli. "Be sure to sign your name on the very next line from where I quit writing, now," he said sarcastically. "That way, I won't have room to add anything to it after you leave."

Pilgrim nodded. "I'd already thought of that," he said. He signed the paper, then picked up his few belongings from the desk. He opened the pocketknife and held it up before the jailer's eyes. "If I'd been planning to kill Hook with a knife, why in the hell wouldn't I have used this one?" he asked.

"It's a whole lot sharper and easier to hide, and the blade is just about as long." When he got no answer, he continued, "Tell me, Tiny, why wouldn't I have used the damn pocket-knife?"

"I don't know," the jailer said. "It ain't never gonna be my damn job to know, either. I ain't gonna be on that jury."

"No," Eli said, "I'm sure you won't be." He pocketed the knife, then followed Benson out of the building.

Big Step backed the buggy away from the hitching rail, then turned it around and headed for the livery stable. As usual at this time of day, both sides of Main Street were crowded with men standing around the many hitching rails. Hardly a one of the bystanders failed to recognize Benson, and most of them either nodded a greeting or threw up their hands and waved.

As the buggy passed the Drover's Saloon, however, it became obvious that Eli himself was now being recognized. A handful of men stood around the front of the establishment leaning against the walls, and Pilgrim had no problem hearing one of them call his name. "You're gonna pay for this shit, Eli Pilgrim!" the man called loudly. "A damn judge might turn you loose, but that ain't gonna cut no ice with the rest of us!" Pilgrim kept his eyes straight ahead and said nothing.

The buggy wheels had barely made another turn when the same man singled out Big Step. "Your day's coming, too, big man!" he yelled. "We know that you bonded Pilgrim out of jail, and that you highfalutin Oxbow people have got plenty of money to buy off a jury for him. Your day's coming, too, Benson!"

Big Step brought the buggy to a halt instantly and stepped to the ground in one fluid motion. He handed the reins to Eli, then moved away from the buggy. He waved his hand at the crowd, motioning for them to scatter. "Everybody move away from the man with the big mouth!" he said loudly. "It sounds like he's got something to say to me!" The crowd dispersed quickly, leaving the man standing alone.

Taking on the well-known gunfighter's crouch, Benson leaned forward and spread his legs slightly apart, then spoke to the man who had been doing the talking: "You said my day was coming, punk, but you didn't say when. Do you feel like you're up to that job this morning?"

The man did not answer the question. Leery of moving a single muscle in haste, he stood with his eyes glued to the boardwalk for a long while, then slowly turned and walked into the saloon.

Benson stood in the street for quite some time after the man passed through the bat-wing doors, then finally climbed back up to the buggy seat and took the reins. He slapped the horse on the rump to get the vehicle in motion, then took one last look at the saloon. "One of them damned smart-alecky Horn brothers," he said. "All mouth and no ass."

"The Horn brothers, huh?" Pilgrim asked. "Do you know which one of 'em he is?"

"Don't know what his real name is," Benson answered. "His nickname is Booger, and I reckon folks've been calling him that for so long that he's actually started believing he is one. He's been known to shoot a few men in his time, but I ain't never heard of him killing anybody that was sober. Like I said, he's mostly mouth."

Eli nodded. "The jailer told me that Digger Hook and the Horn brothers would all be coming after me if I beat my case in court, so that's why I was asking the name of that man you just backed down."

"He's the youngest of the Horns, and I have no doubt that he'd have shown a little more nerve if his brothers had been around." He chuckled loudly. "To tell you the truth, if his brothers had been around, I might not have gotten off the buggy. They're a pretty brave bunch when they've got each other to lean on.

"Tiny told you right when he said they'd come after you if you won the case. Now, I don't intend to let you lose the case, so you can just get ready for 'em. You do know how to use a gun, don't you?"

"I know how to use any kind of weapon, Big Step, but nobody would ever call me fast with a six-gun. I've never had any reason to be."

"Well, you'd better get fast, 'cause you're damn sure gonna have trouble with that bunch after the trial. All it takes to get fast is a lot of practice, and I'll see that you have enough free time for that."

The Horn brothers' conversation died on its own as Benson circled the buggy in front of the livery stable and brought it to a halt. When the rancher and the liveryman were done exchanging greetings, Pilgrim jumped to the ground, saying, "I'm here to pick up my animals and the rest of my stuff, Hank. I'll tie the mule and the buckskin behind the buggy, then ride on out to the Oxbow with Big Step."

"I figured as much," the liveryman said. "Follow me and we'll get your stuff ready to go in short order. I got all of that blood off of your saddlebags and most of it off of the saddle and the packsaddle."

"I sure appreciate that, Hank," Pilgrim said. "Just add all that hard work to the bill, and I'm ready to pay up."

Fry kept walking and said over his shoulder, "The only thing you owe me for is your animals' keep. Three dollars and a half'll take care of it."

"Aw, shit, Hank. It's gotta come to at least twice that much."

Fry stopped in his tracks, then turned around and held out his hand. "Three bucks and a half," he said.

Pilgrim paid the man, then followed him on to the corral.

TRAILING BOTH of Pilgrim's animals, and with his saddle, saddlebags, and packsaddle riding in the back of the buggy, Big Step and Eli were on their way to the ranch less than an hour later. As they crossed the river bridge, Benson asked Eli to show him the exact place where he had pitched his tent, though he did not leave the road after Pilgrim pointed it out. "I've slept under that old tree plenty of times myself," the rancher said. "Me and one of my brothers used to spread our bedrolls under it, then run a trot line all the way across the river.

"The water's a whole lot deeper now, but back then it was shallow enough that you could walk out there and bait your hooks, then walk out again a coupla hours later and take off your catch. I don't think we ever went home a single time without enough catfish to feed everybody on the premises, either." He chuckled, then added, "We employed a lot of Mexicans back then, too, and I think most of them ate about three or four pounds apiece."

"I caught one the first night I was there that must have weighed five or six pounds," Eli said. "At least he was big enough that I ate three meals off of him."

Big Step had nothing else to say about catfish. In fact, he said nothing else about anything for the next hour or so. Long after they had left the main road and turned north toward the ranch, he finally spoke again. "When we get home, I'll set you up in the bunkhouse till I figure out exactly what I'm gonna do with you. I've about decided against putting you to riding line. The Horn brothers and Digger Hook might find out you're up there, and you'd be a mighty easy target for 'em in that flimsy shack."

"Whatever you want me to do, just say the word," Eli said.

Benson nodded, then drove the buggy on home without speaking again. When he arrived at the ranch house yard, he brought the horse to a halt and jumped to the ground, then pointed over Eli's shoulder. "Put the buggy in that shed beside the corn crib, then take out the horse and put his harness in the buggy. Rub him and your own animals down good and put 'em in them first three stalls, then give 'em two scoopfuls of oats and two blocks of hay apiece. Leave their stable doors open so they can water themselves from the trough in the corral. Meet me in the cookshack when you get done."

His very first order as an Oxbow hand, Eli was thinking. "Yessir," he said quickly, then picked up the reins. He was almost smiling as he drove the buggy to the shed. He finished his appointed job in less than half an hour, then headed for the cookshack. Joe Garcia was sitting at a table sipping coffee when Pilgrim entered the building.

"Hey, there, Eli!" the Mexican foreman said loudly. He got to his feet and met Pilgrim halfway to the door. "Big Step told me that he had hired you just a few minutes after I met you, and I've been looking forward to seeing you again." He shook Eli's hand with a firm grip. "Sit down and have a good cup of coffee."

Knowing that he was not about to go anywhere near that coffeepot unless he had been invited to do so by the cook, Pilgrim took a seat on the bench beside the foreman. Baldy King was there quickly with a cup of steaming coffee. "Glad to have you aboard, young man," he said. "It's like I told you the first time you were here: you're the best-looking fellow I've ever seen on these premises."

Eli offered the cook his best smile but said nothing. He had scarcely begun to sip his coffee when King returned to the table. "I've got some doughnuts here to tide you over till suppertime," he said. "Want some?"

Pilgrim smiled again. "I believe I do," he said. "Two or three of 'em, if you don't mind."

The cook laid a tin plate on the table and forked three doughnuts onto it. "Ain't no reason for me to mind," he said. "The Oxbow buys the flour and the sugar, and I've damn sure got to cook something. Doughnuts are about the easiest thing I can think of." Then he returned to his work at the oversized stove.

Pilgrim had just finished eating and was taking his last sip of coffee when Big Step opened the door. "I was looking for you down at the bunkhouse, Joe," he said to the foreman. He walked over to the table and took a seat. "Anyway, I see you and Eli have already run into each other. I want you to point him out a good bunk down there. We're not gonna worry about a permanent assignment for him yet, I want him to just stay close to headquarters for the next few days so he can get the feel of how a cattle ranch operates." He turned to the cook. "Maybe you could use a little help right here in the kitchen, Baldy."

"Oh, yes," the cook answered, chuckling loudly. "I can always use a good onion and potato peeler."

Big Step turned to his newly hired hand. "Would it bother you to work in the kitchen for a while, Eli?"

"No, sir," Pilgrim answered, "it won't bother me at all. Anyway, the kitchen's where the food is, ain't it?"

Big Step nodded. "You'll be getting first crack at it when you work in here, so you should be the best-fed man on the ranch. You won't have to worry about putting on a lot of weight, though, 'cause I don't intend to leave you in here long enough for you to get too fat to work."

Half an hour later, Joe Garcia pointed Pilgrim to a cot in the bunkhouse. "You've already met the fellow who'll be sleeping here in the corner with you," the foreman said. "He told me that he met you on the road the day you came out here looking for work, said he stopped the freight wagon and passed a few words with you. He's pretty much a utility man around here, never knows from one day to the next what his job's gonna be. I'd say he's about your own age."

Eli nodded. "I remember him," he said. "He didn't tell me his name, but he was friendly enough."

"His name is Cliff Cates," Garcia said, "and he's friendly by nature unless somebody gives him some shit. Whenever that happens, I've been told that he can get downright unfriendly in a mighty big hurry. Now, I ain't seen it myself, but people say he can palm that Peacemaker he wears on his hip quicker'n you can blink an eye. They say he hits what he shoots at, too."

Pilgrim smiled, then chuckled softly. "I guess I'd better remember not to rile him, then."

The foreman shook his head. "I reckon I made that sound a whole lot worse than it is. I expect you and Cliff to be big buddies right from the start." He pointed toward the front door. "I've got some other things to look after, so I'll be on my way. You just make yourself at home and introduce yourself to the hands as they come in. You'll hear the bell when supper's ready, then all you gotta do is follow the stampede." He walked through the doorway without looking back.

UNBEKNOWNST TO him, Pilgrim's kitchen assignment was going to last for only one day. After washing up the supper dishes and bringing in wood for the cook's breakfast fire, he headed for the bunkhouse and seated himself on his cot. Cliff Cates, who was already lying on his own bunk, pushed himself up on one elbow. "Did Big Step tell you that he's got a job for you and me tomorrow, Eli?" he asked.

Pilgrim shook his head. "Nope. I haven't seen him but once today, and he didn't say anything to me then."

Cates fluffed up his pillow and lay back down. "Well, he talked to me," he said. "He wants you and me to take one of them big wagons and head for the hills in the morning. Our job is gonna be to cut and haul enough firewood to keep the ranch fires burning for the next coupla years. Baldy'll fix us some lunches and a water jug." He pointed to the gun belt lying in a wooden box at the head of Pilgrim's cot. "Be sure to buckle on that Peacemaker before we leave tomorrow, part of my assignment is to teach you how to use it." He spread his blanket over his feet, then turned over and went to sleep.

Pilgrim lay awake for more than an hour trying to imagine what lay in store for him. Big Step had decided that Eli needed to become proficient with a six-gun, and according to Joe Garcia, he had chosen the right man to do the teaching. The lessons would no doubt begin tomorrow. Eli lay on his back thinking and staring into the darkness, already anxious to see his teacher in action. Just how good was Cliff Cates? he asked himself. Better than Digger Hook or the Horn brothers? The answer was most likely yes, he decided quickly. At least it appeared that Big Step Benson thought so. Eli eventually turned on his side and closed his eyes, knowing that sometime within the next several hours he would have the opportunity to watch an expert gunman at work.

The sun was just rising when the two men finished hitching up the team the following morning. Cates laid two cross-cut saws, two axes, a sledge, and several metal wedges in the bed of the wagon, then climbed to the seat. "Brought an extra saw in case we break one," he said, slapping the horses on their rumps with the reins. He pointed off to his left. "We'll cut the firewood about three miles to the west, then haul it back here before we split it. We'll get pine for the cookstoves, and hardwood for all the heaters and fireplaces." He raised one eyebrow. "You've done all this before, I guess."

Eli nodded. "Since I was about eight years old."

The ride to the timber took more than an hour, and little conversation passed between them. Cates seemed to be in deep thought most of the way. Finally, he pulled the team to a halt at the top of a small rise, about fifty yards from a stand of tall pines. They unhitched the horses and picketed them on good grass well away from the timber, then returned to the wagon.

Cates unbuckled his gun belt and laid it under the seat, then pointed to the trees. "We'll put six or eight of them pines on the ground, then saw 'em into blocks about eighteen inches long. Ain't no hurry about it, so I guess we oughtta figure on it taking us a coupla weeks to get the whole job done." He motioned to the Colt hanging on Eli's hip, adding, "We'll go to work on that thing right after dinner. The first thing I'm gonna have to do is trim that holster up so you can get your gun out of it." He picked up a saw and an ax, then headed for the trees. Pilgrim unbuckled his own gun belt and laid it in the wagon, then picked up the sledge and some wedges, and followed.

They spent the morning felling and sawing up trees, and by noon had at least two wagonloads of blocks on the ground. Cates had become more talkative as the morning wore on and had gradually revealed some of the details of his life. He was now twenty-three years old and had originally come from the Houston area, where his parents had owned and operated a grocery store. He had left home at the age of fifteen and had been on his own ever since.

He had been involved with three cattle drives to Kansas and had walked the streets of both Abilene and Dodge City. He had spent three years working on two different ranches in Dewitt County before coming to his present job. When Big Step Benson finally agreed to hire him, he had moved into the Oxbow bunkhouse the very same day. He had worked as a regular cowboy for the first few months but was now considered a utility man, a man who could be counted on to handle any job on the ranch.

They sat in the shade of a juniper to eat their lunches: three biscuits loaded with ham or pork sausage for each man, along with a large slice of dried apple pie. They ate dinner quietly, then when Cates had washed a final mouthful of food down with half a cup of water, he motioned toward the wagon. "If you'll bring your gun belt over here, I'll take a closer look at it. Offhand, I'd say that holster needs a little work with a sharp knife."

Eli walked to the wagon and returned with both men's gun belts. "I'll look yours over while you're looking at mine, if that's all right with you," he said. "Ain't much to this little holster of yours."

Cates squirted a stream of tobacco juice at a leafy bush, then chuckled softly. "There won't be much of yours left either when I get done with it," he said. "You don't need a big holster to carry a gun around, and you damn sure don't want a big one when you need to get a gun out of it in a hurry." He sat quietly for a few moments, then reached for his pocketknife and picked up Eli's gun belt. "If you don't mind, I'll trim this holster down a little. Having to drag a gun through this much leather to get it out takes time, and you ain't likely to have any of that to spare if you ever get into a gunfight." He pointed to his own gun belt, which Eli still held in his hands. "I'll make your holster about the same size as mine, while you file the front sight off your Colt."

Pilgrim reached for his Peacemaker. "You mean file it off completely?"

Cates nodded. "Down smooth with the barrel," he said. "You don't aim a six-gun before you fire it anyway, you just point it. The last thing in the world you want is that damned worthless sight hanging up on your holster, or maybe the leg of your pants." He pointed to his own gun belt again. "Take a look at my rig, there. The idea is to file off the sight and get rid of some unneeded leather so you can bring the barrel of your gun level with your target with as little effort as possible."

"I've already looked yours over," Eli said, reaching for his own Colt. "Just start whittling on my holster while I get rid of this sight." He retrieved a box of files from the wagon and seated himself on a nearby log. He chose the coarsest file for the first part of the job but would switch to one with finer ridges when he was almost done. He unloaded the Colt, then laid its barrel against the log and went to work. The job took less than twenty minutes.

He returned to Cates to find that the man had cut almost half of the holster away. Eli took a seat on the ground to watch the operation. Since the guns of both men were exactly alike, Cates was using his own Colt to measure what was left of the holster. He slid the weapon back into it now and held it away from him for a better look. "A little bit more," he said, then laid the weapon down and picked up the knife again. "You want a little more than a quarter inch of your cylinder to ride down inside the holster, that way it stays tight enough that it ain't all the time falling out.

"You want your trigger guard to begin at least half an inch above the place where the leather plays out, so you don't go bumping your trigger finger on it. You're gonna be moving as fast as you possibly can, and you want your forefinger inside that trigger guard the very instant your hand touches the holster. Of course, your thumb will automatically be on the hammer, and you'll cock the gun as you jerk it out of the holster." He shaved off one last sliver of leather, then dropped Eli's Colt into the holster and held it up to the light. "I think that about does it," he said. "Strap it on and show me how quick you can get that gun out of it."

Though he felt a little self-conscious about attempting a fast draw in front of a man he had already been told was an expert, Pilgrim buckled on the gun belt. He noticed instantly that the rig felt lighter. He eased the Colt up and down a few times to get the feel of where the holster played out and the trigger guard began, then ripped the gun from his hip and up to an imaginary target.

"Well, pardon me all to hell for thinking you were gonna be slow," Cates said, getting to his feet quickly. "That's pretty damn fast, Eli." Picking up a fist-sized piece of pine bark, he carried it about forty feet away and propped it up against a tall ragweed. "Make another fast draw and see if you can hit that," he said when he returned to Eli's side.

Pilgrim took the shells out of his pocket and loaded the cylinder, then emptied the holster at least as fast as he had the first time. When he fired from the hip, the target went sailing through the weed patch. "Damn!" Cates said loudly. "Don't ever let Big Step find out that teaching you to use a six-gun was all this easy. I want him to think I'm earning my money."

"You'll earn it, all right," Pilgrim said, holstering his Colt. "What I just did sure don't seem like anything special to me."

"It'll get to be something special," Cates said, " 'cause you're gonna be fast. Just stand there and watch me while I show you exactly how fast." He buckled his gun belt around his waist and tied the holster to his right leg with rawhide, then spread his legs slightly apart and leaned his body forward. "Notice the way my body is positioned, Eli. I'm not saying you have to copy my stance, but if you can feel comfortable with it, I believe you'd do well to do exactly that." He pointed to a small oak about fifteen yards away. "Keep your eye about three feet above the ground on that sapling over there."

Pilgrim never actually saw Cates's draw. There was only a blur, then the Colt was spitting flame. Three shots rang out so close together that they sounded almost like one, and Eli thought he saw three chunks of bark fly off the sapling. He stared at the ground for a while, shaking his head. "Bygod that's mighty hard to believe, Cliff," he said finally. "Were you saying you think I'm gonna get to be that fast?"

"At least," Cates answered, "and it won't take you near as long as you think, if you work at it. You've got it over most fellows who are just starting out, 'cause you already know how to hit what you shoot at. You've got the hands for a gun, and you've got the reflexes for a fast draw. If you practice two or three hours a day for the next two or three months, I expect you to be just as fast as me, maybe even faster."

Eli stood shaking his head. "Maybe even faster," he mimicked. "I find it hard to believe that me or anybody else is ever gonna get faster than you, Cliff. Hell, I was watching you real close, and I couldn't even follow your hand with my eyes."

"It won't always be that way, though," Cates said. "You just keep practicing two or three hours a day like I told you, and I'll guarantee you that things'll start looking a whole lot different to you before long. After you begin to put some good speed on your own draw, mine won't seem nowhere near as fast to you as it does right now."

"I'll take your word for that, Cliff," Eli said, "and I intend to practice even more than three hours a day every chance I get." A broad smile crept onto his face as he added, "Besides, I've always felt like I could do anything the next man could, and I just saw you do it with my own eyes. I won't quit till I can do it as fast as you did."

Cates patted him on his shoulder. "That's the spirit," he said, then began to pick up all the pieces of leather that he had carved from Pilgrim's holster. "There's plenty of material here to make you a tie-down. I'll cut it into strings and tie them all together, then we'll use it to tie your holster to your leg. Can't take a chance on it flying up when you need a fast draw. Things like that can get you killed."

Half an hour later, Pilgrim tied his holster to his right leg with the rawhide string his teacher had fashioned. "I can hitch up the team and load the wagon by myself, Eli," Cates said, "and I think you ought to spend that time drawing that Colt and dry-firing it. By that, I mean you should practice with an unloaded weapon most of the time. I've heard of lots of men

accidentally shooting themselves in the leg or the foot practicing with a loaded weapon, and I've seen it happen myself
once. I'd like to see you make it a habit to always practice
with an unloaded gun except when you actually intend to fire
it." That said, Cates picked up the bridles and headed for the
horses.

Pilgrim unloaded his Colt and dropped the shells into his
pocket, then began to draw the weapon as fast as he could,
always bringing the barrel up to bear on the same sapling
Cates had shot into earlier. By the time the wagon was loaded,
he had drawn and dry-fired the Colt no less than a hundred
times, and, just as Cates had predicted beforehand, both the
heel of his right hand and his thumb were blistered. "The
blisters'll turn into calluses after a few days," Cliff had said,
"and they'll probably start aggravating you a little. I even
remember having to use sandpaper on mine a few times."

In answer to Cates's call, Pilgrim finally walked to the
wagon. He unbuckled his gun belt and placed it underneath
the seat, then climbed aboard. "That hand sore yet?" Cates
asked, slapping the horses with the reins.

Eli held up his right hand. "I've got the blisters you promised me."

Cates nodded and said nothing.

Neither man spoke again until they had traveled at least
a mile, then Cates broke the silence. "They haven't set a date
for your trial yet, have they, Eli?"

"Nope. The sheriff told me that it would take place on
whatever date the judge and the prosecutor could agree on.
He said they'd let me know as soon as they made a decision."
He was quiet for a moment, then added, "Big Step said he
was gonna get me a lawyer."

Cates chuckled. "He'll do it, too; and I'll bet he won't
have no problem finding one smarter'n that prosecutor."

"I hope not," Eli said, "I'm probably gonna need all the
help I can get." He rode along thoughtful for several minutes,

then turned to Cates with a question: "Do you know Digger Hook and the Horn brothers, Cliff?"

Cates pursed his lips and rolled his eyes skyward. "I don't guess you could say that I know 'em well, but I've talked to all of 'em at least once during the past few years. I'd say that Digger's gonna turn out to be the biggest problem you have. I don't believe he's as good a gunman as either one of the Horn brothers, but he's certainly the type who'll stir up as much shit as he can. He might not even call your hand himself, but I believe he'll egg them on till they do it." He bit off a mouthful of chewing tobacco, then added, "It's my job to see that you're ready for 'em if that happens.

"Digger's about thirty years old, and about as tall as you are. His real name is Walter; people just call him Digger because he worked for the undertaker for several years. Now, the Horn brothers all look alike to me. Clem's the oldest, then Clayton, then Booger. They're all in their early twenties, and they're all blonds with ruddy complexions. Every one of 'em stands about five ten and weighs about one eighty. I've got a strong feeling that Booger would be the best gunman of the bunch."

"Thank you, Cliff. If I ever see 'em, I guess I'll at least know 'em now."

"You'll see 'em all right. You mark my words."

Twenty minutes later, they threw off the load of blocks at the wood yard, halfway between the main house and the bunkhouse.

13

WHEN PILGRIM was notified on November 1 that his trial was scheduled for the following week, he and Big Step paid a visit to the defense lawyer Benson had hired more than a month earlier. "I've already looked into this thing pretty good," Attorney Will Barney assured the men. "The prosecutor's case ain't worth a hill of beans, so I don't expect the trial to last more'n two or three hours."

"That sounds good to me," Pilgrim said.

"Me, too," Big Step said. Chuckling, he added, "Does that mean we're gonna get a discount on your services?"

Barney, a balding man of average height who appeared to be about forty years old, got to his feet and walked across the room. "Nope," he said. He stood looking through the window for a while, then turned to Eli. "You say you killed Johnny Hook with the same knife he was trying to do you in with? That you just managed to take it away and use it on him?"

"Yes, sir. That's what I'm saying, and that's exactly what happened."

"I believe you," the attorney said, reseating himself behind his desk. "Why do you think Sheriff Beasley didn't?"

"I don't know," Eli answered, "but I certainly told him the truth."

The lawyer was on his feet again, his right hand extended. "Of course you did," he said. "We'll tell him again in the courtroom, then let him try to explain to the jury why he don't believe it." He shook hands with both men, then added, "Ed Poole is gonna prosecute the case, and he ain't much smarter'n Sheriff Beasley. It's like I said before, he ain't got no witnesses, so he ain't got no case. We should be outta there before they ring the dinner bell at Sadie's Restaurant."

"Let's hope so," Benson said. As he and Eli walked through the doorway and out into the street, the attorney walked onto the small porch and called after them: "If you two'll meet me here at eight o'clock Monday morning, we'll all walk over to the courthouse together! You just tell that jury the truth, Mr. Pilgrim, and leave the rest of it to me!"

Eli looked at the man over his shoulder, then waved good-bye. "Yes, sir!" he said loudly. "Nobody's gonna hear anything but the truth from me."

The two men climbed aboard Big Step's buggy, then headed home. Pilgrim felt much more confident about the outcome of his trial since meeting with Will Barney, for the man had literally done everything except promise an acquittal. And though his eyes had more than once come to rest on the tied-down Colt hanging on Eli's right leg, the counselor had failed to mention it.

Pilgrim strapped on the Peacemaker when he put on his pants, nowadays. He had practiced several hours a day since Cliff Cates had first begun to give him instructions back in the summer. More than a month ago, Cates had proclaimed Eli the fastest gun in the county.

The two men had spent an hour working out down by the creek when Cates finally holstered his own weapon and stood shaking his head. "That makes ten times we've drawn against each other," he said, "and the best I can tell, you came out a little bit ahead of me every time." He reloaded his gun, then stood for a few moments with his arms folded. "It's a simple matter of the student outdoing the teacher, Eli. It happens all the time." He shook his head again. "You've got the fastest gun hand I've ever seen, and you can rest assured that there ain't nobody around here gonna match it. Probably nowhere else, either. No reason for you to worry about your marksmanship, either. Anybody who can knock hickory nuts off a fence post like you just did, ain't gonna have no problem hitting a man.

"It's time now for you to start wearing that gun on your hip all the time, just like I do. You ain't got no way of knowing exactly when you're gonna need it, and besides, it takes a little while for your body to get used to the extra weight on that right side. Strap it on as soon as you get up every morning, and you'll be surprised how quick you'll get used to it."

Eli had learned the truth of those words soon enough. He had been wearing the gun during all of his waking hours for only a matter of weeks, but even now he seldom noticed it. Big Step had noticed it, however, and had commented on it. "Cliff told me all about the progress you made on your gun handling, Eli," he said. "He says you've got the quickest hand he's ever seen. Now, bygod if it's any faster than his own, it certainly must be something to see."

"Aw, that's what he told me, too," Eli said, "but I figured he was just trying to make me feel good."

Benson shook his head. "Cliff ain't the type to shoot you no shit, Eli. If he said you were faster'n him, you can count on it. He also says you can hit what you shoot at, and that makes all the difference in the world. Just keep practicing a little bit every day so you can stay loose. I've got a feeling you're gonna need some of that speed before long."

Eli did not see Cliff Cates during the afternoon or at suppertime, and had already retired for the night when Cates seated himself on his own bunk. He took off a boot and dropped it to the floor noisily, saying, "I don't know if the cook just don't like me or was just too tired to heat it up, but that stew he just served me was so damn cold that the grease was already standing on top of it."

Eli chuckled. "I guess Baldy figured you could stir it up," he said.

"Of course I stirred it up," Cates said, "but the damn stuff needed a fire under it. Who in the hell likes cold stew?"

Pilgrim chuckled again. "I sort of developed a taste for it on my way out here from Ohio. After weighing it against the time and effort it takes to hunt up deadwood and build a fire, I remember eating cold stew for breakfast and hitting the road without my morning coffee plenty of times."

Cates dropped his other boot to the floor and stared at Eli for a moment. "Seems like you're having fun hearing about how that cook treated me." Without waiting for another comment from Pilgrim, he asked, "Did you get to see your lawyer today?"

"Yep. I liked what he had to say, too."

Cates nodded. "I've been knowing Will Barney ever since the first year I was in this area," he said. "I had a fight with a fellow in Dressler's Billiard Parlor and messed his head up a little. The sheriff brought charges against me, and Barney took my case even though he knew I didn't have any money. He said getting to make an ass out of Ed Poole in a courtroom was all the pay he needed. He did it, too. Barney didn't have a single witness, but he convinced the jury that I was only fighting in self-defense; that the other fellow started the fight. They acquitted me without ever leaving the jury box."

"I hope I can be that lucky," Eli said.

"I don't think there was any luck involved in my case," Cates said, fluffing up his pillow. "Will Barney is just that damn good." He pulled his blanket up under his chin and turned over, bringing the conversation to a halt.

14

ELI'S TRIAL began at a quarter past nine on Monday morning. Fifty-five-year-old Dewitt County Prosecutor Ed Poole led off the proceedings by announcing that the charge was first degree murder, then went into a hypothetical version of Pilgrim's actions the night of the heinous deed:

"It is obvious to me that the defendant lured Johnny Hook into his tent on the pretext of giving him a place to sleep for the night," he said to the jury, "when his actual intent was to murder him and steal his money. And he carried out that intention with a twelve-inch butcher knife." He picked up a knife from a nearby table and waved it back and forth before the eyes of the panel. "This, gentlemen, is the murder weapon, and you can easily see that it's big enough to get the job done. Now, how the defendant came by this oversized knife is unknown to us, but I think you'll all have to agree that it's a tad larger than the average camper carries around on the back of a pack mule. All the campers I've ever known used a small pocketknife to cut up their food." He walked back and forth in front of the jury box a couple times, then spoke to Judge Tarrington. "Your Honor, I'd like to call Digger Hook to the witness stand."

The judge nodded. "Very well," he said.

Digger Hook took the stand and swore that he and the three Horn brothers had all been in the Elkhorn Saloon with

Johnny Hook the night he died. "Johnny bought drinks for the four of us all night long," Digger testified, "and there at the last, he sat down at the bar with Eli Pilgrim and started buying drinks for him, too."

The prosecutor nodded and waited a few moments for the witness's words to soak in on the jury, then asked another question. "Did it appear to you that Johnny Hook was buying Pilgrim's drinks because Pilgrim was broke?"

"Yes," the witness answered. "That's the only thing we could figure, 'cause every time they ordered up, it was always Johnny who forked over the money for the drinks."

Poole nodded, then continued, "Do you have any idea how much money Johnny Hook had on his person the night he was murdered?"

"Yes. He had a hundred and twenty-five dollars in his pocket when we first started out, so I guess he musta had about a hundred and twenty left by the time the night was over."

"I see," Poole said. "And when the Elkhorn closed, did you and the Horn brothers leave the saloon with Johnny Hook?"

"Oh, no," the witness answered. "Johnny left nearly an hour before the place closed." He pointed to the defendant, adding, "He left with Eli Pilgrim, there."

"Are you saying that Johnny Hook and Eli Pilgrim walked through the front door of the Elkhorn together?"

The witness nodded. "Walked through them bat-wing doors side by side." he said.

Poole dismissed Digger Hook as a witness, then called Sheriff Rone Beasley to the stand. The lawman testified that other than having an excessive amount of blood on the floor, the tent Johnny Hook died in had been neat and orderly, quite unlike a place where a life-and-death struggle had just oc-curred. "You've got to figure that a man's gonna fight for his life, and nothing in that tent had even been kicked over."

"Thank you, Sheriff," Poole said. "Now, I know that you

heard the witness who appeared earlier testify that Johnny Hook had about a hundred twenty dollars on him when he left the Elkhorn Saloon. Now, tell the jury, sir, when you arrested the defendant and went through his pockets, did you find any money?"

"Yes, sir. Mister Pilgrim had a hundred twenty dollars on him."

"A hundred twenty dollars!" Poole repeated loudly. "And when you went through the pockets of the dead man, how much money did you find?"

"None," the lawman answered. "Johnny Hook had no money at all on him."

"No money at all," Poole repeated, then added, "That'll be all, Sheriff. Thank you for your testimony."

The prosecutor next called on Deputy Sheriff Roy Beasley, who echoed his father's testimony word for word. Once the deputy had been dismissed, Poole called the Horn brothers to the stand one right after another. All three men agreed with Digger Hooks's earlier testimony down to the last detail. When the last of the Horns was dismissed, Poole turned and addressed the judge. "Your Honor, we have established both motive and opportunity here, and Sheriff Beasley and his deputy have supplied us with the gruesome details. It's obvious to me, as I'm quite sure it is to the jury, that the defendant, Eli Pilgrim, is guilty of murder in the first degree. The prosecution hereby rests its case."

Judge Tarrington nodded. "Very well," he said, then immediately turned the proceedings over to the defense.

Defense attorney Will Barney had not once objected to the prosecutor's line of questioning, nor had he chosen to cross-examine any of the man's witnesses. Barney now stepped in front of the jury box and offered a jolly greeting to the panel, calling many of them by name. Then he turned his attention to the judge. "Your Honor," he began, "I've got to admit that I feel a little bit foolish at the moment because, considering the reputations of the witnesses the prosecutor has just presented, it appears to me that he don't even have a case. Nonetheless, I'd like to call the defendant to the stand and let him tell us what really happened on the night Johnny Hook met his maker."

"Very well," the judge said, then motioned to Eli. "Please take the stand, Mr. Pilgrim."

Eli spent the next several minutes relating the story exactly as it happened, starting with the moment he arrived at the Elkhorn Saloon on that fateful night. He carried the jury right on through the struggle for the butcher knife inside the tent, then admitted stabbing Johnny Hook an indeterminate number of times. "I was afraid for my own life," he said, winding up the long narration, "so I kept hitting him with the knife till he stopped moving."

"Did you know the man's identity at that time?"

"No, sir. I didn't know who he was till it was all over, not till after I brought the lantern into the tent."

Barney nodded to the defendant, then to the jury. "Now, tell, me, Mr. Pilgrim," he continued, "is it true that you had the dead man's money on you when the sheriff searched your pockets?"

"No. I had my own money, and it came to a hundred twenty dollars. Johnny Hook didn't have any money at all, at least that's what he told me when he asked me to lend him some."

Barney nodded. "And did you, in fact, lend him some money, Mr. Pilgrim?"

"No. I told him that I was neither a borrower nor a lender, but that I would give him a dollar to drink on for the rest of the night. I had already drunk as much beer as I wanted, so I just gave him the dollar and left."

"I see," Barney said, checking to make sure he had the panel's attention. "Let me get this straight," he said. "I mean, let's make sure the jury hears it straight. Are you telling us that you left that saloon all by yourself, that when you walked outta there Hook was still sitting at the bar drinking?"

"Yes, sir. That's exactly what I'm saying."

Barney nodded to the jury, catching each individual man's eye as he did so. Then he turned back to Eli. "Can you tell us approximately what time of night you left the Elkhorn, Mr. Pilgrim?"

"I can tell you exactly what time it was, because I looked at my watch. It was ten minutes to eleven."

"Ten minutes to eleven," the lawyer repeated to the jury. Then he dismissed his client. "That'll be all, Mr. Pilgrim, and we appreciate your testimony." When the prosecutor made no attempt to cross-examine him, Eli stepped down from the witness stand.

Barney stepped to his table and spoke with an assistant for a moment, then addressed the judge again. "Your Honor, I have a witness out in the hall that I'd like to call at this time."

"Very well," Tarrington said.

When the lawyer's assistant returned from the hall he had an old man in tow. "Tell us your name, sir," Barney said to the old-timer after he had been sworn in.

"My name is Owen Aspey," the man answered with a gravelly voice.

The lawyer pointed to his client seated across the room. "Tell us, Mr. Aspey, have you ever seen that man before?"

"Yes, sir. I saw him the night that killing happened over at the campground."

"I see. Can you tell us what time of night that was?"

"Yes, sir. It was about an hour before the liquor store closed at midnight." He pointed to Pilgrim. "I asked that man right there for a quarter, and he gave it to me. Putting that quarter with what little money I already had gave me enough to get me a bottle of whiskey before the store closed."

"I see," Barney said. "Can you tell us who was with the man when he gave you the quarter?"

Aspey sat shaking his head for a moment, then said, "Weren't nobody with him. He was walking down the street by himself when I stopped him and hit him up for the money. He didn't say nothing, just laid the quarter in my hand and kept on walking toward the campground.''

Barney nodded to the jury, then turned back to the witness. "Thank you, Mr. Aspey. I have no further questions.''

When the prosecutor once again made no attempt at cross-examination, Barney dismissed Aspey and asked the judge's permission to bring in another witness from the hall. Two minutes later, Bob Strangelove, a man known to every member of the jury, put his hand on the bible, then took a seat on the witness stand. "You're the owner and occasional bartender at the Elkhorn Saloon, Mr. Strangelove?" Will Barney asked.

"That's correct.''

"I've been told that you know the defendant personally.''

Strangelove nodded. "That's also correct.''

The attorney nodded, then walked around in circles for a few moments. "Tell me, Mr. Strangelove, were you on duty in your saloon the night Johnny Hook was killed over at the campground?''

"Yes.''

"Did you happen to see the defendant in your place of business that night?''

"I sure did. I talked with him quite a while, even drew a few beers for him.''

"Did he have the money to pay for those beers, Mr. Strangelove?''

"Of course he did. He broke a double eagle when he paid for his pitcher.''

Barney turned to face the jury. "Broke a double eagle!'' he repeated loudly.

The attorney walked back and forth in front of the witness stand thoughtfully for a few moments, then continued. "Now, I know that you didn't hear it out there in the hall where you've been, Mr. Strangelove, but Digger Hook and the Horn brothers, namely Clem, Clayton, and Booger, all testified earlier that Mr. Pilgrim was broke; that it was Johnny Hook who had all the money, and that it was him, not Pilgrim, who was buying all the drinks. All four of them claim they saw Mr. Pilgrim and Johnny Hook leave your saloon together, and that Hook had a hundred twenty dollars on him, money that the sheriff found in Mr. Pilgrim's pocket after he was arrested."

Strangelove shrugged, then pounded his fist on the railing. "That's the biggest crock of shit I've ever heard!" he said loudly. "Johnny Hook didn't have a dime. He'd been walking around the room mooching drinks all night. Hell, that's what finally brought him over to the bar where Eli was sitting. Eli bought him a beer or two, then gave him a dollar when he left the building."

"And what time of night was that, Mr. Strangelove?"

"I didn't look at the clock, but I reckon it must have been about an hour before closing time."

"Are you saying that Mr. Pilgrim left the saloon alone, and that Johnny Hook stayed behind?"

"Of course. Hook switched from beer to whiskey after Eli left, and he sat right there on that stool drinking till closing time."

"So, you're saying that Digger Hook and the Horn brothers were mistaken when they said they saw the two men leave your premises together?"

"No!" Strangelove said loudly. "I'm saying they told you a damn lie." He pointed to the four men, who were all sitting in the front row. "That's all they are, Mr. Barney, a bunch of thieves and liars. There wasn't a damn one of 'em in that saloon. It was my turn to tend bar, and I stayed behind that plank all night. If even one of 'em had been in the building, I would have damn sure seen him."

Judge Tarrington bent over toward the witness stand, saying, "I'm going to warn you just this once, Mr. Strangelove; any more such language and you will be held in contempt."

Will Barney spoke quickly. "I have no more questions for this witness anyway, Your Honor. He's dismissed."

The defense attorney called two additional witnesses before resting his case. Hank Fry appeared as a character witness for the defendant, then Barney called Big Step Benson to the stand. "Tell us, Mr. Benson," he said, "how long have you known Mr. Eli Pilgrim?"

"I met him in June of this year," Benson answered.

"Would you say that you know him well?"

"I don't suppose I know exactly what you mean by that, but I know him as well as I need to. He's a good man."

"Do you think he's the type of man who would commit murder for money?"

"Hell, no, he ain't. He never denied that he killed Johnny Hook, just said that he did it in self-defense. I believed him the first time he said it, and I believe him now. Hell, everybody in this courtroom knows what a piece of riffraff Johnny Hook was, and I'll bet you the butcher knife he was killed with is the same damn one he used on that old sheepherder a few years back."

The prosecutor finally hit the floor. "I object to that statement, Your Honor! Johnny Hook was never convicted of a crime in his life!"

"Objection sustained," Judge Tarrington said weakly.

Will Barney threw up his hands. "I'm done with this witness, Your Honor. In fact, I rest my case." He seated himself behind his table and began to look over the notes his assistant had been taking.

When the judge gave the prosecution and the defense fifteen minutes each to charge the jury, Ed Poole was on the floor quickly, spending most of his time trying to discredit the testimony of Bob Strangelove and Big Step Benson. One had only to look at the faces of the jury men to know that it was going to be a hard sell. The prosecutor also seemed to realize it, for he begged the men for a verdict in his favor, then sat down even before his allotted time was up.

Will Barney stood before the jury no longer than three minutes. "I won't take up fifteen minutes of your valuable time," he said. "You're all intelligent men, and you don't need me standing here telling you what you just heard, or failed to hear. I know that it's at least as plain to you as it is to me, that Johnny Hook set out to kill Mr. Pilgrim and rob him, but ended up losing his own life instead. So I'll just take this opportunity to thank you for the proper verdict that I know you're gonna bring back, then get out of your way." He walked to his seat without another word.

The panel was in the jury room for only ten minutes before returning with a verdict. "Your Honor," the foreman began, "we, the jury, find the defendant, Eli Pilgrim, not guilty." When a smattering of hand clapping turned into a rousing round of applause, Judge Tarrington banged his gavel. "Order!" he shouted. The room was suddenly quiet again as several men came around to shake Eli's hand and wish him well.

The smirks on the faces of Digger Hook and the Horn brothers could not be missed as Benson and Pilgrim left the courtroom and walked down the hallway. Both men followed Will Barney, for not only were their guns in his office, their buggy horse was tied to his hitching rail. After Benson had written the attorney a check for his services, he and Eli wasted no time strapping on their weapons and climbing aboard the buggy. "I heard Sadie's dinner bell ring a long time ago," Big Step said, "but I think the best thing you and I can do right now is get the hell out of this town."

"Me, too," Eli agreed. "I didn't like the look on the faces of Digger Hook and the Horn brothers."

"I expect you to eventually get some shit from that bunch," Benson said, "but not today." He whipped the horse to a fast trot, then took the road to the Oxbow.

15

THE NEXT time Eli and Big Step rode the buggy into Cuero was on Christmas Eve. Benson bought gifts for all of the men who lived and worked at the Oxbow, and though Eli himself bought nothing, he tagged along with the ranch manager for most of the day. At midafternoon, they retrieved the horse and buggy from Hank Fry's livery stable, then revisited the stores picking up the purchases Benson had made earlier.

The two men had seen the Horn brothers several times as they walked about the town, and once while he was in the liquor store, Eli looked over his shoulder to see Digger Hook leaning against the wall gazing at him disdainfully. When Pilgrim returned the look with a steely stare of his own, Hook curled his upper lip and shrugged, then stepped through the doorway to the street.

Even after Benson's shopping was done and the Oxbow men were returning to the livery stable afoot, Hook and the Horns had ridden past them laughing. "Just ignore the sons of bitches, Eli," Big Step had said. "It's obvious that they're trying to pick a fight, but I don't like the odds. Just let 'em think we're afraid of 'em; they'll get a little braver one of these days." Even as Benson was speaking, Hook had let out a rebel yell and led the Horn brothers down Main Street at a hard run. When they reached Esplanade, all four men turned south and left town at a gallop.

Benson and Pilgrim crossed the bridge an hour later, and the sun was still two hours high when they left the main road and took the cutoff leading to Oxbow. They had traveled about a mile when Big Step brought the buggy to a halt at the top of a small rise. He pulled the stopper from a bottle of whiskey with his teeth, saying, "For quite a while now I've been wanting to take a drink and a piss both, and this looks like as good a place as any." He took a big swallow from the bottle, then handed it to Pilgrim and jumped to the ground. Eli punished his own throat with the fiery liquid for a moment, then jumped off the buggy beside his boss. The men now stood side by side relieving themselves.

Neither Eli nor Big Step heard the shots that brought them down. Pilgrim felt a hard blow to his forehead that was reminiscent of a man's fist, then his head was suddenly spinning around wildly. A moment later he blacked out completely, then fell in a heap beside the still body of Big Step Benson.

Their assailants rode out of the trees quickly. The first thing Digger Hook did was put a bullet in the buggy horse's brain. "Don't want that son of a bitch to go running out to the Oxbow pulling an empty buggy," he said. "If we leave the damn horse lying right here with the dead asses of his passengers, there probably won't nobody come looking for 'em till some time tomorrow."

Digger Hook's voice was easily recognizable to Pilgrim, for Eli had suddenly regained consciousness. Nonetheless, he lay with his eyes closed feigning death, for he knew that the slightest movement on his part would prove to be fatal. He had only to continue listening to ascertain that all of the Horn brothers were present, for they were talking among themselves freely, and he had committed the sound of all three voices to memory during the trial. "We want people to believe that somebody just killed these bastards to rob 'em, Clayton," Eli heard Clem Horn say. "Get all the money outta their pockets, and anything else you find worth having. Get their guns, too; we can take 'em up to Gonzales and sell 'em for good money.

I've been wanting to leave this damn town anyway, and I reckon this is gonna give me a good excuse."

Eli passed out again after hearing those words and regained consciousness on his own bunk four days later. "Nice to see you among the living again," Cliff Cates said when Pilgrim opened his eyes.

Eli pushed himself to a sitting position and put his feet on the floor. Then he began to stammer. "Lord . . . I'm thirsty. Am . . . I . . . is Big Step all right?"

Cates, who was sitting on his own bunk facing Pilgrim, began to shake his head. "We buried him two days ago," he said. "He took a rifle bullet right between the eyes." He got to his feet quickly. "Just sit where you are, old buddy; I'll get you some water." He was back moments later with a bucket and a gourd dipper. "A man can't live very long without this stuff," he said, handing Eli a dipperful. "I got quite a bit of it down you with a spoon last night and again this morning. You fought me pretty hard, but at least you kept on swallowing it."

Pilgrim emptied the dipper twice, then dropped it back into the bucket. "I remember lying in the road beside the buggy, Cliff." He touched the bandage on his forehead, then grimaced and drew his hand away quickly. "They shot me right there."

"They sure did," Cates said. "Doc Peterson put that bandage on, and said for us to leave it there. He said the bullet didn't go through your head at all, said it hit you on the right side of your forehead, then circled around under your scalp and came out just above your right ear. Funny how a bullet could stay under a man's scalp like that and go halfway around his head before it comes out." He chuckled softly. "Old Doc was right, though. He said from the start that you'd be out for about three more days, and that he'd be mighty surprised if you didn't come back around today. Well, here you are, bygod, talking and sitting up just as straight as you please."

"How'd I get here?"

"Hank Fry brought you," Cates said. "He just happened to come along the next morning after you and Big Step were ambushed. After he found out that you were still alive, he got you home and on your bunk in a hurry. I went to town and got Doc Peterson myself; brought him out here in the spring wagon, and took him back the same way." He smiled broadly. "He told me right from the start that it wasn't time for you to leave us yet. He said your heartbeat was the strongest one he'd ever heard, and that he'd bet a hundred dollars you were gonna make it."

Hank Fry had indeed been the man who found Pilgrim and Benson on the road. The hostler had ordered six head of horses for Big Step two weeks before and had been on his way to Oxbow to tell him that the animals were now at his livery stable. Fry had come upon the buggy and the dead horse at seven o'clock in the morning. When a closer look revealed the unconscious Eli Pilgrim and the rapidly decomposing body of Big Step Benson, Fry had lifted Pilgrim to the back of his saddler and headed for Oxbow at a hard run.

"Joe Garcia and Adam Sweeney took another horse and went back for the buggy and Big Step's body," Cates said. "Joe said that he and Adam found the tracks of four horses in that little stand of trees about a hundred yards north of the road. He said that's where the shooting came from; that the four men rode right on down to the buggy and killed the horse, then went through your pockets and robbed both of you. Even took your Colts and gun belts. Rifles, too.

"Garcia brought Big Step's body home, and Adam Sweeney went on to town to inform the sheriff of the bushwhacking. Beasley and his deputy came out here later on in the morning. They spent most of their time in the house talking with Mr. Benson, then came in here to your cot and stood around staring at you for a while. Beasley said he found the same horse tracks in the trees that Garcia and Sweeney found, and that he would be carrying out an investigation of the matter."

"I've already seen an example of his damned investigating," Eli said.

Cates made no further comment for a while, then continued: "We buried Big Step beside his brothers at four o'clock the next afternoon. I know you've seen the headstones up at the Benson graveyard, it's on that little rise about three hundred yards above the main house." He was quiet for a while, then added, "I reckon whoever shot you fellows must have made a pretty good haul. I know that Big Step always carried a fat roll on him, and Joe says his pockets were empty when he was found."

"Big Step wasn't shot for his money!" Eli said emphatically. "Neither was I!" He pulled on his boots, then picked up the water bucket and left the building. He set the bucket on the washstand just outside the doorway, then walked up the hill to the Benson graveyard.

Once there, he seated himself cross-legged on the ground and stared at the freshly turned mound of earth till he grew misty-eyed. Then he began to talk to his departed friend: "They didn't give us no chance to fight, Big Step, and I don't intend to give them no chance, either. I know exactly who the sons of bitches are, and I'll promise you right now that I'm gonna put every one of 'em in the ground with you. Maybe you'll see 'em there. If you do, I hope you'll kick their goddamn asses up under their shoulders at least twenty times a day." He got to his feet and put on his hat, then took one last look at the mound and walked away. "Good-bye, my friend," he said over his shoulder.

A few minutes later, Pilgrim opened the door to the cookshack to see that Joe Garcia and Adam Sweeney were already seated at a table eating. Both men dropped their spoons noisily as Eli stepped inside. "Somebody just woke up our sleeping giant!" the diminutive Sweeney said loudly, sliding off the bench with his right hand outstretched. He grasped Eli's hand

and began to squeeze his shoulder and pat him on the back. "Doc Peterson said he thought you'd come back out of it today, and he was right. I'll bet bygod you're hungry, too."

"Of course, he's hungry," Baldy King said, hugging Eli like a long lost son. He pointed to the nearest table. "Take a seat right there and let me see what I can do about filling you up." Pilgrim headed for the table, and the cook returned to the stove.

Joe Garcia shook Eli's hand and expressed his elation at seeing him up and around again, then followed him back to the table. "I don't reckon I talk to the Lord near as often nowadays as I ought to, Eli," he said, "but I've been begging Him to pull you through this. Now, if you'll excuse me, it seems to me like I oughtta take a minute to thank Him for answering my prayer." He crossed himself with a forefinger, then bowed his head and moved his lips silently for several seconds. When he raised his eyes again, he pointed to the big iron pot that the cook had just pulled over the stove's firebox. "Baldy's got the best stew there that anybody on this ranch has ever tasted," he said. "I shot a goat yesterday afternoon, and most of it wound up in that damn pot. Ain't that right, Baldy?"

"No, Joe," the cook answered. "I don't reckon I used more'n about nine or ten pounds of meat. The rest of the goat's out yonder in the smokehouse."

"Oh," Garcia said. "I guess it just seemed like it had that much meat in it because it was so good. Anyway, if it's all right with you, I think I'll have another bowl of it myself when you get it heated up again."

"You're the boss," King said, then began to stir the stew with a large wooden spoon.

Joe Garcia was indeed the boss: Oliver Benson had known of his son's death for only a few hours when he walked to the cookshack and informed the small dinner crowd that the former foreman was now the new ranch manager. With dry eyes and a countenance of granite, the baldheaded old-timer stood beside the stove and spoke to the eating men firmly, an unmistakable touch of sternness in his tone. "Ain't nothing none of us can do about my son not being with us no more," he said, "but, that don't change the fact somebody's got to do his job." He pointed across the room to Garcia. "As of right now and from this day forward, Joe Garcia will be the manager of Oxbow Ranch.

"Now, if anybody has a problem with that, just tell Joe or me either one, and you can draw your pay. Most of the crew is out working and can't hear what I'm saying, but I expect you fellows to pass the word on to 'em. Remind 'em, too, that I consider Mr. Garcia's knowledge of the cattle business to be without equal. From now on his word shall be taken as gospel by every man on this ranch, and I expect his orders to be carried out with no exceptions." He nodded curtly to signal that the speech was over, then left the building and closed the door behind him.

Now, as Baldy King set a bowl of stew before Eli, he also informed him that he was sitting beside the new ranch manager. Pilgrim was neither shocked nor surprised, for he had decided some time ago that Garcia was probably the most knowledgeable man on the ranch. "Glad to hear that, Joe," he said, offering a handshake. "They couldn't have chosen a better man."

Garcia gripped the hand firmly, then released it quickly. "I just hope I can do something to earn Mr. Benson's confidence."

"All you gotta do is keep right on doing what you've been doing," Sweeney said. "Hell, you've been calling most of the shots on this ranch anyway. I reckon a few men resented it before, but now you've got authority. When you want a man to do something all you gotta do is tell him so. Ain't nobody around here gonna give you no shit, now."

"I hope not," Garcia said, picking up his oversized spoon.

Pilgrim inhaled his first bowl of stew and asked the cook for another. "Joe sure didn't lie about that stuff, Baldy," he said. "I'm not even sure two bowls are gonna be enough to satisfy me."

King accepted the empty bowl for a refill. "Try four bowls, then," he said. "I've got several gallons of it here."

Eli did not eat four bowls, but he did finish off a third. By the time he dropped his utensils in the dishpan and thanked the cook, both Garcia and Sweeney had vacated the premises. "Best stew I ever tasted, Baldy," Pilgrim said. "See you again about daybreak." Then he stepped through the doorway.

When Eli returned to the bunkhouse, Cliff Cates was lying on his cot reading a book. He laid it aside, then raised up and swung his feet to the floor. "I reckon you went up to visit Big Step," he said. "Did you stop by the cookshack and put something in that empty belly?"

Pilgrim nodded. "Best stew I ever tasted," he said. "I might have stretched my stomach out of shape permanently."

Cates patted his own midsection. "I ate two bowls of that stuff even before Baldy got it done. It tasted mighty good half-raw." He sat quietly for a few moments, then asked, "Have you given any thought to how you're gonna go about replacing your guns?"

"I've given it a lot of thought," Eli answered, "but that don't mean I've come up with any good ideas. I don't have any money; the thieves took care of that. In a way, that part of it's my own damn fault, though, 'cause I've been carrying all of my money around in my pocket ever since I've been in Texas. I always intended to put it in the bank, but I just never got around to doing it. I don't have any way of knowing whether any of the stores'll sell me a Colt and a rifle on credit or not."

"I'd say that it would probably run against their policies," Cates said. He sat gazing at Eli quietly for a moment, then chuckled, adding, "You've got a mighty damned honest face, though. It could be that one of the hardware stores'll load you up on anything you want for a dollar down and a dollar a week."

Pilgrim smiled. "I'll probably have to ask some of 'em about that eventually," he said.

Cates reached for his boots. "Maybe not," he said. He pulled on his footwear and picked up the lantern. "I've got a bunch of stuff in the storeroom that I'll go check out. Got an extra gun belt that's in pretty good shape if the rats haven't eaten it up. I'll take this lantern with me, 'cause it might be dark before I get back. You just lie there and rest yourself. You need to gain back your strength just as quick as you can." He walked through the front doorway without looking back.

Pilgrim had heard many of the hands ride in from their jobs some time ago, and he knew that they would make the cookshack their first stop, then hurry on to the bunkhouse to begin their nightly game of draw poker. Eli avoided that game like the plague, for he had heard several arguments at the table that would have surely turned into fisticuffs if cooler heads had not prevailed.

When the riders finally showed up in the bunkhouse, Eli knew immediately that the word had spread that he had regained consciousness. Every man who walked through the doorway headed straight to the back of the room and Pilgrim's bunk. "It's good to see you sitting up instead of stretched out," Jack Harmon said, pumping Eli's hand. "Bygod, you look to me like there ain't never been nothing wrong with you."

"That's about the way I feel, Jack," Pilgrim said. "I walked around outside some this afternoon, and I seem to be about as strong as I've ever been. My legs seem to be a little stiff, that's all."

"Good," Harmon said, then walked away so some of the other hands could get to the cot. During the next twenty minutes, Eli shook hands and passed a few words with the entire crew, then watched as about half of them assembled around the card table.

Even as the game began, Cliff Cates walked through the front door with the lantern in one hand and a Colt Peacemaker in the other. A faded brown gun belt was lying across his shoulder. When he reached the back of the room, he set the lantern on the floor and laid the Colt and the gun belt on Eli's cot. "Ain't neither one of these things very pretty," he said, "but they're still in good working order. I just quit using the Colt because I let a gun salesman convince me that a new one would fit my hand better. I'd already bought the new one before I figured out that the handles on the two guns were exactly the same size." He picked up the belt and pointed to several faded spots on the leather. "I know a fellow in town who'll dye the belt and holster both for about thirty cents, then I can take my knife and trim up that holster; make it exactly like the one you had before."

Pilgrim looked at the floor for a few moments. "You're a true friend, Cliff," he said finally. "I don't know when I can pay you for this stuff, but I'll get around to it as soon as I can."

"Forget it, Eli. I'm not using it, and probably never would again. If you can be satisfied with it, it's yours."

For the first time in his adult life, Eli Pilgrim actually hugged another man. What made it seem even more like the thing to do was that Cates hugged him just as tightly. "I won't be forgetting it, Cliff," Eli said. "You'll see." He looked the Colt and the belt over again, then said, "This stuff is gonna be just fine. Maybe I can get a big enough advance on my pay to buy me another rifle. A man would have to be crazy to go riding around without a long gun in this country."

Cates shook his head. "With the kind of enemies you have, it would be out of the question. I don't believe getting you another rifle is gonna be a big problem, though. Rusty Trout tried to sell me one less than a week ago, and I know he's still got it. He's spending the night with his mother in Cuero tonight, but he'll be back in the cookshack for breakfast in the morning. We'll talk with him then."

"Rusty's always been pretty friendly with me, Cliff," Eli

said. "It could be that he'll sell me the rifle on credit. I wonder what kind of shape it's in."

"Good condition, is what he said. He said that the stock is scarred up and some of the bluing has faded on the barrel, but that the gun shoots true every time. It's a Henry just like the one you had, only it ain't as pretty. He wants fifteen dollars for it, but if he happens to lose money in a poker game in Cuero tonight, he might take a little less for the gun tomorrow. I know he didn't take it to town with him, 'cause I saw it in the storeroom when I was out there." He pulled off his boots and swung his legs up to his bed. "Take that rifle out and shoot it a while tomorrow. If you decide you want it, I'll be more'n happy to lend you the money to buy it."

Pilgrim stretched out on his own cot and pulled up the covers. "Like I said a little while ago, Cliff, you're a true friend." He was asleep in short order.

16

THE NEW year was now more than a week old, and Joe Garcia had still not assigned Pilgrim a job. Though Eli occasionally washed dishes, mopped floors, and brought in firewood for the cook, most of his daylight hours were spent in the woods practicing his fast draw. He had resigned himself to the fact that he had a job to do, and he did not intend to put it off much longer. His body strength had returned completely, and the only sign that he had recently been laid up for a while was a red welt running across his forehead and around the side of his head.

He had not only acquired Rusty Trout's Henry rifle but had bought a double-barreled, ten-gauge shotgun from him as well. Though neither weapon was pretty, both were in top working order, and Eli considered the twenty-five-dollar price he had paid for them to be one of the best deals he had ever made. Of course, he now had an outstanding loan, but Cliff Cates had assured him that the money did not have to be repaid this month, or even this year.

During the middle of the week, after he had been out behind the barn for two hours practicing the fast draw and dry-firing, Eli walked into the cookshack at ten o'clock in the morning for a cup of coffee. When the cook set the steaming liquid in front of him, he also delivered a message. "Mr. Oliver says to tell you that he wants to see you in the house when you have a chance to get up there. I wouldn't put that off very long, Eli."

Pilgrim shook his head. "No," he said. "I won't put it off at all."

Ten minutes later, Eli rapped his knuckles against the doorjamb at the main house. A lady affectionatelly called Miss Emily by the Oxbow crowd, who was the old man's live-in cook, housekeeper, and caretaker, answered his knock. A tall, auburn-haired lady who was less than half Benson's age, she had been in his employ for more than two years and was totally devoted to him. Whether the two had a sexual relationship or not was anybody's guess, but every man living at Oxbow believed that if Oliver Benson still needed and wanted one at his age, it was unlikely that Miss Emily would say no. She pushed the door open widely now. "Are you Mr. Pilgrim?" she asked.

When Eli answered in the affirmative, she directed him to a large room that apparently served as a combination office and library. Bookshelves ran the length of the carpeted room on two sides, and a large oaken desk occupied one corner. Eli was directed to a cushioned chair on the near side of the desk. "Mr. Benson is occupied with his bath at the moment," the lady said, "but he'll be with you as soon as he can." Then she disappeared so quietly that Pilgrim did not hear her leave.

Oliver Benson entered the room just as quietly several minutes later. Eli had just helped himself to a magazine and was busy scanning the pictures when the old man spoke from somewhere behind him. "Thank you for coming, Mr. Pilgrim. I've been wanting to talk with you for quite a while now, and I finally decided that it might as well be today."

Eli jumped to his feet quickly.

"No, no," the old man said softly, "just keep your seat."

When Pilgrim had reseated himself, Benson walked behind the desk and did likewise, saying, "I never was one for beating around the bush, Mr. Pilgrim, so I'll just ask you straight out. Do you know who shot you and Robert?"

Eli looked the old-timer in the eye and answered quickly. "Yes, sir," he said. "Our assailants were Digger Hook and the three Horn brothers."

"I see," Benson said. He shuffled some papers back and forth on the desk for a few moments, then suddenly decided to deposit all of them in one of the drawers. "Did you see all of 'em with your own eyes?"

"No, sir," Eli answered, "but that was only because I was afraid to open my eyes. You see, I regained consciousness about the time they rode up to the buggy, but I had to lie there acting like I was dead to keep 'em from finishing me off. I could hear and understand their conversation just as well as I can hear you right now, and I not only recognized their individual voices from the day of the trial, but they were actually calling each other by name."

"Let me get this straight," Benson said. "You're saying that you heard every one of the four men speak, and that you heard every one of their names called?"

Pilgrim nodded. "Yes, sir," he answered. "I also know which one of 'em shot me, and who shot Big Step."

Benson nodded. "Keep talking," he said.

"Well, right after I heard Digger Hook laughing about shooting the buggy horse, Booger Horn started talking about how quick the rifles had brought us both down. 'Pilgrim stood around for a second or two after Digger put a hole in his head,' he was saying, 'but Benson fell like a ton of bricks when Clem popped him.' Then I heard Clem Horn tell his brother Clayton to take all our money so people would think somebody killed us just to rob us. He told Clayton to take our guns, too, said they could sell them up in Gonzales.

"I was lying on my face, so I just stayed still and held my breath while he took my money out of my pocket. I must have passed out again right after that, 'cause I don't remember any more about it."

The old-timer drummed his fingers against the desktop for a moment, then sat looking through the window. "I'd say you remembered about as much as you needed to, my boy," he said softly. "It sounds like Digger Hook pulled the trigger on you, and Clem Horn murdered my son."

"There's absolutely no doubt in my mind about that, sir. Of course, I consider Clayton and Booger Horn to be just as guilty as the two riflemen."

"Yes, of course," Benson agreed. "They were all in it together." The old man was quiet for what seemed like an eternity to Pilgrim, then put his elbows on the desk and cradled his chin in his hands. "What do you intend to do about it?" he asked.

Pilgrim did not hesitate. "I intend to kill 'em," he answered.

"All of 'em?"

"Yes, sir. All of 'em."

The old man sat quietly for another extended period of time. "Have you considered giving all this information to Sheriff Beasley?" he asked finally.

Eli shook his head several times. "I didn't consider it for long," he said. "For some reason the sheriff decided that he didn't like me right from the start, even tried to get me convicted of murdering Johnny Hook when he knew very well that I wasn't guilty. No, sir, when I get ready to go after Digger Hook, Rone Beasley won't know it till after the fact."

Benson raised his eyebrows. "And when do you intend to do that?"

"Any day now," Pilgrim answered. "I've been thinking about going hunting him tomorrow."

"I see. Have you ever killed anybody, Mr. Pilgrim?"

"Yes, sir. I never lost any sleep over it, either, 'cause I knew it was the right thing to do."

Benson nodded. Then, without another word, he pulled out a drawer and laid a stack of double eagles on the desk. "I know that you're broke and that you even had to borrow money to replace your guns, my boy, so I want you to put this two hundred dollars in your pocket.

"I'll guarantee you that, after you shoot Digger Hook, you're gonna have to chase the Horn brothers all over Texas. There ain't no way in the world that they'll hang around here after they hear that you've planted another one of their cousins." He pushed the money across the desk. "Put this in your pocket like I told you. Manhunting costs money, and if you happen to run out, just get word to me."

Pilgrim sat staring at the coins. When the old man nodded and pushed them a little farther across the desk, Eli picked them up and dropped them into his pocket. "I wouldn't spend this much money in a coon's age," he said.

"Of course you will," Benson said. "You can't find a man when you're out sleeping in the damn woods; you've got to stay in hotels and hang out in saloons, just like they do. All that costs money, and—" He reached into the drawer again and extracted more coins. "On second thought, here's another hundred. I believe you'll be needing it, too."

Eli pocketed the third hundred with no hesitation. He was now in possession of more money than at any other time in his life. He got to his feet. "Like I said, Mr. Benson, I'll probably go looking for Hook tomorrow. If I find him, you'll hear about it pretty soon no matter how it turns out."

Benson was on his feet also. "Hell, I already know how it's gonna turn out. Cliff Cates has done told everybody on this ranch how good you are with a six-gun. He claims you're better'n he is, and if that's really so, there ain't no doubt in my mind how Digger Hook's gonna end up." He made a shooing motion with his hands, adding, "Now, get on out there and do what you've got to do. Just don't let that son of a bitch get the drop on you. One more thing: I think Cliff Cates ought to go along with you to keep a lookout for the rest of that bunch."

"Yes, sir," Pilgrim said, heading for the doorway. "I'll see what Cliff thinks about that."

Eli did not even discuss his plans with Cliff Cates. He felt that dealing with Digger Hook and the Horn brothers was his own problem and something that he must handle alone. Deliberately waiting till after Cates had ridden out to whatever job Garcia had assigned him to the following morning, Pilgrim roped and saddled his buckskin. He spent most of the next hour fashioning a scabbard for his shotgun, then tied it on his saddle.

That done, he mounted and rode out of the barnyard. He now had two long guns on his saddle, the Henry under his right leg, the ten-gauge under his left. Both weapons were loaded and ready for action, as was the big Peacemaker on his hip. He had added a sixth shell to the cylinder of the Colt when he buckled on his gun belt this morning.

He stopped at the cookshack and had a cup of coffee with Baldy King, never mentioning the fact that he was about to begin his search for the man who had put the purple scar on his head. When informed that Pilgrim was going into town, the cook handed him a quarter. "I've had a hankering for some chocolate candy for a coupla weeks, now," he said. "Nub Lewis's grocery store's usually got it on sale for fifteen a bag. You'll be doing me a big favor if you'll stop by there and pick up a bag of it for me."

Pilgrim pocketed the coin. "I'll be glad to do it, Baldy," he said, then left the building. Moments later, he remounted and kicked the buckskin to an easy canter. His first stop would be Hank Fry's livery stable, for he could think of no other man who was as likely to know what was going on around the town.

When he reached the slope where the ambush had occurred, he rode into the grove of timber to have a look. The tracks of the assailants' horses were still there, though none had any particular meaning to him. He followed them down to the road, then sat with his hat in his hand for a few moments in reverence to Big Step Benson. When he kicked the buckskin in the ribs again, the little animal took him to the main road quickly. After crossing the big bridge an hour later, he turned off Esplanade at Sutherland's store, then made a half-circle around the town to the east. A short while later he rode around Hank Fry's corral, then through the big barn's open doorway. "Tell me who I'm looking at," the liveryman said, slamming a stable door. "The last time I saw you, you didn't look like you'd ever sit on a horse again."

Pilgrim jumped to the ground quickly. "I feel as good as I ever have, Hank," he said, offering a handshake, "and one of the reasons I'm here is to thank you for hauling me out to Oxbow after you found me on the road."

Fry gripped the hand firmly for a moment, then chuckled. "What else was I gonna do?" he asked. "You looked as help-less as a newborn babe." He pointed to the office, adding, "The coffeepot's still on the stove." He tied Pilgrim's animal to a post, then led the way.

When Fry had poured coffee for both men, he motioned Eli to the room's only chair, then seated himself on the edge of the cot. "You've told me one of the reasons you came to town this morning," he said. "Is there something else on your mind?"

Pilgrim took a sip from his cup, then nodded. "I've got some business with Digger Hook and the Horn brothers," he said.

"I can't say that I'm surprised to hear that," Fry said, getting to his feet. He walked to the window and stood look-ing up the street for a few moments, then continued to talk. "I've been told that the Horns have pulled up stakes, but Digger Hook ain't gonna be hard to find.

"Fact is, he left his horse with me for several hours one day last week, but I ain't got no way of knowing when he'll be back. I saw him twice yesterday, once in the morning and again at midafternoon." He pointed through the open door-way. "I was standing out there at the hitching rail when he came riding down the road from the east. He stared at me like he'd never even seen me before, then rode on up the street at a trot. I saw him again a few hours later when I went up to the restaurant to eat dinner." He refilled his coffee cup, then added, "Actually, I didn't think he'd ever even slow down at my place after I testified in your behalf at the trial, but he did."

Pilgrim nodded. "I know you didn't have any way of knowing it, Hank, but he's responsible for this scar on my forehead. I regained consciousness while he and the Horns were riding down to the buggy and, while I was playing dead, I heard Booger Horn laughing and describing the whole show. He said Hook shot me, and that Clem Horn killed Big Step." He drained his coffee cup and set it on the table. "They were all in it together, though, and Clayton and Booger Horn are just as guilty as the other two. I intend to treat 'em all alike if I ever come face to face with 'em."

"You say I didn't know it?" Fry asked. "I reckon that might be right, but if you believe I didn't think it, you're wrong. To tell you the truth, there was never any doubt in my mind about who shot you and Big Step. Hell, they're the only ones around here who had it in for you."

"I hope so," Eli said.

At that moment, a middle-aged man brought his horse to a halt just outside the doorway, then dismounted and helloed the building. The liveryman responded quickly. After a short conversation with Fry, who unsaddled the big gray and led it down the hall to a stable, the man walked up the street and disappeared inside the Drover's Rest. Pilgrim believed that he had seen him before but could not put a name on him.

A short while later, Fry returned to the office and reclaimed his seat on the edge of the cot. "Where do you intend to go looking for Digger Hook, Eli?"

"I haven't decided yet," Pilgrim answered, "but I'd be willing to deal with him wherever I find him. The most important thing is that I catch him alone. I don't feel lucky enough to take him and the Horn brothers on at the same time."

"Casey Eden told me that the Horns have left this part of the country," Fry said. "I reckon he oughtta know, 'cause he lives right close to 'em over on Willow Creek. He's a nosey sort of man who makes it his business to find out everybody else's business, so he probably knows what he's talking about." He knelt beside the cot and pulled a double-barreled shotgun out from under it, thrusting it at arm's length above his head. "Anyway, bygod, I reckon you might have a friend or two around here, yourself."

"Thank you, Hank." Pilgrim got to his feet and refilled his coffee cup, then reseated himself. "Do you think Hook'll ever leave his horse here at the stable again, Hank?"

"I don't know," Fry said, "but I reckon I know what you're thinking. There ain't no other place in town where you'd be as likely to catch him alone, as you would right here."

Eli nodded. "Yep, that's what I was thinking, all right."

"I'd almost bet that he'd show up sometime today or to-morrow," Fry said. "Hell, if he don't come to you, maybe you oughtta go to him. He's the type who's not gonna miss a day in the saloons. I'm not saying he gets drunk every day, but he likes to be where the action is.

"Now, even if you did find him in one of the saloons, that don't mean you'd have to fight somebody else in order to get to him. It's true that most of his friends are members of the sporting crowd, but I don't believe there's a man among 'em who'd stand up with him in a gunfight."

Even as Pilgrim and Fry sat discussing the man, Digger Hook rode around the north side of the barn and dismounted at the hitching rail. He tied his animal, then pulled a bag of smoking tobacco out of his vest pocket and began to blow on a book of cigarette papers, walking toward the building with his eyes downcast as he did so. After only a few steps he raised his eyes and came to a sudden halt, for Eli Pilgrim was now standing in the doorway.

Hook dropped the tobacco and the papers to the ground, then stood with his mouth open for a moment. "Whatcha . . . whatcha think—"

"Today's payday, Hook," Eli interrupted. Standing with his legs apart and his body leaning slightly forward, he pointed to the scar on his forehead with his left hand, adding, "And it seems like the right time for you to finish what you started."

"I didn't start nothing. I—"

Pilgrim interrupted again: "Go for that gun on your hip, you son of a bitch!" Even as Eli spoke, his own Colt was spitting flame. His first shot took Digger Hook in the chest, and his second landed six inches lower. Hook had cleared his holster, but even as he tried to raise his shooting arm, his weapon fell from his hand. He stood staring at Pilgrim for a few moments, then staggered backward and sat down on the ground. He glanced at the blood leaking from his chest, then lay down on his back. He did not move again.

As Eli holstered his weapon, Sheriff Beasley and his son Roy dismounted at the hitching rail. Pilgrim had not noticed the lawmen coming down the street, for Digger Hook's presence in the yard had demanded his full attention. "I knew it," the sheriff said, handing his horse's reins to his son. "I knew damn well it was gonna come to this." He trotted over to the body and got down on one knee, his ear on Hook's chest. "This man's still alive!" he said loudly, getting to his feet quickly. "Roy, go get Doc Peterson, and be quick about it!"

The deputy stepped into the saddle and headed up the street at a gallop, leading the sheriff's mount for the doctor to ride.

"Well, there weren't but two of them Hook boys," the sheriff said to Pilgrim, "and it looks like you've done killed 'em both. I say that because Digger don't look to me like he's gonna make it."

Eli pointed to his scar. "Hook and the Horn brothers bush-whacked me and Big Step Benson on Christmas Eve, Sheriff, but I believe you already knew about that. I came to town looking for him this morning, and as you can see, I found him."

Beasley locked eyes with Eli for what seemed like a full minute, then walked back and knelt beside the fallen man. He was still there when the deputy and Doc Peterson arrived. Sliding out of the saddle with his bag in his hand, the doctor quickly shooed the sheriff away and got on his knees beside the wounded man. It took him only a moment to determine that Hook was conscious. "It's easy to see that you've been hit in the lung, Mr. Hook," he said, "and if you ain't right with your maker, now's the time to do some tall talking. Is there anything you want to say to the Almighty?"

Sheriff Beasley elbowed his way past the others. "Speak up, Digger," he said. "Tell us the truth about that shooting out on Oxbow Road. Did you shoot Eli Pilgrim?

Hook spoke hoarsely through a mass of bloody froth that had accumulated on his lips. "Yes," he said.

"Who all was in on it with you?" When he got no answer, the lawman bent over closer to Hook's ear, repeating the question loudly.

"Ho . . . Horn brothers. Clem . . . Clem shot Big Step Benson. He—" His chin dropped to his chest, and his eyes turned to glass. Digger Hook was dead.

"Bygod that settles it!" the lawman said loudly, addressing Pilgrim. "I never thought I'd see the day that I'd say this, but I reckon bygod that puts you in the clear." He pointed to the body, adding, "He even said that Clem Horn killed Big Step Benson."

Eli nodded. "I already knew that, Sheriff. I regained consciousness after they shot us, and I heard 'em talking about it."

"Well, the least you coulda done was come into town and tell me about it. I coulda rounded 'em up and put 'em in jail."

Pilgrim pointed to the body. "Hook just told you about it himself," he said. He walked back through the doorway and untied his buckskin from a post.

Hank Fry followed Eli inside the building and said to him softly: "If you'll go back out to the Oxbow and stay there for a day or two, I believe I can find out everything you need to know about the Horn brothers. My friend Casey Eden not only knows 'em, he also knows one of their uncles who hates their guts. The old man'll probably know exactly where you oughtta go looking for 'em, and I'll bet he's just dying to tell you."

Pilgrim nodded. "That sounds good, Hank. You want me to come back two days from now?"

Fry shook his head. "Meet me at the campground about an hour after dark tomorrow night. That'll give me all the time I need to get hold of Casey."

Eli nodded. "I'll be there," he said. He handed Fry an eagle, saying, "Give this to the undertaker and tell him to put Digger Hook in the ground." He mounted the buckskin and spoke to nobody as he rode past the growing crowd of gawkers. He would stop to pick up a bag of chocolate candy for Baldy King, then head for Oxbow.

DIGGER HOOK had been in the ground for two weeks now, and Pilgrim had not shaved his face since the day of the shooting. A thick, black beard now hid his face and part of his neck, and a man who did not know him well might have had a problem identifying him. He had grown the beard on the advice of Cliff Cates, who believed it would make him harder to recognize. "A man oughtta play every card he's got," Cates had said, "and if you've got a beard covering up everything but your eyes, the Horns ain't gonna know who in the hell you are till you're breathing right down their throats." Eli had stopped shaving his face that very same day. The beard was now fifteen days old, and the incessant itching had already begun.

Today, he was taking up the hunt for the Horn brothers. Hank Fry had not only met him at the campground two weeks ago, but had brought one of the Horn brothers' maternal uncles, named Elmer Jude, with him. Jude had been eager to talk and had given Pilgrim enough information to put him on the road. "Ain't no doubt in my mind that them boys did exactly what you're thinking they did," Jude had said. "Ain't neither one of 'em worth the goddamn powder it would take to blow his brains out, and never has been. They worried their pa into committing suicide more'n five years ago, and now they're about to drive my sister crazy. Maybe if you kill all three of the no-good bastards, she'll sell that cabin and come on back home."

According to their uncle, there was a variety of places where the men might possibly find a safe haven. "They've got distant cousins all over South Texas and West Texas, too," Jude had said. "Now, I can't say how many of them kinfolks would actually give 'em the time of day, but there's certainly a bunch of 'em out there. If it was me looking for them boys, I believe I'd check out Uvalde. Old Duke Hayden's got a ranch there called the Double D, and he's a second cousin to 'em. I don't think he's ever been around 'em long enough to know what a lousy bunch they are, so he just might take 'em on if they asked him for work. Anyway, I believe it would be worth a try."

"Thank you, sir," Pilgrim had said. "I'll certainly keep all that in mind." He was thoughtful for a few moments, then asked, "Do you know of anybody they might be acquainted with in Gonzales?"

Jude chuckled loudly. "I know damn well they're acquainted with the town marshal up there. He locked their asses up one weekend, and it was several days before their pa could get 'em outta jail. I don't remember exactly what he charged 'em with, but he damn sure wasn't gonna be rushed into turning 'em loose. The marshal's name is Jake Saw, in case you want to talk with him about it."

Jude talked so long that Eli was finally obliged to sit down beside the lantern and write the information on a small pad that he had brought along for that very purpose. By the time the meeting was over, he had written down the names of a dozen different towns and twice as many people, and the list was tucked away in his pocket at this very moment.

The first place he intended to check out was Gonzales, an old town of much renown that lay thirty-five miles north of Cuero. "Get their guns, too," Pilgrim had heard Clem Horn tell his brother Clayton the day of the bushwhacking, "we can take 'em up to Gonzales and sell 'em for good money." For that reason, Eli would make the bustling little town his first stop. He would also have a talk with Marshal Jake Saw.

Cliff Cates helped Eli balance the packsaddle on his stripe-legged mule, then waved good-bye as Pilgrim rode out of the corral. Halting at the cookshack long enough to pick up a large sack of grub that Baldy King had put together, Pilgrim then remounted and headed across the open plain behind the main house. Cates had informed him that Gonzales was directly north of Oxbow, and that if he would ride cross-country for two or three hours, he would save at least ten miles. "Just keep riding due north," he said. "You'll run into the country road right after you cross Little Dry Creek."

Eli rode by the Benson graveyard and spoke to Big Step, then continued on toward the thick clusters of cedar and juniper that he could see in the distance. He had no intention of riding into Gonzales in broad daylight but would make camp a few miles before reaching town. Then he would ride in after dark. Although he had little hope of finding any of the Horns there, he would certainly not dismiss the possibility. He had heard Clem Horn mention going there with his own ears, and, for all he knew, the man just might be dumb enough to try to start a new life in a town only thirty-five miles from where he had committed a cold-blooded murder.

Pilgrim had long ago promised himself that he would not give up the hunt until he had personally dealt with all three of the Horns, and today he renewed the vow. He had as much time as it took, he had decided, and he did not intend to get himself killed by trying to rush things. He would go after them diligently and deliberately, and he did not expect to be back on Oxbow soil until after the hunt was over.

Although he had the money to sleep in some of the better hotels, Eli intended to spend many of his nights in the woods. He had everything on the pack mule that he was likely to need, and although the weather was unseasonably warm at the moment, and he was riding along in his shirtsleeves, he had a fleece-lined coat behind the cantle and a thick bedroll and several extra blankets on the mule. And he was also loaded for bear. He carried a twelve-shot Henry rifle and a double-barreled, ten-gauge shotgun on his saddle, and a Colt Peace-maker hanging on his right leg. The rifle and the shotgun were both ready for action, and the Colt had five live shells in its cylinder. And he was plenty capable of hitting a hickory nut at a considerable distance with any of the weapons, for he had done that very thing on more than one occasion.

The pack animal was also carrying a two-man tent. Eli had been forced to discard the one Johnny Hook died in, for even though he had scrubbed it with a stiff brush and hot soapy water, the bloodstains refused to budge. The one he now carried had been on the ranch for several years, but according to Joe Garcia, it had never been used. "Them tents just lie out there in the storeroom year after year," the foreman said. "Put one of 'em on your pack mule, 'cause I'd say that you're damn sure gonna need it before winter's over. We don't have the snow and ice like you grew up with back in Ohio, but I'll tell you right now, when it does get cold in Texas, bygod it's cold."

"I believe you, Joe," Eli had said, then headed for the storeroom. He had noticed that several one-man tents were also in the building, but chose the larger one because it would not only accommodate himself and his bedroll but the rest of his belongings as well. He had set it up to try it out that very day. It was of a much higher quality than the one he had brought from home. Not only did it have a small dome that could be removed to reveal a smokehole, it also had an extra sheet of fitted canvas that could be used as a floor. He had decided right away that he would use the tent, and use it often.

Eli carried a two-week-old full-page article from the Cuero newspaper in his saddlebag. Written by the paper's ed-itor, it began with the death of Johnny Hook and the subse-quent trial and acquittal of Eli Pilgrim, then continued with Pilgrim's killing of Johnny Hook's brother, Digger, at Hank Fry's livery stable. With his dying words Digger Hook had confessed to ambushing Eli Pilgrim and Big Step Benson on Oxbow Road, the article stated, and he had also implicated Clem, Clayton, and Booger Horn in the dastardly deed. Benson had died from a bullet wound to the head, and Pilgrim had recovered only after several days of suffering. Several witnesses, including Sheriff Rone Beasley, had heard the confession, and the lawman had immediately proclaimed the shooting to be justifiable homicide.

The article ended by stating that the Horn brothers had obviously left the area, for no one had seen any of them since the day of the bushwhacking. It quoted Sheriff Beasley as saying he intended to see that the U.S. marshal tracked them down and brought them back to Cuero to stand trial.

Eli laughed when he first read the last paragraph, for he knew that Sheriff Beasley had no control whatsoever over the district federal marshal and probably did not even know the man. Knowing that he himself would not wait around for a U.S. marshal or anyone else to act, Eli had folded the entire page and put it in his pocket, for there might come a day when he would need to show it to authorities in some strange town.

Just as Cliff Cates had promised, Eli ran into Gonzales Road shortly after crossing Dry Creek. Due to the heavy rains that had fallen several days ago, the creek did not live up to its name this morning. Even so, the water was no more than a few inches deep, and after drinking their fill, his animals splashed across it with no coaxing from him.

He had been on the road for less than a mile when he met a man headed south on a tall roan. Pilgrim moved his Peacemaker up and down in its holster a few times, then kept his right hand close to his gun butt as the rider drew near. The man appeared to be unarmed, and at a distance of forty yards, Eli could tell that he had never seen him before. A redheaded six-footer who was a little on the scrawny side, the man drew alongside Pilgrim and brought his animal to a halt. "Good morning," he said with a raspy voice. "Going up to Gonzales?"

Pilgrim nodded curtly. "I'm headed that way," he answered.

"Mighty good town," the man said, grinning from ear to ear. "Fact is, I pretty well expect to live out the rest of my days there." He pointed south. "I'm on my way to Cuero right now to try to buy the house I'm living in. I've been renting it for the past year, but the family that owns it lives down there. I've got a feeling that they'll sell it to me if I offer 'em enough money."

Pilgrim stifled a chuckle. "I've got the same feeling," he said. "Good luck to you." He kneed the buckskin and rode on up the hill. When he looked over his shoulder a few moments later, the redhead had already disappeared around the curve.

He ate two biscuits filled with ham about noon, washing them down with water from one of his canteens. Other than the two times he stopped to relieve himself, however, he traveled steadily all day long. The sun was less than two hours high when he reached a roadside sign reading that Gonzales was only two miles away. He watered his animals at a creek about a quarter mile past the sign, then crossed the shallow stream and left the road.

Green grass was practically nonexistent in the area at this time of the year, and since the pack mule carried a large sack of grain on its back, Pilgrim tied his animals very close to where he dropped his bedroll. He tied nose bags filled with oats on their heads, then smoothed out his campsite. He would set up the tent even though the night was clear, for anyone who might be passing on the road would have no way of knowing whether it was occupied or not. With the mule standing close by, he believed that any onlooker would think it was. He intended to ride the buckskin into town later, and he wanted a fire burning at his campsite while he was gone. He set up the tent within a matter of minutes, then began to gather up some thick chunks of wood left over from earlier camp-fires.

He put his coffeepot on the fire at sunset, then took the empty nose bags off his animals. As darkness closed in, he sat eating more biscuits and ham, washing them down with strong coffee.

When he had finished eating, he put all of his belongings, including his rifle and his shotgun, inside the tent. Then he built up the fire and banked it with rocks on all sides. He tied his mule to a nearby sapling, then mounted the buckskin. When he had ridden to the road, he sat his saddle for a few moments looking back at his campsite. No doubt about it, he was thinking as he gazed at his camp in the glow of the fire-light, a man on the road would simply suspect that some tired soul had stopped off and gone to bed early, and that he most likely had a small arsenal in the tent with him. A wise man would keep right on riding, or at least spread his own bedroll a respectable distance away.

Twenty minutes later, Pilgrim brought his buckskin to a halt on the edge of Gonzales. He sat looking down the street for several minutes as he tried to get the layout of the town in his mind. He could see that the main street was two or three blocks long, with at least two others running in the op-posite direction. Even from where he sat, he could identify the saloons and bawdy houses, for all were lit up brightly, and a small crowd of men stood around in front of the nearest one.

Since the saloon with the crowd was on the left-hand side of the street, Eli guided the buckskin as close to the right-hand boardwalk as possible. With the men standing in the glow of light shining through the windows and over the bat-wing doors of the saloon, he knew that none of them could see him as he rode down the dark side of the street. Even though he could see all of the men clearly, however, he rec-ognized nobody.

He rode on to the north end of town, then dismounted

and tied his horse at the hitching rail of a darkened hardware store. Then he began to walk past a few of the smaller saloons, slowing down long enough each time to look over the top of the bat-wing doors. Though all of the bars were crowded with drinkers, Eli always backed off quickly, for he recognized none of the men.

After several minutes he returned to his horse and remounted, then rode back down the dark side of the street. When he came even with the well-lighted saloon again, he sat his saddle till the men out front ended their discussion and decided to go back inside. Then he tied his horse and hurried over to the bat-wing doors. He mentally counted at least a dozen men at the bar but had never seen any of them before. He whirled and crossed the street at a trot, then mounted and rode out of town. He must get a good night's sleep, for tomorrow was going to be another busy day.

The fire was still burning brightly when he reached his campsite. He stripped the saddle from the buckskin's back and carried it into the tent, then snuffed out the fire with several handfuls of dirt and cold ashes. Then, after looking around him well enough to ascertain that there were no other campers in the immediate area, he crawled into the tent and stretched out on his bedroll. He was asleep in a matter of minutes.

He slept soundly. When he finally crawled out of the tent to relieve himself, he could see that the sky had already taken on a pinkish hue in the east. He sat down on his bedroll long enough to pull on his boots, then went about rekindling his fire. Once he had coaxed a flame to life, he headed for the creek with his coffeepot in his hand. A few minutes later, he was sitting on the ground watching his morning coffee boil.

18

THE TOWN of Gonzales, often called the "Lexington of Texas" because the first skirmish of the Texas revolution had been fought there, had been settled in 1825 by an American impresario named Green C. DeWitt, and named for Rafael Gonzales, then governor of Coahuila/Texas. And though designed by the Mexican government, the town's streets had nonetheless been named for saints.

It was past nine o'clock, and the town had already come to life when Pilgrim rode into Gonzales for the second time. He came to a halt at the edge of town and sat his saddle for a while looking the place over, just as he had the night before. Then, pulling the brim of his hat down low over his eyes, he kneed his horse and rode on down the street.

When he reached the middle of the block, a small building constructed of squared logs drew his attention. "New And Used Firearms," the sign out front read, then went on to inform one and all that a wide assortment of ammunition could be bought inside. Pilgrim brought the buckskin to a halt and sat thinking for a few moments, then guided the animal across the street to the establishment's hitching rail. He dismounted and greeted an old man passing by on the sidewalk, then stepped inside the store. A middle-aged man with a full shock of gray hair stood behind the counter. "Come in, young fellow," he said, "and thank you for stopping by my place. My name's Clyde Kelso, and if there's something I can help you with, I'd be tickled to death."

Pilgrim smiled, then walked to the counter. "I don't guess you could actually call me a customer," he said, " 'cause I can't think of anything I need. I just saw your sign outside, and thought you might be the right man to ask for some information."

"Ask away," the man said.

Eli leaned closer. "Did anybody happen to come by your place trying to sell some guns right after Christmas?" When the man took his time about answering, Pilgrim added, "It would have been one, two, or even three blond-haired men, and the guns would have been a Colt Peacemaker and a twelve-shot Henry rifle."

"Sure did," Kelso said. "I bought both of 'em the day after Christmas; got 'em from a blond-headed man about thirty years old." He took a few steps and reached for a rifle standing in a gun rack.

Pilgrim raised his hand quickly, causing the man to halt his motion. "Don't pick it up just yet," Eli said, "not till after I've described it well enough for us to know if it's the one I'm looking for." He held a forefinger against his temple for a moment as if it might help his thinking, then added, "There's a chip of wood missing on the right-hand side, right where the hand-piece fits against the barrel, and there are two big dents right in front of the trigger guard on the same side." He pointed to the rack. "Will you look and see if that's the same rifle you've got over there?"

Kelso stood shaking his head. "I don't have to look," he said. "I've already noticed the dents and the chipped hand-piece. Would you mind telling me why you're looking for the rifle?"

"No, sir," Pilgrim said. "Not at all." He told the merchant about the ambush on Christmas Eve; that one man had died in the incident, and that he himself had been wounded. "They stole all of our money and our guns, too," he said. "I heard one of 'em say they would bring the guns to Gonzales and sell 'em. That's why I decided to talk to you after I saw your sign outside."

Kelso reached into a box behind him and laid Pilgrim's Colt and gun belt on the counter. "Is this yours, too?" he asked.

Without touching the weapon, Eli nodded. "Absolutely," he said. "A fellow I work with at the Oxbow Ranch trimmed that holster up for me." He stood at the counter thinking for a few moments, then added, "If there's some way that we can work up a trade, I'd certainly like to have my guns back. My pa bought that Henry for me when I was ten years old."

Kelso chuckled softly. "Hell," he said, "if you was to go to the sheriff with it, he'd probably make me give 'em back to you for nothing. He sure did that once before, when I bought a stolen plow and some hand tools." He smiled broadly. "You damn right we can work up a trade. What did you have in mind?"

Pilgrim unbuckled the gun belt from his waist and laid it on the counter. "I had in mind trading you this outfit and the Henry on my saddle, for my old guns back. Of course, I wouldn't mind paying you a little boot if you don't want too much."

"Would you mind bringing the Henry in here so I can look at it?"

Pilgrim spun on his heel and headed for the hitching rail. Moments later, he laid the rifle on the counter. "It don't look quite as good as the one they stole from me," he said, "but it shoots just as true."

Kelso picked up the weapon and turned it from side to side. He worked the lever action twice, and two live shells fell out on the counter. "Damn," he said, "you didn't tell me it was full up and ready to go. Do you carry it around like that all the time?"

"No," Eli answered, "not all the time. Just when I'm hunting."

Kelso chuckled. "And I reckon you're hunting the men who killed your boss and stole your guns. Right?"

Pilgrim nodded. "Right," he said.

"Well, I hope to hell you find 'em, but I can't tell you much. The man who sold me the guns was by himself. Like I said before, he looked to be about thirty, and his face was kinda red, I mean a whole lot redder'n most light-headed people. Didn't say nothing about where he came from or where he might be going." Even as the man was talking he had been scrutinizing the weapons Eli had laid on the counter. "Seems to me like there oughtta be at least five dollars difference in the value of the two Colts, and about ten dollars difference between the two Henrys. Now, if you feel up to giving me fifteen bucks to boot, I reckon we've got us a trade."

Without another word, Pilgrim laid an eagle and a half eagle on the counter, then strapped his old gun belt around his waist. When he had transferred the shells from the Colt on the counter to the one that was now on his hip, he finished unloading the rifle and pointed to the gun rack. "If you'll hand me the Henry, I'll load it up and be on my way."

"Yes, sir," Kelso said, dropping the money into a drawer. He handed the rifle over, then stepped back with his arms folded across his chest. "The guns you traded me are gonna be a lot harder for me to sell, but to tell you the truth, I'm right glad to see you getting back what's yours."

"Me, too." Pilgrim said. "Now, would you direct me to the town marshal's office?"

"Be glad to," Kelso said, pointing. "Keep going west till you get to the courthouse, then turn north. You'll see Marshal Saw's office on the right-hand side of the street." He stood blowing for a moment on a book of cigarette papers to separate them, then snapped his fingers as if he had suddenly remembered something important. "I just thought of something that fellow who sold me the guns said. I don't know whether this'll mean anything to you or not, but he said he'd probably be needing a rifle that had a longer shooting range where he was going."

Eli stood digesting the man's words for a while: "A longer shooting range," he repeated to himself. Horn was no doubt headed for flat, open country. Uvalde!

"Thank you, Mr. Kelso," Pilgrim said, "and good luck to you." Moments later, he shoved the rifle he had grown up with into his saddle scabbard, then mounted the buckskin and took up the slack in the pack mule's lead rope.

The town marshal was standing outside his office leaning against the wall when Eli rounded the corner and pulled up at the hitching rail. A square-jawed, brown-haired man who appeared to be about thirty-five years old, he stood almost as tall as Pilgrim and was probably twenty pounds heavier. He nodded a greeting as Eli came to a halt and dismounted, but said nothing.

Pilgrim tied his animals and stepped up on the boardwalk. "I was wondering if I could talk with you a few minutes, Marshal," he said. "I'll try not to take up too much of your time."

The lawman chuckled and smiled broadly. "My time don't seem to be all that valuable this morning," he said. "In fact, I couldn't think of a single thing that I needed to be doing, so I've just been standing out here watching the world go by." He jerked his thumb toward the closed door, adding, "I've got some soft seats inside the office."

Once inside the building, the marshal offered a handshake. "I'm Jake Saw," he said, "and I'll be more than happy to help you if I can."

Pilgrim grasped the hand. "Eli Pilgrim," he said, "from Oxbow Ranch down at Cuero."

The lawman gripped the hand firmly, then released it. "I recognize the name from all the newspaper stories, Mr. Pilgrim," he said. "The Gonzales paper made a lot of hay out of your problems with the Hook brothers and the Horn brothers." He pulled out a cushioned chair for Eli, then walked behind his desk and seated himself. "Now," he said, "what brings you to this town?"

Pilgrim told him about the ambush on Oxbow Road, and the conversation he had heard between the Horn brothers. "I came to Gonzales looking for the Horns, Marshal, any or all of 'em. I know that at least one of 'em was here the day after Christmas, 'cause he sold my guns at Clyde Kelso's gun shop. I traded Kelso out of 'em this morning; he gave me a deal that I thought was reasonable, too."

The marshal nodded. "I'm glad you found your guns so easily," he said. "Now, as for the Horn brothers, I know 'em, all right, but I haven't seen any of 'em for about a year and a half." He scratched his head for a moment, then added, "It's been exactly that long, 'cause I remember it was the first week of July, the year before last. All three of 'em ganged up on an old drunk and damn near beat him to death in front of one of the saloons over on Main Street.

"They were still kicking the poor fellow in the ribs and holding his face down in the mud when I got there. I put all three of 'em in jail and kept 'em there for nearly a week. Their pa finally came up from Cuero and hired 'em a lawyer. The lawyer presented me with a court order next morning, and I had no choice but to turn 'em loose. If it had been left up to me, the bastards would still be in jail."

Pilgrim nodded. "And Big Step Benson would still be alive," he said. He was on his feet now. "I didn't really expect you to know where the Horns are, Marshal; I just decided to check with you because I was already in Gonzales. I'll be on my way now, so good luck to you."

"Good luck yourself," the lawman said. "I think you're the one who's gonna need it."

Pilgrim stepped off the boardwalk and untied his animals, then mounted and headed toward Main Street. Uvalde was several days' ride west of Gonzales.

He rode to the end of Main Street, then took the road to San Antonio, which, according to his map, was about the halfway point between Gonzales and Uvalde. He expected to set up camp in Uvalde County in about six days. By pitching his tent on the Frio River, he could very easily stay out of sight during the daytime, then still be no more than an hour's ride from the town of Uvalde after dark.

Once the sun went down he could ride into the settlement and prowl around at will. By taking his time and keeping to the shadows, a man could often move about completely unnoticed during the night hours. And Pilgrim was in no hurry. He was a young man with enough money in his pocket to live on for at least a year, and he seriously doubted that the same could be said for any of the Horns.

He fully expected to find one or all of the brothers around Uvalde, for Elmer Jude had made it plain that he thought they would head for Duke Hayden's Double D Ranch. Jude had said that he had no reason to believe Hayden knew his cousins were thieves and social outcasts, adding that "The Duke" himself was known as an upstanding citizen. "A man of unquestionable character" was the way Jude had described the rancher, something Eli would certainly remember.

Clem Horn had told Kelso that he expected to need a rifle with a longer shooting range than the Henry, which probably meant that he was heading for an area that was flat and relatively treeless; a place where sneaking up on a game animal for a close-up shot would be difficult. And even though the Henry could hardly be called a short-range rifle, it had nowhere near the shooting range of some of the buffalo guns, a few of which could knock an animal down from a distance of a mile or more. Horn had probably had the Sharps or the Spencer in mind when he mentioned a long-range rifle, and Pilgrim had already been told that Uvalde County was made up of terrain where such a weapon would offer a shooter an advantage.

He stopped at a roadside spring an hour before noon, then put the nose bags on his saddler and his pack mule. He gave each of the animals a small portion of oats, knowing that he would be more generous with the grain once the day's traveling was over. He gathered up an armload of kindling and started a fire, then filled his coffeepot with water and dropped in a handful of grounds. He laid out two biscuits and cut off a big slice of cheddar cheese, then leaned back on his elbows to wait. Dinner would be ready in about fifteen minutes.

Once the coffeepot had come to a boil, he snuffed out the fire with handfuls of dirt, then began to concentrate on his food. Even as he sat eating, two canvas-covered freight wagons drawn by four-horse teams pulled off the road and halted at the spring. Headed west, the vehicles were driven by two men who appeared to be about Pilgrim's own age. Each of the men wore a high-crowned hat pulled low over his eyes, and both sported thick, black beards.

In spite of the fact that Eli could not see much of their faces, he nonetheless gauged the men to be brothers, for not only did they move around the same way as they jumped to the ground and began to unhitch their teams, it also sounded as if they were speaking with the same voice when they offered a greeting. "How're you doing this morning?" they asked almost in unison. Then the taller of the two added, "I reckon we better enjoy this pretty weather while we can, 'cause winter's gonna be hitting us any day now."

Pilgrim got to his feet. "I'm doing very well," he said, "and I believe you're right about the weather. I sure never have seen anything like it before. Back where I came from, folks start looking for a hole to crawl into about the first of January."

"And where might that be?" the man asked.

"Ohio," Eli answered.

Nodding curtly, the man led his horses up the hill and let them drink from the spring's runoff, then brought them back to the wagon. "Never been to Ohio myself," he said, "but I've heard about all that snow and ice. Don't want me none of that stuff."

Eli shook his head. "I can't say that I liked it either," he said.

Neither of the drivers spoke again till after both teams had been watered and rehitched to the wagons. Then the second man climbed to the seat and untied the reins from the brake pole. "Going far?" he asked, looking at Pilgrim.

"Going to Uvalde," Eli answered.

The man backed the team up a few yards so he could turn the wagon around, then pointed west. "We're going to San Antonio on this run, and to tell you the truth, I don't envy you one bit on your trip to Uvalde. If that place ain't the end of the world, I'll damn sure pay for lying." He slapped one of the horses on its rump with the reins, then the big vehicle rolled out onto the road. His partner was close behind, and the wagons were out of sight in short order.

Eli sat beside the ashes of his campfire sipping coffee till the pot was empty, then mounted and headed west at a trot. When he overtook the freight wagons a few minutes later, he turned off the road and took to an open field, waving to both drivers as he passed. "Good luck in Uvalde!" the smaller of the two men called out loudly. "I'd say you're damn sure gonna need it!"

Once he had passed the wagons, Pilgrim returned to the road and continued on at a trot. Since he had received two warnings about Uvalde within the past few minutes, he was wondering what might be wrong with the town. Had the man doing the talking had some kind of unpleasant experience there, or could it be that he simply did not like the looks of the place? Eli knew that either instance was possible, for how many towns had he himself ridden into that he disliked for no particular reason? More than a few, he said to himself.

It could be that he would like Uvalde for the same reasons the freighter did not, Pilgrim was thinking, but whether he liked the town or not mattered little to him. He had no intention of taking up residence there. He would be there only long enough to take care of business, then he would return to his job on the Oxbow Ranch. He kicked the buckskin to a faster gait. He wanted to put at least another twenty miles behind him before the day was done.

AT MIDAFTERNOON six days later, Pilgrim forded the Frio River and pitched his tent between two large mesquite trees. It was an excellent campsite, and some thoughtful soul had even built a fireplace by banking several flat rocks in a circle. Eli put the nose bags on his animals, then walked around till he had gathered up an armload of deadwood. After coaxing a flame from a handful of kindling, he set his coffeepot and a potful of lima beans on the fire. He had a loaf of bread in his pack that he had bought at a grocery store earlier in the day.

The town of Uvalde was less than five miles to the west, but he would not go there until after nightfall. Nor did he intend to rent a hotel room there. He would stay right where he was for however long he remained in the area, for he could ride into town whenever he chose, then head back to the tent anytime he took a notion. A man could learn a lot by traipsing around a town at night, and if he was careful and stayed in the shadows, he could keep his chances of being spotted and recognized to a minimum. And Pilgrim would be careful.

The sun was still two hours high when he decided that his beans were done. He had just dished up a plateful and poured himself a third cup of coffee, when he had company. Riding down the east bank of the river astride a tall sorrel, the man brought the animal to a halt about ten yards from

Pilgrim's fire. "Howdy," he said, beginning to blow on a book of cigarette papers that he had taken from his vest pocket. "Have you been here long?"

"No," Pilgrim answered. "Probably less than three hours."

The man had a three-day growth of brown beard and appeared to be about twenty-five years old. He selected a paper, then rolled up a cigarette and touched it with a burning match. "Well, I don't reckon the boss minds if a fellow camps here overnight," he said, blowing a puff of smoke to the wind. "Of course, if a man was to start putting up something permanent, that would be another matter altogether. You expect to be gone within the next day or so?"

Pilgrim set his plate and his coffee cup down on a large rock, then got to his feet. "I don't know exactly when I can get on the road again," he said. He pointed to his mule. "Old Zebra there has sorta come up lame. Might be a few more days before he can travel."

"Well," the man said, sliding from his saddle, "which hoof is it? Let me take a look at it."

Eli shook his head quickly. "That won't be necessary," he said, "I've already done everything that could be done. He had a rock buried in the frog; I just dug it out and cleaned it up a little. He'll be fine in a day or two."

"All right," the man said, leaning against his horse. "Whatever you say."

Pilgrim pointed to the fire. "Plenty of beans and coffee there," he said. "You're more than welcome."

The man took a tin cup out of his saddlebag. "I don't want no beans," he said, "but I believe I could handle a little of that coffee." He reached into the saddlebag again. "I've got sugar here, too. I always carry some with me, 'cause most people I run into ain't got none." He walked to the coffeepot and filled his cup, then stirred the sugar in with a spoon that he had also been carrying in his saddlebag. "Where you coming from?" he asked as he sat down cross-legged beside the tent. "You been riding around looking for work?"

Pilgrim chuckled, then shook his head. "I've been riding around all right," he said, "but I'm sure not looking for work. I guess you could say that I took a leave of absence from the job I already had. I just wanted to see some of the country, and this winter seemed like a good time to do it."

The man sipped his coffee noisily, then chuckled softly. "I don't know why I even asked you that last question," he said. "There ain't no opening on the Double D, nohow, and I ain't got the authority to hire a man even if there was."

"The Double D?" Pilgrim asked. "This is the Double D Ranch?"

"Sure is," the man answered. He refilled his cup and re-seated himself, then offered a handshake. "My name's Alf Hand," he said, "and I've been working here a little over three years. You sounded like you'd heard of the Double D before. Is that right?"

Pilgrim shook the man's hand. "My name's Jim Smith," he said, "and, yes, I have heard of the Double D before. I don't remember exactly who, but I believe somebody once told me that it was a good place to work."

"It is a good place to work," Hand said. "Of course, like I said before, there ain't no opening right now. The boss had to turn down some of his own kinfolks a while back. Three of his cousins came riding in from somewhere east of here needing work, but Mr. Hayden didn't have no place to put 'em. He made a job for one of 'em, but the other two hung around for one night, then kept on riding. The Duke put the youngest one, the one they call Booger, to work up at the northeast line shack. He won't really have to know much to handle that job."

"Booger," Eli repeated softly. "That sure is an unusual name."

"Well, I don't guess that's his real name," Hand said, "but that's what all the Haydens call him: Booger Horn."

Booger Horn, Eli repeated to himself. He had struck pay

dirt. "I used to live in a line shack," he said. "I had to do an awful lot of hard riding, but that didn't bother me much. The hardest part of it was having to do my own cooking."

"Well, he's gonna have to do his own cooking, too, but he won't have to do much hard riding. The river ain't no more'n fifty yards east of that line shack, and I believe it'll turn the cattle back." He dashed his coffee grounds toward a bush, adding, "No, sir, he ain't gonna have no hard job a-tall."

Pilgrim changed the subject. "I guess the Double D's a pretty big outfit," he said. He pointed south, then north. "Probably runs for at least a dozen miles in both directions."

Hand smiled. "It would if we were sitting in the middle of it," Hand said, "but we ain't. I reckon it's somewhere around twenty miles to the southern border, but the line on the north side ain't more'n four miles from here." He pointed north. "On the far side of that rise up yonder is a long, level valley that eventually turns into a wooded area. Right there in that big stand of timber is where the property line is, and it's more'n fifteen miles to the western border." He was on his feet now. "Yes, sir," he said, "I reckon you could say that the Double D is a pretty big spread. I wouldn't take nothing for my job here, either."

"I know what you mean," Eli said. "If a fellow's got a job he likes he'd better hang on to it, 'cause good ones are hard to come by these days."

Hand nodded, then walked to his horse and dropped his cup and his spoon in the saddlebag. He picked up the reins and stepped into the saddle, then spoke again: "I've got to be going now," he said. "I hope your mule's hoof heals up in a hurry, and you enjoy your vacation. You take care, now." He kicked his animal in the ribs, then headed west at a canter.

Pilgrim stood watching till the man disappeared among the junipers and the cedars, then he dumped the cold beans back into the pot. After stirring the pot a few times, he refilled his plate and his coffee cup, then reseated himself on the ground. Unable to believe that things were working out so easily for him, he sat enjoying his hot meal. He had been dreading making an appearance in Uvalde, and had been immensely glad to learn that he probably would not have to. Alf Hand had not only told him where to find Booger Horn but exactly how many miles it was to the line shack.

As soon as Pilgrim had finished eating, he poured the remainder of the coffee on the fire, then struck his tent. He could easily travel another four miles before calling it a night. The fact that he would have to travel part of that distance after dark would actually work in his favor, for he did not want to take a chance on Booger Horn spotting him.

Alf Hand had said that the Double D property line was located on a hill in heavy timber, and it seemed logical that the line shack was also there. Knowing that both sides of a river were usually made up of the same type of terrain, Eli supposed that the east bank of the Frio was also timbered. He would travel north on the east bank till he came to a big stand of hardwoods, then make camp. There he would remain until it was time to take care of business.

He saddled the buckskin and loaded the pack mule, then forded the Frio and turned north. The sun was no more than one hour high, then the protection of darkness would be upon him. The moon would be in its first-quarter phase, offering enough light for him to see where he was going but not enough to give away his presence.

When he had ridden over the rise, he found himself in the long, level valley that Hand had mentioned. And though the moon had already replaced the sun that had slipped over the western horizon, Eli could see no farther than a few yards in any direction. He moved closer to the water, for the river was his only means of keeping his bearings. He stayed within seeing distance of the water till he came to the hill, then rode into the timber for about two hundred yards.

He dismounted and tied his animals to a ten-foot sapling, then dropped his bedroll in the levelest place he could find.

Then, with his shotgun in his hand, he began to weave his way through the trees toward the riverbank. Looking west, he could see where the timber ended and the river began, for it was much like seeing a light at the end of a tunnel. He moved from one tree to another stealthily till he came to the river-bank, then suddenly came to a halt. There, across the river and about two hundred yards away, was the unmistakeable glow of lamplight shining through a window. He nodded with satisfaction. He had no doubt that he was now looking at Booger Horn's current place of residence.

He stood behind the trunk of a big cypress, thinking. Should he ford the Frio and kick the door to that shack in right now? No, he decided quickly. It was very possible that a kick would not open the door, which would put him in a vulnerable position. And did he know for sure that Horn was alone in the shack? No. Though logistics dictated that the man would indeed be alone, Eli was unwilling to bet his life on it. He backtracked to his bedroll. He would stay away from the shack till after he had done some scouting during the light of day. He spread his bedroll a few yards from his animals and was asleep in minutes.

When he opened his eyes again, he could see that the sky was already taking on a pinkish hue in the east. Knowing that the timing could not have been better, he pulled on his boots, then walked a few steps to relieve himself. He put on his fleece-lined coat and buttoned it up to his chin, then picked up his shotgun and his spyglass. After walking about a hundred fifty yards, he found himself beside the same cypress tree that he had stood behind the night before. Daylight was coming on fast now, and he could already see the timber on the west bank of the river. He moved behind the tree and sat down on the ground cross-legged.

Twenty minutes later, there was enough light for him to make out the back side of the line shack. The small building had been built with twelve-inch boards, and the door was ob-viously on one of the other three sides. Remembering how the lamp had shown through the window the night before, Eli knew that it was on the south side. He was hoping that the door was also on the south side, so he could see Horn when the man stepped into the yard. From his present position, all he could see was the east wall.

When he saw smoke coming from the flue a few minutes later, Eli knew that Horn was in the process of fixing his breakfast. Pilgrim kept his eyes glued to the shack. He was still sitting behind the tree holding the small telescope to his eyes when he saw a door open on the south side of the building. When a man stepped into the yard and stood stretching and yawning, Eli had no problem identifying him as Booger Horn. Though he could seen no barn or corral, Eli nonetheless supposed that the man's horses were somewhere on the south side of the building, and that he was about to feed them and get them ready for a day's work.

When Horn moved out of sight in a northwesterly direction, Pilgrim kept the telescope on the spot where he had last seen the man. Five minutes later, Horn reappeared and reentered the shack. Eli lowered the spyglass and nodded. The man had just fed his horses, he was thinking, and would very soon be eating his own breakfast. After that, he would saddle one of his mounts and head west, for as Alf Hand had said, there was no reason for him to patrol the eastern boundary. The Frio River worked very well as an artificial barrier.

Half an hour later, Horn was back in the yard. He disappeared once again, then reappeared five minutes later astride a small sorrel. He dismounted and spent a few moments inside the shack, then remounted and kicked the little horse in the ribs. He guided the animal around the building, then headed west. He was out of sight quickly. Eli had no doubt that the man would be gone for most of the day.

Knowing that he would build no fire this morning, Pilgrim returned to his bedroll. He put the nose bags on his animals, then sat down to his own breakfast of bologna sausage, cheddar cheese, and soda crackers. Even after he had eaten as much food as he needed, he sat for a while longer washing oatmeal cookies down with water from his canteen.

Half an hour later, he mounted the buckskin and led the mule out of the timber. He allowed the animals to drink their fill at the river, then trotted them back up the hill. He tied the mule to the same sapling, then remounted the saddler. He had some scouting to do.

He kicked the horse to a canter and rode out of the trees on the south side. He forded the Frio where the water was no more than knee-deep to the buckskin, then hurried the animal up the opposite bank. He turned north till he was well into the trees, then dismounted and tied the saddler to a low-hanging tree limb. He moved his Peacemaker up and down in its holster a few times, then pulled his shotgun out of the boot and walked toward the line shack. Though he had just seen his quarry ride off to the west, Eli nonetheless moved along soundlessly, almost creeping. A man never knew what he might come upon in the woods, and besides, moving about quietly had long since become second nature to him.

A few minutes later, he came to a spring that had been boxed in with wide boards. The tracks and the droppings scattered around it left no doubt as to where the animals did their drinking, and a tin cup was turned upside down on a nearby rock. He circled the spring, then came upon a tin-roofed shed that was adjacent to a small corral. Even from where he stood he could see that the pole enclosure held only one horse. That would be Booger Horn's relief animal, Pilgrim was thinking, and the man would be back to switch mounts sometime between midmorning and noon. When that happened, Eli intended to be waiting.

He stood watching for a few moments, then walked up the hill to the line shack. A twist of the knob opened the door, and he took in the scene at a single glance: a cast-iron stove stood in the northwest corner, and a small table and two chairs took up most of the south side. Two bunks had been built against the east wall, and both were well supplied with blankets. A rifle, appearing to be a .22 caliber, leaned against the wall in the southeast corner. Eli closed the door, then took up his vigil behind the shed. He had no way of knowing if his wait would be long or short.

Sitting cross-legged and consulting his watch on a regular basis, his wait could hardly have been called a long one. He had just stood up to stomp some feeling back into his feet when he heard hoofbeats in the distance. The time was nine-thirty.

Completely hidden from the oncoming rider by the crib, Eli stood where he was for a few moments, then began to slowly circle the structure as the man got closer. By the time Horn pulled up at the corral gate, Pilgrim was at the northwest corner of the crib.

Horn dismounted and opened the gate, then led his mount into the corral. He stripped the saddle and the bridle, then watched the tired animal walk away with its head hanging low. He hung the bridle on the fence post and dropped the saddle just outside the gate, then took a few steps toward the line shack.

Pilgrim suddenly stepped around the northwest corner of the crib, a double-barreled, ten-gauge shotgun pressed against his shoulder. "Stop right there, Horn!" he said loudly. "Pull that Colt out of its holster with your thumb and forefinger, and let it fall to the ground!" When Horn hesitated, Pilgrim shouted, "Now!"

The man complied, then raised his arms high above his head. "What's the meaning of this?" he asked. "Wha . . . who're you?"

Eli took his time about answering, but finally spoke. "Are you telling me that the beard fooled you, Horn? Are you saying you don't recognize your old friend, Eli Pilgrim?"

Watching the man like a hawk watches a rabbit, Eli could easily tell when the realization of who he was facing finally hit him. "Eli . . . Pil . . . Pilgrim," the man stammered, then grew tight-lipped. He stood quietly for a few moments, then started over. "I'd already decided to come back up to Cuero next week and get all that stuff straightened out.

"I didn't have nothing a-tall to do with that shooting, and I tried everything I knew to talk the rest of 'em out of it. They didn't listen to me, but I decided yesterday that I was gonna come back up there and clear my name. Now, Digger Hook was the man who shot you, Mr. Pilgrim, and my older brother Clem is the one shot Big Step Benson." He chewed on his lower lip for a moment, then added, "I'd even be willing to go back to Cuero and testify to that in court. I can tell the law where to find both of my brothers, too."

Pilgrim stood staring at the man for a few moments, then spoke through clenched teeth. "Let's just pretend that I'm the law," he said, "then you can tell me where to find Clem and Clayton Horn. You'd better not lie to me, either."

Horn shook his head. "Ain't got no reason to lie," he said. "Like I told you before, I had already decided to come back up there and clear my name."

"Well," Eli said with raised eyebrows, "start talking."

"Clayton headed straight for Webb County," Horn said. "He spent more'n a year in Laredo once before, and he's been talking about going back ever since. Pete Caldwell owns a ranch and several other businesses down there, and he'll be the man who can tell you exactly where Clayton is."

Pilgrim continued to hold the double barrel in line with Horn's face. "And Clem?" he asked.

"Clem's always wanted to catch on with a trail herd headed north. He ain't never done it before, but it sure ain't nothing he couldn't do. He's been around cattle all his life."

When nothing else was forthcoming, Eli punched the air with the shotgun. "And just where is he figuring on catching on with that trail herd?" he asked.

"He said he was gonna go down around Edna, first. He knows a few people there, and he didn't seem to have no doubt that he could get work. Probably be able to get a job easy enough two or three months from now. That's about when everybody'll start putting their trail herds together."

The longer he looked down the twin barrels at Horn, the more disgusted Eli became with the man. Not only had he lied about trying to talk the others out of the bushwhacking, he was now willing to sell his brothers out in order to save his own skin. "There's something you oughtta know before we part, Horn," Pilgrim said. "I happen to know that you didn't try to talk anybody out of anything. You stood there beside that dead buggy horse talking about how long it took me to fall when Digger Hook shot me. I heard it with my own ears, mister. You laughed and bragged about how quick Big Step fell when Clem shot him, and you thought it was funny, you son of a bitch. If it hadn't been for the fact that you thought I was already dead, you'd have put a bullet in my brain yourself."

Even as Pilgrim was talking, he was squeezing both of the shotgun's triggers. The big weapon knocked Booger Horn end over end, then rolled him up against a fence post like a rag doll. Eli did not need a closer look to know that the man was dead. Nobody lived over two loads of double-aught buckshot in the face. He put the spent shells in his coat pocket and reloaded the weapon. Then, after checking to see that the dead man's horses had enough water in their trough to last them till the supply wagon came by, he headed for his own horse at a trot.

An hour later, Pilgrim rode out of the trees and led his pack mule down the hill. Booger Horn had said that his brother Clayton had gone to Laredo, and that Clem would most likely be hanging around the town of Edna. Since Laredo was closer to Eli's present position, it would be his first stop. He followed the Frio River for a few hours, then when it began to snake around in an easterly direction, he forded it and headed cross-country. Laredo was about a week's ride due south.

He had filled both of his canteens and allowed his animals to drink their fill before leaving the Frio, for he knew that water might soon become a scarce commodity. As he rode along he was consulting his map, which showed that the Nueces River was only a few hours' ride to the west. And although it eventually turned back to the east, it ran south all the way across Zavala County. He could follow it for a few days, then ride southwest till he came to the Rio Grande if that became necessary. The Rio Grande would not only furnish him with all the water he needed, it would lead him straight to Laredo.

He made a dry camp the first night, and when he had not come upon a creek or a spring by midmorning of the next day, he turned west and urged the buckskin to a ground-eating trot. His animals needed water, and according to his map, the Nueces was less than ten miles away. After holding the same pace for about two hours, he topped a small rise and saw a long line of green cypress trees at the bottom of a long slope.

The pack animal seemed to sense the water before the buckskin did, for the little mule was suddenly abreast of Pilgrim, trotting along with its ears laid back and its nose pointed toward the river. When the saddler finally smelled the water, however, he took the slack out of the lead rope very quickly. Both animals were soon drinking noisily from the shallow Nueces.

Pilgrim refilled both of his canteens, then stood beside his horse consulting his map again. In about forty miles the river would make a sharp turn to the east, and that's where he would leave it. A day's ride in a southwesterly direction would then take him on to the Rio Grande, bringing his water problems to an end. He returned the map to his saddlebag, then remounted and forded the river. He knew that he would eventually have to be on the west bank anyway, and this was probably the shallowest place he was going to find.

He headed downstream at a fast walk, a pace that he held for the remainder of the day. An hour before sunset, he rode into a small grove of mesquite trees and dismounted. He could easily see that he was not the first man to choose the place for a campsite, for the ashes of a large number of campfires were scattered about. Someone had even left a small pile of deadwood, about enough for him to boil his supper coffee and cook breakfast in the morning. He smiled at his good fortune, then began to fill the animals' nose bags with grain.

After gathering up several handfuls of twigs, dead leaves, and grass, he soon had a fire going under his coffeepot. He laid out a bag of soda crackers, two tins of fish, and a can opener, then led his pack mule and his saddler a few yards farther down the river. By the time he had picketed the animals and returned to the fire, his pot had come to a boil. He poured himself a cup of coffee, then opened both tins of fish. Then, thanks to the many companies that had within the last several years began to offer meat and fish in tin cans, he sat down to his meal. He ate a few handfuls of crackers and all of the fish, then threw the empty cans over his shoulder. The food had not only been quick and convenient, it had tasted good, and he expected to add several additional cans to his pack at the first opportunity.

He kicked dirt over the fire just as night came on, then spread his bedroll in a nearby clump of bushes. After making sure that all of his weapons were close to hand, he crawled under his blankets. Then, using his heavy coat for a pillow, he lay in the darkness for a long time, thinking. Had his brothers and his mother made any headway toward putting their own company together? he asked himself. Had they already bought more property and acquired more hogs?

His mother had seemed to be set on the idea. She had called the shots in the family since Eli could first remember, he was thinking, and he seriously doubted that his brothers would disagree with her now. If either of the boys voted against expanding the operation it would be Justin. His vote would quickly be overridden by his oldest brother, however, for Lawton had never been known to argue with his mother about anything. Eli hoped they did expand the farm and start producing their own brand of bacon and sausage. And if he had not decided to leave home, he would have cast his vote to do exactly that.

He also wondered if his mother had ever attempted to close the gap between herself and Uncle Neely. Two of the finest people who ever drew a breath, he was thinking; two people sorely in need of each other, and both of them too proud to mention it. After thinking on it a little longer, he decided that, sometime before the year was out, he was going to write a letter to each of them. "Since you live less than a mile apart," the letter would read, "it should be easy for both of you to walk halfway across the hill and give each other a hug. Then, finding a preacher should be a simple matter." He chuckled, then turned over and went to sleep.

The next time he opened his eyes he could see the sun

coming out of the Earth a few miles to the east. He pulled on his boots and walked a few steps to relieve himself, then sat back down on his bed. He slipped on the coat that he had used for a pillow, even though the morning was not uncomfortably cool. He doubted that he would see many cold days on this trip, for, according to what he had been told, winter sometimes passed Southwest Texas by. All of which would suit him very well, for he had seen enough cold weather back in Ohio to last him a lifetime.

He walked downriver and moved his animals to new grass, then built up his fire. While the remainder of last night's coffee was reheating, he sliced several potatoes into his skillet, then added a few small chunks of smoked ham. Twenty minutes later, he sat down to a breakfast that was considerably better than the average trail fare.

When he had finished eating, he kicked dirt over the fire, then walked to the river and washed his skillet. He readied his pack, then headed downriver with the bridles in his hand. He had deliberately saved this chore till last, for he wanted his animals to graze as long as possible before beginning their workday. Half an hour later, he mounted the buckskin and yanked on the pack mule's lead rope.

According to his map, there was a small town about ten miles ahead called Hugo Springs. If the settlement had a grocery store, he would try to replenish his supply of tinned meat and fish there. Maybe he was becoming spoiled, but he saw no reason in the world why a man should have to cook his supper after traveling all day; not when he could simply open a few cans and heat up their contents, then sit down to a meal that tasted about the same. No, sir, he would not be doing quite as much cooking in the future, for recently he had even seen an advertisement in a magazine for canned beans. The ad had been hawking not only the beans but canned cherries and peaches as well. He nodded at his thoughts. He would check into the matter when he reached Hugo Springs.

Though the road along the river was at least as good as

most, he met only one wagon during the next two hours. A large freighter drawn by a four-horse hitch was headed north with a load of green two-by-fours. Pilgrim yielded the right of way, and the two burly men sitting on the seat waved a greeting as the big vehicle rolled by. Pilgrim answered with a wave of his own arm, then guided his animals back on to the roadway.

He reached Hugo Springs at midmorning. As he sat his saddle beside the welcome sign, he could see about everything the town had to offer. About a dozen buildings lined both sides of the short street, but the most prominent establishment, and the one sporting the largest sign, was "Bolen's Grocery." Two boardwalks ran the length of the town, and even from where he sat Eli could see a man sitting in a rocking chair in front of the store. Pilgrim kneed the buckskin on down the street, coming to a halt at the store's hitching rail. Sitting on the porch about twenty feet away, the man eyed him for a moment but said nothing.

Eli dismounted and tied his animals, then spoke. "Is this your store?" he asked, pointing.

Exceptionally skinny, with gray hair sticking out on all sides of his hat, the man appeared to be about forty years old. And although he was seated, it was easy to see that he was well over six feet tall. He smiled, then nodded. "Belongs to me and the bank," he said, getting to his feet. He headed for the doorway, adding over his shoulder. "Come on in: you'll be my first customer of the day."

Pilgrim followed him through the doorway. "What I'm looking for is some canned stuff," he said. "Tinned meat and fish. Fruit and vegetables too, if you happen to have 'em."

"Sure, I got 'em," the man said. He pointed to the middle aisle. "All of that stuff on the lower shelf is priced at a nickel a can. Had to cut the price in order to sell 'em, 'cause everybody that saw 'em thought they were old. That ain't really the case at all. Now, it's true that the cans have got a certain amount of rust on 'em, but they're actually newer'n a whole lot of that other stuff there.

"A deliveryman that weren't too bright in the head stacked 'em up on the porch out there one day when the store was closed, and it rained on 'em. They sat there with that water on 'em all weekend, and the rust just naturally took 'em over. That stuff is just as good as it was when it was brand-new, and I'll guarantee you that there ain't no rust on the inside of the cans. I opened up two of 'em myself and looked."

"Yes, sir," Eli said, heading down the aisle. "I believe you." Within minutes, he had set aside an assortment of goods from the lower shelf, some tarnished with rust, some not. "I've got fourteen cans here," he said to the grocer, who was now standing at the head of the aisle.

"Yes, sir," the man said. "Let me get you a box."

"I won't need one," Eli said. "If you'll help me take the cans out to my mule, we can do it in one trip." He handed the man a dollar. "Take your money out of this, and I won't have to come back in."

The man complied, and a few minutes later, Pilgrim rode on through the town. The road ran parallel to the river, sometimes within a few feet of the bank. In fact, it ran too close in a few places, for portions of it had been washed away by heavy rains and high water. In those areas, the wide-wheeled freight wagons had simply taken to the treeless prairie, and other traffic had been quick to follow.

He rode at a fast walk for the remainder of the day, and at sunset dropped his bedroll, saddle, and packsaddle on the ground at a wide bend in the river. He would camp here for the night, for his map showed that the river made a sharp turn to the east. He would head southwest in the morning, riding across a long stretch of arid land where the presence of water would be questionable. He would try to coax the mule and his saddler into drinking a little more than usual in the morning, and would not slow down till he reached the Rio Grande.

He put the nose bags on the animals, making a mental note that he had only enough grain left for one more feeding. Getting another sack of oats should be no problem, however, for his map showed that a town called Diego Wells was about thirty miles ahead of him. The town lay on the east bank of the Rio Grande and, judging from the size of its dot on the map, had a sizable population. A lot of people meant a lot of horses, he was thinking; therefore at least one feed store.

He found kindling and deadwood easy enough, and soon had a fire going. After putting a pot of coffee on to boil, he laid out a bag of crackers and the two cans that he intended to open for his supper. The labels on both the beef and the beans claimed they had been canned in Chicago, and Eli supposed that was true. He had certainly never heard of a commercial cannery anywhere else.

When his coffee came to a boil, he pulled it off the fire and poured half a cup of cold water in the pot to settle the grounds. Then he dropped the empty nose bags on the ground and led his animals about forty yards downriver, where the grass was greener and more plentiful. He picketed them on forty-foot ropes, then returned to his fire and poured himself a cup of coffee. He opened the cans and poured their contents in his skillet, then seated himself on the ground cross-legged to wait for his supper to heat. A short time later, he ate a meal of beef, beans, and crackers, then sat around till daylight faded, munching on oatmeal cookies and sipping coffee.

He finally carried his bedroll to a patch of tall weeds thirty feet away, then returned to the fire and snuffed it out with several handfuls of dirt. A few minutes later, he pulled off his boots and stretched out under his blankets, all of his weapons close to hand. He was asleep quickly.

He was up at the crack of dawn next morning, and restarting the fire he had smothered the night before was an easy matter. He heated up his leftover coffee and another can of beef, and ate breakfast just as the sun was rising. He took his cup, coffeepot, and skillet to the river and washed them, then returned them to his pack. Wanting to get an early start, he headed downriver to get his animals. He fed them the last of the grain, then mounted and headed cross-country.

He had been riding for about two hours when he came to a wagon road that angled in from the north, then continued on in a southwesterly direction. After a look at his pocket compass confirmed that the road was running the way he needed to go, he guided the buckskin onto it. Any doubts that he might have had as to its destination disappeared about an hour later, when he came to a roadside sign reading that the town of Diego Wells was twenty miles straight ahead. Nodding with satisfaction, he kicked the buckskin to a trot.

He reached the river about an hour before he reached the town. The sun was still about three hours high when his animals picked up the pace of their own accord, leaving no doubt in Pilgrim's mind that they smelled water ahead. He let them continue at a fast trot till they topped a small rise, then he himself could see the water. A few minutes later, both man and beasts drank their fill.

The first building he came to when he reached Diego Wells was the livery stable. When he dismounted in the wide doorway, he was met by a tall, middle-aged man who was obviously of Mexican descent. "How do you do, sir?" the man asked in perfect English. "Can I help you?"

"I believe you can," Pilgrim answered, offering up the buckskin's reins and the pack mule's lead rope. "I was hoping I could leave my animals with you for the night."

"Of course," the man said, offering a handshake. "My name is Jose Alvarez, and taking care of livestock is my specialty."

"My name's Pilgrim," Eli said, then pumped the man's hand a few times. "As far as I know, I'll only be in town for one night. You got oats for sale?"

"No, sir. Got plenty of shelled corn and hay, but I haven't had any oats since way back before Christmas."

Eli nodded. "Just feed 'em and hay 'em tonight and in

the morning, then I'll put a bushel of corn on the pack mule tomorrow, if you don't mind."

"If I don't mind?" the man asked with a chuckle. "Of course I don't mind, sir. The corn will be sacked up and waiting for you in the morning."

Pilgrim nodded, then motioned to the saddle scabbards. "How about my long guns?" he asked. "Is it gonna be safe for me to leave 'em here?"

"Absolutely," Alvarez said. He pointed toward an enclosure that Eli took to be the office. "I sleep right there in that room, and I'll put your guns in the corner behind my bed. Ain't nobody gonna even know they're in there."

"That sounds good," Eli said. He jerked his thumb toward the town. "Is there a place to rent a room down there?"

"Two hotels and a boardinghouse," the hostler answered. "If I were you, I'd stay at the Grande Hotel. Now, the place ain't actually all that grand, but they've got a restaurant and a saloon there, and that oughtta come in handy. If a fellow wants a drink and something to eat to go along with his bed, he don't have to go off somewhere else looking for 'em."

Eli nodded. "I think I'm in the mood for some supper and a drink both, Jose. How far to the hotel?"

"About two hundred yards," Alvarez answered, then pointed south. "Just keep walking in that direction, and you'll see it on the right-hand side of the street. There's a big sign out front."

Pilgrim draped his saddlebags across his shoulder and headed toward town. "I'll be back about sunup in the morning," he said over his shoulder. He walked at a fast clip till he reached the hotel, then pushed the door open and stepped inside. A young man not yet out of his teens offered a big smile from his seat behind the counter. "Come right in, sir," he said, getting to his feet. "Thank you for stopping at the Grande. Can I help you?"

Pilgrim walked across the room and laid his saddlebags

on the counter. "I've been on the road for quite a while," he said. "You got a room with a good bed?"

"Yes, sir," the young man said, his smile remaining constant. "Every bed in this building is a good one. You want to sleep upstairs or downstairs?"

"Makes no difference to me," Eli said. He spun the register around and signed "Jim Smith" in big letters, then stood waiting.

"I'll put you in number eight, then," the clerk said, handing over a key. "It's down the hall there on your right."

Moments later, Pilgrim let himself into the room and relocked the door. He walked straight to the bed and pulled off his boots, then fluffed up the pillow and stretched out. He was asleep quickly.

When Pilgrim awoke the room was dark. He pulled his watch out of his pocket and struck a match, then cursed softly as he read the time: ten minutes to midnight. He had intended to eat supper in a restaurant and have a few beers before going to bed, but his body had obviously decided otherwise. "Ain't no use in setting a particular time to go to bed," he could remember his mother saying on several occasions, "your body'll tell you when it's time." Knowing that his mother had known what she was talking about, he blew out the match and laid the watch on the bedside table, then turned over and went back to sleep.

Daylight was showing around the edges of the window shade the next time he opened his eyes. Feeling like he might never want to go to sleep again, he was on his feet quickly. He washed his face and put on his hat, then pulled on his boots and walked into the lobby. An old man sat behind the counter this morning. "Is the restaurant open?" Eli asked.

"Two hours ago," the old-timer answered, pointing to a door that opened off the north side of the room. "You'll be getting there at the right time, too, 'cause the early-morning rush is over with."

"Thank you, sir," Pilgrim said as he walked across the lobby. "I sure like the sound of that." He pushed the door open and stepped inside the restaurant. There were only two customers in the building, both of them sitting at the counter. Eli walked to a table and seated himself. A young waiter was there quickly. Pilgrim waved away the bill of fare he was offered and spoke softly: "Just bring me some flapjacks and sausage," he said, "and I'll have a cup of coffee while I'm waiting."

"Yes, sir," the waiter said, then headed for the kitchen.

After he had finished his breakfast, Pilgrim ordered another cup of coffee. He looked at his watch again, then sat shaking his head. He was still trying to figure out why he had slept so long. His first nap had been seven hours long, then he had slept another eight hours without even waking up to take a piss. He had originally intended to doze off for half an hour or so, then get up and walk around the town for a while. Had his body been all that weary without his realizing it? Obviously, the answer was yes.

He finished his coffee and paid his way out of the restaurant, then headed for the livery stable. The hostler met him at the door. "Thought maybe you'd backed out on leaving us this morning, Mr. Pilgrim. Most traveling men are up and gone long before this time of day."

Eli chuckled. "Most days I would be, too," he said. "Seems like I suddenly took on some kind of sleeping sickness."

The hostler laughed loudly. "Same thing happens to me every weekend. I sleep all day Sunday, and don't really wake up good till after I've been working an hour or two on Monday morning." He pointed down the hall. "I guess you're ready for your saddler and your mule."

"Yep," Pilgrim answered. "I should've been on my way two hours ago." He seated himself on a bale of hay.

Alvarez led the animals down the hall a few minutes later. Tying the mule's reins to a post, he began to saddle the buckskin. "I'll take care of that, Jose," Eli said, getting to his feet. "Just bring my packsaddle out here, then we'll put it on the mule together."

The hostler laid the saddle back on the rack. "Yes, sir," he said, heading for the office.

A few minutes later, they tied a small sack of shelled corn on each side of the pack animal, then Eli reached for his purse. "How much is the damage, Jose?" he asked.

"A dollar sixty," Alvarez said. "If you'd been down in Laredo, they'd have charged you about two sixty."

"I sure don't doubt that, Jose," Eli said. "Your price seems reasonable to me." He threw a leg over the saddle, then led the mule through the doorway. "You take care, now," he said over his shoulder. He had ridden only a few steps when he pulled up and twisted his body around in the saddle. "By the way," he said, "how far is it to Laredo?"

Alvarez smiled broadly. "Forty miles, as the crow flies," he answered, "and you're gonna get there damn near as the crow flies. That's about the straightest stretch of road I've ever seen."

"Thank you," Eli said. "Sounds good to me." He guided the buckskin onto the road, then rode out of sight quickly.

He held the animals to a steady walking gait for the remainder of the day, and two hours before sunset rode into a thick stand of mesquites a hundred yards east of the river. As dodging limbs became more difficult, he dismounted and led the buckskin deeper into the trees. Once he was confident that his camp could not be seen from the river or the road, he tied the mule and the saddler to the same sapling, then put on their nose bags. Once they had eaten he would water them, then lead them back to the thicket. They would spend the night tied to the sapling. Eli knew that horse thieves abounded in the area, and he had little doubt that the animals would bring a good price across the river in Mexico.

He found a level spot about forty feet away, then dropped his bedroll to the ground. He had no problem finding wood for a fire, for dead mesquite limbs, both large and small, were lying almost everywhere. He would make a pot of coffee immediately, for he certainly had no intention of using a fire after dark.

He gathered up fuel and kindled a blaze between two flat rocks, then walked to the river and filled his coffeepot. He poured in a handful of grounds and set the pot on the fire, then laid out the cans he intended to open for his supper. He put his rifle and his shotgun on his bedroll, then went about unburdening his animals. He laid both the saddle and the packsaddle close to his bed, then seated himself on the ground beside the fire. He sat eating a sardine and an oatmeal cookie while he was waiting for the coffee. The combination tasted much better than it sounded.

He snuffed out the fire with dirt as soon as the coffee came to a boil, and was done with his meal in less than half an hour. He led the mule and the saddler to the river and watered them, then retied them to the sapling. No reason to put them on picket ropes, for not only was there no green grass in the area, there was little grass of any color. They would be just fine, however, for Eli had fed each of them a hefty portion of shelled corn, and he had plenty of grain to repeat the process in the morning. He would be in Laredo before dinnertime tomorrow, anyway. A sign he had passed only a few minutes ago read that the town was twelve miles ahead.

He did not intend to make his presence in Laredo any more obvious than was necessary, but neither did he plan to sneak into town. He would put his animals up at the livery stable like any other traveler, then find lodging for himself. He would wait till after nightfall to do most of his prowling, but if he decided that his man might be in any particular establishment, he would not hesitate to go in after him. Besides, he had decided that the beard might have done the trick, for after all, Booger Horn had failed to recognize him in broad daylight. Even at a distance of less than fifteen yards.

He stretched out on his bedroll as darkness closed in, and the only sounds he heard were those made by the restless mule. He got up once during the night to relieve himself, then slept the remainder of the night away. When he awoke to see a pink glow in the east he was lying under both of his blankets, and try as he might, he could not remember spreading the second one over his bedroll. He had gone to sleep using it under his head for a pillow, but had obviously woken up enough to spread it over himself as the night grew cooler. Smiling, he snuggled deeper under the warm covering to await full daylight.

He built a fire at sunup, then led his animals to the river to drink while his coffee was reheating. When he returned, his breakfast amounted to half a bag of oatmeal cookies and three cups of coffee. He saddled the buckskin and buckled the packsaddle on the mule, then mounted and headed downriver. He expected to be in Laredo within the next three hours.

Established by a Spanish land grant in 1755, Laredo became the county seat when Webb County was organized in 1848. Due to its close proximity to Fort McIntosh, which had also been established in 1848, and the fact that it was a major crossing on the U.S.–Mexican border, the town was located in a well-traveled, diversified area. Laredo itself had existed under seven flags.

Nuevo Laredo, founded in 1755, lay just across the Rio Grande in Mexico. Pilgrim was hoping that he would not have to cross the river, for he could count all of the words he knew in Spanish on the fingers of one hand.

He topped the hill above Laredo an hour before noon, then sat his saddle looking down into the town for a while. Finally, taking his spyglass out of his saddlebag and putting it to his eye, he could make out the lay of the town. In close proximity to the river, the streets were narrower than those he was used to seeing, and the buildings, most of which were made of adobe, were much closer together. He shoved the small telescope back into his saddlebag, then kneed the buckskin on down the hill.

Livery stables were almost always a hundred yards or

more from the town proper, and Laredo was no exception. As Eli pulled up at the stable's hitching rail, he could see a familiar name a short distance farther down the street: a large sign proclaimed that the unpainted building to which it was attached was a feed store belonging to Pete Caldwell. Pilgrim read the sign and nodded. "Pete Caldwell," he said to himself, the same man that Clayton Horn had come to the area hoping to work for.

"You look like a traveling man, mister," a red-haired, teenaged boy said as Pilgrim dismounted. "Everybody calls me Red, and I guess you can see why. You gonna leave your stock with us for a while?"

Eli nodded and handed over the reins, neglecting to mention his own name. "I'm gonna leave 'em for a while," he said.

The boy took the reins. "We got corn and we got oats," he said. "Whatever you order, is what they get."

Eli chuckled. "They're about like me," he said, "they're a little bit partial to oats."

"Oats it is," the boy said, then led the animals through the wide doorway. He stripped the saddle from the buckskin and laid it across a wooden rack, then began to unbuckle the packsaddle from the mule. "Gonna be in town long?" he asked.

"I don't have any way of knowing yet," Eli answered, "but you look like a fellow who'll take care of my animals no matter how long I decide to stay."

The boy giggled like a schoolgirl. "You're right about that," he said, then changed the subject. "Anything you leave here at the stable is gonna be safe, now." He pointed to the office door, on which a thick hasp and a heavy padlock were plainly visible. "Ain't but one key to that door, and it stays in my pocket. I sleep there in the office, too; so if you ever happen to need your animals in the middle of the night, all you gotta do is peck on the window."

Pilgrim nodded, then moved out of the way as the boy

led the animals toward the stables. He stood looking down the street till the young man returned, then spoke again. "I see the sign on top of that feed store up the street, Red. Is that the same Pete Caldwell who owns a ranch around here?"

The boy nodded. "Same man," he said. "His spread is about ten miles south, and it's called the PC. I reckon he just decided to use his own initials when he named the ranch. He owns a lot of other stuff around here, too. I think he's part owner of the bank, and I know for sure that the Riverside Saloon is his." He chuckled, adding, "No sir, old Pete Caldwell ain't doing no worrying about where his next meal is coming from."

"I wouldn't think so," Eli said. Pointing to the office, he changed the subject. "You gonna keep my long guns in there?"

"Yes, sir," the boy said, nodding several times. "I even lock that door when I walk back to the stables or the corral. Ain't nobody gonna mess with nothing in there."

Pilgrim laid his saddlebags across his shoulder. "Is there any particular hotel that you'd recommend?"

"I never have slept in any of them myself, but I'd say that the Border Hotel's probably the best one. At least, it's the best-looking one. As far as I know, Pete Caldwell might own it, too." He pointed through the doorway. "It's on the corner at the end of the first block."

A few minutes later, Eli stepped inside the hotel. A silver-haired man with a ruddy complexion sat behind the counter. "Come in, son," he said, getting to his feet. "Tell me what I can help you with."

Pilgrim walked to the counter. "I need a room for the night," he said. "You got a vacancy on the second floor?"

"Sure do," the old-timer said, spinning the register around for Eli to sign. "Two hotels besides us in town, and you could have chosen one of them. Thank you for stopping at the Border. Our rooms are eighty cents a night; same price the other two places charge."

Pilgrim nodded. He laid the money on the counter, then signed his newly adopted alias in the book.

Pointing up the staircase to the second floor, the clerk handed him a key. "Room two-twelve," he said.

Moments later, Pilgrim let himself into the room and re-locked the door. He stepped to the window and saw that he had a good view of the street below, then drew the shade. There was a washpan and a pitcher of water on a small table, and a foot-square mirror hanging on the wall. He washed his face and dried it on the flimsy hotel towel, then combed his hair with his fingers. He brushed the dust off his hat with the corner of a blanket, then headed for the door. He had seen a restaurant a few doors up the street that he wanted to visit.

"Aunt Jenny's Restaurant," the sign out front read. Pil-grim took a quick look in all directions, then entered the build-ing. There was another sign just inside the door stating that a man could get all the catfish he could eat for thirty cents. Eli smiled, then found himself a table. "I'll have the fish," he said to a young waiter who had seemingly appeared out of nowhere.

"Yes, sir," the youngster said. "One fish platter." Then he was gone to the kitchen.

After only a few minutes, Eli sat eating a dinner of ketchup-covered catfish, brown beans, and fried potatoes. He enjoyed the food immensely, and when he brought his empty platter to the young man's attention a short time later, it was refilled immediately. Even after Pilgrim had finished eating, he had another cup of coffee, for whoever had brewed the strong liquid had done it exactly right. He left a nickel on the table for the waiter, then paid his way out of the building.

Back out on the packed earthen sidewalk, he began to look around for the Riverside Saloon. The mere name of the place told him that it was most likely on the south side of town, beside the river, so he began to wander along in an easterly direction. Just around the corner the street curved back toward the riverbank; then he could see the oversized watering hole.

Noticing that all three of the horses at the hitching rail wore the PC brand, he stood in front of the building for a few moments, thinking. If Clayton Horn happened to be inside, would the man be able to identify him? It was altogether possible, he decided, but the answer was most likely no. After all, his brother had failed to recognize Pilgrim in broad daylight, and the lighting inside the saloon would be considerably dimmer. Besides, Eli's hair grew almost to his shoulders now, and the thick beard covered almost everything except his eyes. He nodded at his thoughts, then stepped forward and elbowed his way through the bat-wing doors.

The men who probably owned the horses at the hitching rail were sitting side by side on three barstools. Pilgrim walked around the end of the bar and seated himself on a stool directly across from them. One of the men twitched a finger at Eli, then took a sip of his beer. Pilgrim acknowledged the greeting with a nod, then spoke to the bartender. "I'll have a beer," he said, then laid a coin on the bar.

"A pint of good beer brings a pound of good cheer," the man said, making an obvious effort to make his raspy voice sound musical. "One good beer coming up." He drew the foamy liquid, then slid the mug down the bar beside Eli's elbow. "Ain't seen you around here before, so I'd bet that you're just passing through."

"You'd win your bet," Pilgrim said, "unless I come across something I like around here." He reached for the mug and took a sip.

The bartender took Eli's quarter and laid his change on the bar, then went about the chore of washing and polishing glasses. He was a tall, stoop-shouldered man with gray temples and a receding hairline, and he appeared to be about forty years old. "My name's Joe," he said. "When you need another brew, just sing out."

Pilgrim sat sipping his beer and taking in the layout of

the room. The bar itself was about thirty feet long and shaped like a horseshoe. There was a stage and an oblong dance floor along the back wall, with an unpainted piano resting on a riser between them. A door on the west side of the building most likely led to a dressing room for the female performers, he decided quickly, and there was a staircase against the same wall leading to several second-story rooms. A man needed no explanation as to what went on upstairs.

Overall, the saloon appeared to be about a hundred fifty feet long and at least half as wide. Eli believed that it would comfortably seat about a hundred men, and he had little doubt that it was sometimes filled to capacity. Especially on the weekends. He had just bought his second beer and touched the mug to his lips when one of the men sitting across the bar spoke to him. "Heard you talking to Joe about maybe coming across something you like around here," he said. "You looking for work?"

Pilgrim shrugged. "I haven't actually made up my mind, yet," he said. He took another sip of his beer, then set the mug down noiselessly. "Why do you ask? Are you looking for some help?"

"No, no," the man answered, shaking his head emphatically. "The last thing the PC needs right now is another hand. Mr. Caldwell hired a drifter a few weeks ago that he didn't need no more'n he needed another hole in his head. He ain't worth a shit for nothing, but I reckon the old man just put him on the payroll for old times' sake. He worked for the PC once before, but everybody says he wasn't worth a shit then, either."

Pilgrim sat staring into his beer mug. Pete Caldwell had hired a drifter a few weeks ago, the man across the bar was saying, and the fact that the new hire had turned out to be something less than a good hand went right along with Eli's opinion of Clayton Horn. Pilgrim decided to go fishing. "You say Mr. Caldwell hired a man a few weeks ago," he began. "Is he a redheaded fellow about six feet tall, who rides a big gray gelding and answers to the name of Jack Hamilton?"

"No, no," the man said. "He's about six feet tall, all right, but he rides a jug-headed piebald. He claims his name is Clayton Horn, and I figure that's probably the only thing he's ever told any of us the truth about."

Eli knew that he had hit pay dirt without even trying. Hoping the fact that he was lying did not show on his face, he spoke quickly. "The reason I asked about your new hand," he said, "is because I met a man named Jack Hamilton a few weeks ago who said he was coming down this way hunting work. I just thought he might have caught on out at the PC."

"Nope," the man said. "If he's anything like that joker we got, we don't want him out there, either. I mean, a man is supposed to wait till payday to do most of his whiskey drinking, but that Horn fellow seems to think a man oughtta get drunk every day." He pointed to a particular stool farther down the bar. "Clayton Horn sits right there at that post and closes this place up two or three nights a week."

Pilgrim drummed his fingers against the bar a few times, then upended his beer and got to his feet. "I've enjoyed talking with you," he said, speaking to the man who had fed him the information. "Maybe we'll see each other again." He walked through the front doorway, then headed for the Border Hotel at a fast clip.

AFTER LYING on his bed for a few minutes reading a magazine he had bought in the hotel lobby, Pilgrim suddenly got to his feet. He stood at the window staring down at the empty street for a while, then pulled the shade. He emptied the shells out of his Colt and laid them on the bed, then began to dry-fire the weapon. He made his fast draw from many different positions, making an all-out effort to increase his speed with each pull.

After emptying the holster fifty times or more, he reloaded the weapon and seated himself on the edge of the bed. Deciding that he had lost nothing due to lack of practice, he sat on the bed for a long time, thinking. Was he as fast as Cliff Cates? he asked himself. He thought back to the many times he had watched his teacher at his best, then smiled. Yes, he said softly. And then some.

The man at the Riverside Saloon had told Pilgrim as much as he needed to know about his quarry. Clayton Horn was employed at the PC Ranch and came to town to get drunk every chance he got. On one of his trips to the saloon in the very near future, he was going to find Eli waiting for him. The fact that Pilgrim knew exactly what to expect from Horn would keep him from stumbling into a vulnerable position.

Supposing that many men had died because they tried to rush something, Eli intended to take his time; he would make his move only after determining that his knowledge gave him the upper hand.

He was on the street again an hour later. And though the day was a little on the chilly side, he had left his fleece-lined coat in the hotel room for good reason. Although the garment would have made him a little more comfortable, it also restricted the movement of his arm, and the fact that it hung down past his holster would have made a fast draw an impossibility.

Walking down the opposite side of the street from the Riverside Saloon, he continued on till he reached the livery stable. "Just thought I'd pick up another shirt while I'm down here, Red," he said to the young hostler who appeared in the doorway. "It's a little bit cool for the way I'm dressed, but not quite cold enough for a big coat. I've got one shirt in my pack that fits me a little too loose anyway, so I've just decided to put on two shirts."

The youngster pointed toward the office. "Help yourself," he said.

Pilgrim put on the second shirt, then returned to the doorway and seated himself on an upended nail keg. "Do you own this stable, Red?" he asked.

The boy shook his head. "Not by myself," he said. "Ma says it's family owned, so I guess that's what you'd call it. Pa built it the same year I was born, and he ran it till he died from pneumonia two years ago. Ma was gonna sell it after he died, but I told her I could run it just as good as he did. I've done that, too, 'cause Pa was crippled, and he got around mighty slow.

"I've got two sisters and one younger brother, but they don't ever come down here nowadays. Business fell off a lot right after Pa died, but a lot of men have got to where they trust me to shoe their horses here lately. The stable makes a pretty good living for us, now."

Eli nodded. "How old are you, Red?"

The youngster smiled and stuck out his chest. "Turned seventeen last week."

"Seventeen's plenty old enough to shoe a horse," Eli said. "You look to me like a fellow who could do about anything he set his mind to."

"That's what I've always told Ma and my sisters," the youngster said, "and so far, I've been able to do everything I've tried. I spent an awful lot of time watching Pa."

Pilgrim got to his feet and patted him on the back. "You're a good man, Red. You just keep up the good work." He pointed toward the office. "I remember you saying you sleep in there. Didn't you tell me that if I need my animals during the night all I have to do is peck on that window?"

The youngster nodded. "That's right," he said. "Just make sure you keep pecking till I answer you, so you'll know that I'm awake."

"I'll remember that," Pilgrim said, then left the building. Walking down the opposite side of the street, he spotted a piebald saddler tied at the Riverside's hitching rail long before he reached the saloon. "He rides a jug-headed piebald," the PC hand had said of Clayton Horn. Pilgrim crossed the street for a closer look. There, standing at the same rail as the three PC horses was a large piebald bearing the Rocking S brand. Eli had seen the brand around Cuero many times and knew that it belonged to Joe Sealy, who owned a ranch in northern DeWitt County.

He recrossed the street almost at a run, then stood for a few moments leaning against the wall of a building, contemplating his next move. Finally, he headed for the Border Hotel at a fast clip. He was in his room no more than one minute, for he had come only to retrieve his coat and his saddlebags.

Back on the street, he headed for the livery stable again. "You didn't stay gone very long," the redhead said when Eli arrived at the office. "Did you forget something?"

Pilgrim pointed toward the corral. "I'm gonna be needing my animals just as soon as you can get 'em out here, Red.

Move along now; like I said, I'm in a big hurry."

The youngster was on his feet instantly. "By golly, you must be," he said. "You can take your pack outside and wait for me by the door. I won't be long." He grabbed a coiled rope from a peg on the wall and disappeared down the hall.

Twenty minutes later, Pilgrim mounted the buckskin and led the pack mule through the doorway. He had shed one of the shirts and now had it and his coat tied behind his saddle. When he reached the Riverside Saloon, the piebald was still standing at the hitching rail. Pilgrim sat his saddle for a few moments, then dismounted and tied his own animals. He had made his decision: Clayton Horn was inside this watering hole, and Eli intended to go in after him. He took the clipping of the newspaper story from his saddlebag and shoved it into his pocket, then stepped up on the sidewalk. After a quick look in all directions, he elbowed his way through the batwing doors.

The three PC hands were sitting right where they had been before, and there was only one other customer in the building: Clayton Horn sat a few stools down the bar from the other hands, his right shoulder leaning against a post. He turned his head slightly and took a quick glance toward the front door, but showed no sign that he recognized the man who had just walked through it. As Horn concentrated on his drink, Pilgrim walked on to the bar. He handed the bartender the newspaper clipping. "Read that, Joe," he said almost at a whisper. "Then you'll understand what I came in here to do."

The bartender had read no more than half of the article, when he laid it on the bar and stood staring at Horn. "I'll be damned," he said.

Pilgrim waited no longer. He stepped into the aisle and spoke to his quarry: "Get off that stool, Clayton Horn, and make your play! My name's Eli Pilgrim, and I've been on your trail ever since you bushwhacked me and Big Step Benson!"

"Pilgrim . . . You . . ." Horn stammered. He looked behind himself in an effort to calculate his chances of getting behind the post, then obviously realized that the move would involve taking at least three steps. "What . . . what if I don't want to fight?" he asked finally.

"It's the only chance you've got, you son of a bitch!" Pilgrim said loudly. "I'm gonna count to three, then I'm gonna start shooting! One . . . two . . ." Horn dived headfirst into the aisle and drew his Colt in one fluid movement, but took a shot in the chest even as he was in the air. As he tried to raise his shooting arm, he received another slug in his mouth. The man dropped his gun and never moved again.

"Couldn't have happened to a more deserving fellow," the same man who had talked to Pilgrim earlier in the day said quickly. He nodded at Eli, adding, "I mean, you just done a favor for the entire human race."

Pilgrim picked up the newspaper article and shoved it in his pocket, then laid a double eagle on the bar. "Here, Joe," he said. "Give this to the man who cleans up this mess and puts that bastard in a hole."

The bartender dropped the coin into his vest pocket. "Hell, I'll do it myself for this kind of money." He pointed toward the street. "You be careful, now."

With his six-gun still clutched in his fist, Pilgrim walked out of the saloon backward. Even as he stepped through the doorway he heard one of the men behind him say, "Did you see that draw, Ellis? I mean, did you see how quick that fellow emptied that damned holster? I'll tell you . . ."

Pilgrim rode through town at a canter, then headed northeast. There was one more Horn brother, hanging around the town of Edna.

THE MOON came out before sunset, and Eli continued to ride for another two hours after daylight had disappeared. He had hoped to come upon a creek or a spring, but it was not to be. Finally, he pulled off the road into a small grove of stunted mesquites and dismounted. He unburdened his animals and tied them to a limb, then put on their nose bags. He ate no supper, just stretched out on his bedroll and covered himself with his blankets and his heavy coat. He was asleep in a matter of minutes.

He was awake at daybreak and had no problem starting a fire for his coffee. He poured all of the water from one of his canteens into the pot, then added a handful of grounds. A short time later, he sat washing soda crackers and cheddar cheese down with strong coffee. He ate half of his oatmeal cookies, then divided the other half between the buckskin and the mule.

He drank the last of the coffee mainly for its water content, for he could very easily see that he was in dry country. He saddled the buckskin and buckled the packsaddle down on the mule, then consulted his map and his pocket compass. According to the map, he was at least forty miles from the Nueces River, which he believed might be the closest source of water. He had another canteenful for himself, but none for his animals.

The compass showed that the wagon road was running southeast, while the Nueces River was located northeast of his present position, across the remainder of Webb County and a few miles into Lasalle County. He doubted that the road would ever turn back north. Anyway, if it did, he would probably come upon it again in a few hours. Knowing that his animals had walked even farther without water on a few occasions, he guided the buckskin out into the parched prairie and headed cross-country at a fast walk.

Thankful that the morning was cold, he buttoned his coat up under his chin and held the same pace hour after hour. One more thing in his animals' favor was the fact that the terrain was relatively level, with no hills or mountains to sap their energy and make them even more thirsty. No, sir, there was no question in his mind that they could make it to the Nueces without a drink. He himself could, if need be.

It was close to noon when he realized that he was about to run into the road again. He had just topped a small rise when he saw it off to his right, angling in from the south. The road was headed due north now and would no doubt cross the Nueces River in a few hours. He chuckled softly and guided the buckskin onto it. Not only had he played it safe by traveling cross-country, he had saved his animals a little work. He dismounted and relieved himself in the ditch, then remounted and rode on.

As the afternoon wore on, he began to pick up a few pieces of deadwood here and there and put them on the pack mule. When he finally reached the Nueces two hours before sunset, he had plenty of fuel for a fire. He allowed his animals to drink their fill, then forded the river. He had deliberately refrained from feeding them this morning because he knew the oats would make them thirsty. Now that water was no longer a problem, he gave them heftier portions of grain than usual, then set about building a fire for his coffee.

Even as he was coaxing a flame from a handful of twigs and dead grass, he saw a covered wagon coming down the road. With a middle-aged couple and a young boy dressed in overalls sitting on the seat, the vehicle was headed south. The driver guided his team off the road, then brought the wagon to a halt about forty yards past Pilgrim's fire. "Howdy!" the man said loudly, then jumped to the ground. Not waiting for a reaction from Eli, he added, "I've prodded these mules just as far as I intend to this day!"

Pilgrim waved a greeting and said nothing.

When the lady and the youngster began to unhitch the team, the man walked to Eli's fire with a double-barreled shotgun cradled in the crook of his arm. "I've gotta try to find something to eat before dark, 'cause we're down to nothing but a few potatoes." He pointed north. "You reckon a man might be able to jump a rabbit on this side of the river?"

Pilgrim nodded. "Maybe," he said. "I believe you'll improve your chances if you stay in that tall grass close to the riverbank."

"That's what I was thinking," the man said. "I've got to make sure one shot does the trick, cause I ain't got but one shell. It's loaded with bird shot, so I don't reckon I could pull down nothing bigger'n a rabbit, nohow." He turned to leave.

"Ain't that a ten-gauge you've got there?" Eli asked.

The man halted. "Sure is," he said over his shoulder.

Pilgrim was on his feet quickly. He rummaged around in his saddlebag for a moment, then came up with two shotgun shells. "Here's some double-aught buck," he said. "Put one of these in that other barrel in case you happen to jump a deer."

The man backtracked and accepted the shells. He held one of them up to the light. "I believe that'll bring a buck down, all right."

Pilgrim nodded. "I know it will if you don't have to take too long a shot. I can't even remember how many deer I've brought down with a ten-gauge."

The man loaded the second barrel of the big Greener and put the other shell in his pocket, then nodded. "I certainly thank you, young fellow," he said, then crossed the road and headed upriver. He was a big man, a few inches shorter than Eli but considerably thicker. The heavy wool coat he wore made him look even bigger than he was. Pilgrim sat watching till he disappeared in the trees and undergrowth.

Eli filled his coffeepot at the river, then poured in a handful of grounds and set it on the fire. He opened a can of fish and a can of beans, then sliced up some cheese. After laying out a bag of soda crackers, he leaned back on his elbows to wait for his coffee to boil.

Twenty minutes later he had just begun to sip on a cup of coffee, when the young boy approached his fire. "Sure smells good," the youngster said, pointing to the coffeepot. "You got enough to spare me a cup?"

"Got more than enough," Pilgrim said, reaching into his pack for another cup. He handed it to the young man, adding, "Just help yourself."

The young man filled the cup to the brim and seated himself on the ground cross-legged. "My name's Willy Hayes," he said, "and my parents are named Oscar and Emily. We've been on the road all the way from northern Arkansas, and we've about run out of everything. Pa went to try to shoot a rabbit for supper. Sure hope he gets a big one, 'cause there ain't none of us et nothing today."

Pilgrim pointed to his pack. "I've got a little extra food in there, and I'd be more than willing to share it with you folks. If your pa don't have any luck on his hunt, just tell him that you're all welcome to eat with me."

The boy shook his head. "I wouldn't think he'd do that. I ain't never seen him accept anything from anybody. He'd probably raise Cain with me right now if he knew I was drinking your coffee."

"Well, I'm sorry to hear that, Willy," Pilgrim said. "I was always taught to share and share alike when somebody was temporarily down. You folks are more than welcome to eat right here with me, and I want you to tell your pa that."

"I will, but like I say, it probably won't do no good."

Pilgrim took another sip of his coffee. "How about your ma, Willy? How does she feel about accepting help from somebody else?"

"She don't never say nothing about it; don't never argue with Pa about nothing."

Eli took another cup from his pack and poured it full of steaming coffee. "Take this to your mother, Willy. Tell her I've got some extra food over here in case her husband fails to shoot some game."

The boy took the cup. "Yes, sir," he said. "I'll bet she'll be glad to get it, 'cause we've been outta coffee for more'n a week." He headed for the wagon at a trot.

Without appearing to do so, Eli kept watch on the woman out of the corner of his eye. The lady seated herself on the wagon tongue, and she did drink the coffee. Five minutes later, Willy brought the empty cup back. "Ma says to tell you she appreciates the coffee, and that she'll be asking the Lord to bless you. She's always saying stuff like that."

"That's fine, Willy, and I think it's a good thing to say."

The boy had no more than reseated himself when they heard the report of the ten-gauge farther up the river. Judging from the sound, Eli believed that it was the double-aught shell that had discharged, for it was packed with a heavier load of powder. "Your pa might have got a deer. Willy, 'cause I believe that was one of the big shells we just heard."

"Sure hope so," the boy said. Good-sized deer would feed us for a long time."

About twenty minutes later, Oscar Hayes crossed the road, his shotgun lying across one shoulder and a hindquarter of a deer across the other. "What the hell do you think this is, Willy?" he said to his son. "Didn't you hear this shotgun? Didn't you know I'd be needing some help? The truth is, you simply didn't give a damn, did you? You get more like them lazy-ass cousins of yours every day. Ain't worth a shit for nothing now, and ain't never gonna be." He pointed toward the wagon. "Get up off your ass and get that ax out of the back of the wagon. Walk straight down that riverbank till you come to the dead doe. Chop off the other hindquarter and get it back up here to your ma just as fast as you can. Don't you let your shirttail touch you till you've got that done, neither." The boy jumped to his feet and went about the task at a hard run.

Ignoring Pilgrim, Oscar Hayes walked on to his own campsite. Eli could hear the man barking orders to his wife as he handed her the venison, but could make out none of his words. As the lady busied herself with the meat, Hayes finally grew quiet and seated himself on the wagon tongue.

Pilgrim opened his beans and fish and ate it all right out of the can. He really had no preference over whether it was hot or cold, for it tasted about the same either way. Topping it off with several slices of cheddar cheese and two more cups of coffee, he considered his supper to be well above the average trail fare. He snuffed his campfire well before dark and leaned his shoulders against the trunk of a nearby tree.

The boy returned with the hindquarter of venison a few minutes before dark and delivered it to his mother. Her fire was burning brightly, and Eli could smell deer steaks frying in the pan. Yes, sir, the Hayes family was going to eat well tonight, and tomorrow night, as well.

Moments later, Oscar Hayes approached Eli's camp. "Want to thank you for giving me that shotgun shell, mister. There ain't no way in the world that I'd have ever brought that deer down with my bird shot."

Pilgrim shook his head. "No," he said. "I wouldn't think so."

"Well, I just want you to know that I appreciate it, and if there's anything I can do to make it up to you, all you gotta do is ask."

Pilgrim sat quietly for a while, then decided to speak up bravely. "One favor you could do for me, sir, is to start talking to that son of yours in a more civilized manner. I mean, all that rough talk is gonna eventually take its toll on that boy. I heard you telling him that he wasn't worth a shit now and was never gonna be. Hell that ain't no way to talk to a boy, Mr. Hayes. Best way I know of to make sure he don't give a damn how he turns out is to keep belittling him. You need to brag on him, keep telling him how much better he's gonna be."

"Oh, hell, I know that. I reckon the wife reminds me of it every day, but I keep forgetting. Just keep letting my temper get away from me and the first thing I know I'm jumping down his throat about something that don't amount to a hill of beans." He cupped his hands around his mouth and called out to his son: "Willy, come over here a minute, son."

The boy trotted over and stood before his father. "I want to apologize for the way I talked to you a little while ago, son," Oscar Hayes began. "You know I don't really intend to be mean to you, but I guess it takes something like this fellow here pointing it out to me before I really realize how bad I must sound sometimes. Please forgive me, son, 'cause I love you more'n anything in the whole world."

The boy was on his knees instantly with both arms around his father's neck. "It's . . . all right, Pa," he said. "I know you don't hate me. Anyway, you treat me good most of the time." He kissed his father's forehead. "I love you too, Pa."

Pilgrim was on his feet now. He poured a tin cup full of coffee grounds and handed it to the boy. "Take this to your mother, Willy. Tell her I've got some sugar if she needs it."

"Yes, sir," the young man said. "I bet she needs it too, 'cause I know she ain't got none." He left for the wagon at a trot.

When the two men finally got around to introducing themselves by name, Hayes pointed southwest. "Any water between here and Laredo?" he asked.

"I didn't see any," Eli replied. "Of course, I traveled cross-country most of the way, and it could be that I'd have come upon a spring if I'd stuck with the road. My advice to you would be to count on about a fifty-mile dry run, though."

Hayes nodded. "That's about what I expected. I reckon we'll make it all right, though, I guess you noticed that we've got a water barrel on the wagon. Got two washtubs we can fill up too, if we need 'em."

"I believe I'd fill the tubs if I were you. Half of the water'll probably slosh out, but I'll bet your mules'll be needing the other half before they get to Laredo. Is that where you're intending to light?"

"No, we're just heading to Laredo so we can be near the Rio Grande. We'll follow the river on down to Mission from there. We've got another two weeks of traveling ahead of us yet, but we've got a little money. We'll buy a few supplies and some mule feed in Laredo, then we'll be fine. I've got work waiting on me in Mission, so we'll be set once we get there."

"Good," Eli said. "I'll bet you're gonna like the climate, too, 'cause I've been told that winter just about passes that place by."

"That's right," Hayes said, "and I reckon that's the only reason I'm getting hired. Even with good weather, looking after three hundred acres of fruit trees is probably gonna be a full-time job, though."

"I would imagine," Pilgrim said.

Their conversation was interrupted by young Willy Hayes, who announced that supper was ready. "Ma cooked a steak for you, too, sir," he said to Pilgrim.

Eli shook his head. "Thank the dear lady for me and tell her to feed it to her husband. I ate every bite I could hold only a few minutes ago."

"I'll tell her," the boy said, then looked at his father. "She says to come on right now, Pa."

"Well, I guess bygosh I heard that," Hayes said, getting to his feet and dusting off the seat of his pants. "Thank you again for the shotgun shells, Mr. Pilgrim, and God be with you." Both father and son could soon be seen sitting in the glow of the campfire with plates in their hands.

Pilgrim dragged his bedroll off into some bushes and stretched out. Ten minutes later, he was sound asleep.

Eli was sitting beside a campfire at daybreak drinking the remainder of last night's coffee. He ate a can of sardines and a few slices of cheese, then began to put his pack together. Even though he made no special effort to move about quietly as he saddled the buckskin and buckled the packsaddle on the mule, nobody stirred at the Hayes wagon. The sun was just breaking over the distant rise in the east when he forked his saddle and led the pack mule away from the campground. A glance over his shoulder told him that the Hayes family was still sawing logs.

Water for his livestock would no longer be a problem. He would travel parallel with the Nueces all day and camp at a place called Three Rivers tonight. His map showed that there was an abundance of water from there on to Edna, and he expected to be on the road for about three more days.

He came upon a community called Easonville at ten o'clock in the morning and visited a small general store. He bought several cans of meat and a roll of German sausage, along with another bag of oatmeal cookies. A dozen hen eggs filled out his order, then he bought a sack of oats at the feed store. When he left town, he had everything he needed to see him on to Edna.

When he reached Three Rivers two hours before sunset he was glad that he had picked up a little deadwood along the way. There were four covered wagons already camped nearby, and not a single piece of bark could be seen on the ground. No dead grass, nothing that would burn. It appeared that all of the people in the wagons had brought their own kindling, however, for there was a cookfire burning in every camp.

Eli selected his own campsite and dropped off his wood, then unburdened his animals and put on their nose bags. He filled both his coffeepot and his cooking pot at the river, then kindled a fire. He discarded two of the eggs that had broken during the day's jostling ride, then put the other ten in the pot to boil. He would soon enjoy a supper of boiled eggs, cheese, German sausage, and oatmeal cookies washed down with strong coffee. And the same menu would prevail when he woke up in the morning.

A few of the other campers waved a greeting to Pilgrim during the afternoon but none spoke. All of which was fine with Eli, for he was not exactly in a talking mood. Even as his coffee and his eggs boiled, he lay beside the fire looking at his image in a small mirror that he carried in his pack. The beard was more than an inch long now and covered almost everything except his eyes. Would Clem Horn recognize him on sight? Eli believed there was a good chance that the man would not, for neither of his brothers had. Besides, the beard was even longer now.

Pilgrim had no intention of betting his life that Horn would not recognize him, however. He would be very careful where he went, especially during the daylight hours. Clem Horn was known to be a heavy drinker, and that bit of information told Eli where he would most likely find his man. He would keep a close eye on the town's watering holes and go right in after his man if the need arose. He was tired of traveling and ready to put the entire matter of the Horn brothers behind him. He was also eager to get back to the Oxbow Ranch and some kind of regular routine.

He arrived in the town of Edna at two o'clock in the afternoon three days later. As he rode down Main Street, the first building he came to was the Frontier Hotel. He tied his animals at the hitching rail and stepped inside. A skinny old man sat behind the counter. "Come in, young man," he said. "Can I help you with something?"

"I believe so," Pilgrim said. "I need a room for at least one night."

The old man nodded. "You've got your choice of upstairs or downstairs," he said, "all of 'em rent for eighty cents a night."

"I'll sleep upstairs," Eli said, signing Bill Alexander to the register.

The clerk handed him a key, saying, "You'll be in room two twenty-two. It has a padlock on the outside of the door, and you can bar it from the inside while you're in the room. I hope your stay is a pleasant one."

"Thank you," Pilgrim said. "Now, can you direct me to the livery stable?"

"Sure," the clerk said. "Just keep riding down Main Street for three blocks, and you'll run right in to Joe Preston's livery."

Eli nodded, then spun on his heel and headed for the hitching rail. A few minutes later he dismounted in front of the stable. "Thank you for stopping by, young man," a muscular gentleman of about fifty years old said as he stepped into the wide doorway. "I don't mind admitting that business ain't been too good lately, and every little bit is appreciated."

Pilgrim offered a pleasant smile. "I'm glad I could help out, then," he said. "If you'll grain my animals and put 'em up for the night. I'll appreciate it. I don't know how long I'll be around, but I sure don't intend to go anywhere else today."

The hostler pointed toward the pack mule. "You want anything outta that pack before I lock it up?"

Eli shook his head. "No, sir. I assume that my long guns'll be safe too, is that right?"

"Absolutely. It'll all be under lock and key."

Moments later, Pilgrim headed back up the street with his

saddlebags across his shoulder. Though he passed several places where a man could buy a drink, the most prominent watering hole was called the Texas Saloon. Located on an oversized corner lot, the establishment took up almost half a block. It had four hitching rails in front, as well as a large parking lot across the alley in the rear. Eli walked down the side of the building so that he could see into the parking lot, then turned and headed back to the hotel. Once inside his room, he barred the door and lay down on his bed. He was asleep in a matter of minutes.

He slept for two hours, then woke up refreshed. He washed his face and hands and brushed his hat with the corner of his blanket, then stepped out into the hall. A short time later, he was sitting in a restaurant across the street eating a bowl of chicken and dumplings. He was served a slice of the best apple pie he had ever eaten for dessert, and the waiter was careful to keep his coffee cup full. Eli left a dime beside his empty bowl to show his appreciation.

He stood outside the restaurant leaning against the wall for a few minutes trying to decide what to do next. Finally, he decided to take a look at the inside of the Texas Saloon. He crossed the street and walked to the corner, then elbowed his way through the bat-wing doors. Although the saloon was large, even by Texas standards, there was only one bartender on duty.

The forty-foot bar had stations for three additional attendants that were most likely needed on weekends, or when a bunch of drovers came through. Located on the Lavaca River, the town of Edna was right on the old Bill Johnson Feeder Trail, and did much business with the herdsmen during the trail-driving season. Eli believed that the saloon would comfortably seat at least a hundred men, and had no doubt that it was often filled to capacity. He stood just inside the doorway for a few moments, then walked to the bar and took a seat on a stool. "I'll have a beer," he said to the bartender, a redhead who appeared to be barely out of his teens.

"Yes, sir," the barkeep said, then drew a beer and placed it beside Eli's elbow. "That'll be a nickel," he said.

Pilgrim laid the coin in his hand, then took a sip of the foamy brew. Wiping his mouth with the heel of his hand, he nodded to two drinkers who were seated directly across the bar from him. His greeting was returned by both men. "Just passing through?" the older of the two men asked.

"Actually, I'm just prowling around the country," Eli answered. "Don't know exactly where I'll end up."

The man smiled and shook his head a few times. "I reckon that's what I've always wanted to do," he said, "but I never could figure out no way to make a living at it."

Pilgrim chuckled. "I didn't mean to imply that I'm making a living at it," he said. "I reckon I'll eventually have to stop somewhere and go to work if I expect to keep on eating."

The man sipped at his whiskey glass, then said, "I don't reckon a fellow who really wants to work could be in a better place than right here a few weeks from now. It's probably a little early yet, but I hear that some of the trail bosses are already signing up a few men for the trail drives this spring. If this pretty weather holds out. I believe that most of 'em'll be leaving for Kansas a little earlier than usual this year. Fact is, the grass is pretty good out there right now."

Pilgrim drained his beer mug. "I figured that some of the bosses might be gonna hit the trail early this year; one of Clem Horn's brothers told me that Clem was already down in this area figuring to sign on with somebody."

"Clem Horn's done signed up with Collin Mayhew," the second man said. "He done that more'n a month ago." He upended his drink. "Is Clem Horn a friend of yours?"

Eli shook his head emphatically. "No, no," he said. "I did know one of his brothers, though." He caught the bartender's eye. "Give me another beer here," he said, "and give those two gentlemen over there whatever they're drinking."

The bartender was quick to comply, then stood by till Eli forked over a quarter. Pilgrim sipped at his beer, then asked another question. "After a fellow signs on for a trail drive, who feeds him till it's time to go to work?"

The first man answered the question. "I reckon you could say that varies. In Clem Horn's case, he's eating off of Collin Mayhew. Mayhew's got a mighty big spread, and his foreman can always use another hand if he wants to. Anyway, I doubt that old man Mayhew even knows Horn. Rag Phillips is the man who does all the hiring out there. I understand him and Clem Horn have been friends for a few years. I know for a fact that they sometimes drink together, 'cause I saw 'em doing it right here in this saloon three nights ago."

Pilgrim was quiet for a while, then directed another question to the same man. "Would you have any idea when they might be back in here? I might want to talk with Mr. Phillips about a job."

The man chuckled. "Rag Phillips might not be back in here between now and Christmas," he said, "but you can bet your ass that Clem Horn won't stay away that long. I'd say that he'll be in here again just as soon as he gets his hands on a little money. I don't reckon he's the one you want to see, though, 'cause he ain't got the authority to hire nobody. Best thing you can do is just ride south on Wolf Creek Road till you come to the Mayhew Ranch cutoff. It ain't but about two miles from there to ranch headquarters. I'll guarantee you that Rag Phillips'll take the time to talk to you and if he decides to use you, he'll probably sign you up right on the spot."

Pilgrim upended his beer mug for the final time. "I just might do that," he said. "Right now, I've had my limit for the day, so I'll be getting on out of here." He slid off his stool and walked through the bat-wing doors. He stood in front of the building for a few minutes, thinking. The drinker at the bar had said that Clem Horn would be back in the saloon again as soon as he came by some money. How hard would it be for him to borrow a dollar or two from one of his fellow workers? Not very, Eli decided. Tomorrow would be Saturday, and Pilgrim had a feeling that his man would be in this very saloon. He nodded at his thoughts, then headed down the street toward the livery stable.

"Have you done seen all the sights of our big city?" Joe Preston asked as Eli walked through the doorway.

Pilgrim chuckled. "Most of 'em, I guess. Actually, I've been sitting up at the Texas Saloon drinking beer and talking to some local men. Just thought I'd come back down here and kill a little time, if you don't mind. It's too damn early to go back to that hotel room."

"Anytime's too early for that unless a man happens to be sleepy. I can't think of many things that are as boring as sitting around in a hotel room in the daytime. I have to go to San Antonio on business every once in a while, and that's the main part of it that I dread. I mean, sitting around waiting on somebody else to make up his mind about something will eventually put you to talking to yourself." He pointed toward the office. "Coffee's on the stove, and it ain't had time to get bitter yet."

Pilgrim followed him into the office and accepted a tin cup filled with coffee. The hostler seated himself on the side of his cot, then pushed out the room's only chair for his guest. "My name's Joe Preston," he said, offering a handshake. "What's your name, and where'd you come from?"

"I'm Bill Alexander," Pilgrim said, "and I live up at Cuero. Been traveling around a lot during the past month and a half. Not headed anyplace in particular."

Preston chuckled. "That sounds like fun," he said. "I ain't never been in no financial position to do it, myself."

"Me either," Eli said. "I just decided to do it anyway."

They made small talk for another half hour, and Pilgrim had just finished his second cup of coffee when he decided to start digging. "Do you know a man named Clem Horn, Joe?" he asked.

Preston shook his head. "Not very well, 'cause he don't say much when he's in here. He has left his horse with me a few times, though: tall gray with black mane and tail. He a friend of yours?"

"No," Pilgrim answered. "A fellow up in Cuero just told me to look him up if I was ever down this way."

"Well, he ain't hard to find. He stays out at Mayhew's spread, and visits the Texas Saloon at least a couple times a week. Tomorrow's Saturday, so I'd say you could find him up there about any time after two o'clock in the afternoon."

Pilgrim got to his feet. "Thanks for the coffee and the information, sir. I'll check out the Texas about two o'clock tomorrow afternoon. See you later." He walked through the doorway and headed back up the street.

Eli had walked only a short distance when he decided that he might not have to wait till tomorrow to find his man. He saw the tall gray with the black mane and tail even before he reached the Texas Saloon's hitching rail. The animal was standing alone, which meant that Clem Horn might be the only customer in the oversized watering hole at the moment. Pilgrim inspected the horse to find a brand that he had never seen before. Did the animal belong to Horn, or somebody else? He pondered the question for only a few moments, then decided there was only one way to find out.

He stepped up on the boardwalk and elbowed his way through the bat-wing doors. He spotted his man instantly, sitting halfway down the bar with his shoulder leaning against a post. Horn glanced in his direction, then cast his eyes back to his drink. No doubt about it, Pilgrim was thinking, the man had not recognized him.

Eli nodded to the red-haired bartender, then continued to walk forward. When he was twenty feet away from his man, he halted and spoke loudly. "I'm here on behalf of Big Step Benson, Horn! Remember him?"

"Who . . . wha—"

"I'm Eli Pilgrim, so you might say that I've come back from the dead. Get off that stool and defend yourself you no-

good son of a bitch; it's the only chance you've got of coming
outta this alive!''

Though he was decidedly at a disadvantage, Horn made
his play. He scooted off his stool and reached for his weapon,
but died before he even cleared leather. Eli had pumped two
shots into him before he hit the floor. His right leg went into
a convulsive spasm for a moment, then he lay still.

Pilgrim backed away from the body, then took the newspaper article from his pocket and handed it to the bartender.
"Read that, Red, then you'll know what this is all about."

The redhead read the article, then handed it back. "I
reckon you got your man, all right," he said, " 'cause that's
damn sure Clem Horn lying there."

"Of course it is," Pilgrim said. "I'd seen him before up
in Cuero."

"You a bounty hunter?"

"Hell, no. Far as I know, there ain't even a bounty on
him. Him and three others of his ilk shot my boss and me
from ambush and robbed us. I lived over it, but my boss died.
It's over now, he was the last one of the bushwhackers left."
He glanced toward the front of the building. "Looks like
somebody would be coming in here by now. Don't you think
somebody heard them shots?"

"I doubt it," the bartender said. "This building's awful
tight." He stood with his tongue in his cheek for a moment,
then added, "Now, if I was you, I'd lay enough money to
bury Horn on the bar there, then get the hell out of this town.
Ain't no telling how many people you might have to fight if
you keep on hanging around."

Pilgrim laid a double eagle on the bar and walked to the
front door at a fast clip. Once on the boardwalk, he headed
for the livery stable at a slow trot. He would get his animals
and stop at the hotel long enough to pick up his saddlebags,
then head northwest toward Cuero.

HE RODE steadily for more than three hours, and it was well after dark when he pulled off the road and made a dry camp. He tied the buckskin and the mule to a bush and put on their nose bags, then spread his bedroll beside his packsaddle. He would take the empty bags off the noses of the animals in half an hour, then leave them standing where they were for the remainder of the night. Moments later, he stretched out without even taking off his boots, his shotgun and his Colt both close to hand.

He lay motionless for a long time thinking about his recent manhunt. He had now dispatched all three of the Horn brothers, and he felt no remorse whatsoever. Whether he was supposed to feel anything or not he had no idea, but deep down he was glad that they were all in the ground with Big Step Benson. He was also wondering what made men like the Horns tick. They had been three able-bodied men of at least average intelligence, who simply chose to live a life that most folks would have called pointless.

According to what Eli had been told, none of the three men had ever held any one particular job for more than a few weeks at a time, and all were reputedly involved in the many unsolved burglaries and robberies that had taken place in DeWitt County in recent times. And though the Horns were respected by hardly anyone, most folks blamed local law enforcement for the fact that none of them was ever jailed or even charged with the crimes. Pilgrim himself was among those who attributed that fact not to the dumb luck of the Horns but to the lackadaisical manner in which DeWitt County law enforcement operated.

Half an hour later he got up to relieve himself, then took the nose bags off his animals and stretched out again. He was asleep quickly.

AT MIDAFTERNOON two days later, he left the main road and took the cutoff to the Oxbow Ranch. In just five more miles, he would be home. When he reached the area where the ambush had taken place, he pulled up and sat his saddle for a few moments. With his hat in his hand, he spoke softly to his departed friend. "It's all over for the Horns now, Big Step. Maybe you've done seen 'em, and if you have, I hope you're giving 'em a hard way to go." He put on his hat and headed for Oxbow headquarters at a fast trot.

Half an hour later, he tied his animals to the hitching rail at the cookshack. "Well, I'll be goddamn!" Baldy King said through the open door. "A bunch of us were talking about you while we were eating dinner today." He got to his feet, adding, "Come on in this house and get yourself something to eat."

Eli stepped through the doorway and shook the cook's outstretched hand. "Good to see you, Baldy. I mean, it's just good to be back home."

"Good to see you, too," King said. "I've got turkey and dressing on the back of the stove, if you're hungry."

"Hungry as a bear," Eli said quickly, then seated himself on the bench.

The cook served him a large platter of food, then cut a thick slice from a newly baked loaf of bread with a sharp knife. He set a cup of coffee at Pilgrim's elbow, then seated himself on the opposite side of the table. "Well, we all know where you've been," he said. "How did you come out?"

Eli took a sip of the coffee. "I accomplished what I set out to," he answered.

"You . . . you mean you killed all three of them sons of bitches?"

Pilgrim nodded. "All of them," he said.

The cook sat quietly for a few moments, then drummed his fingers on the table. "Well, I'll be damned," he said. "Did they put up a fight?"

Pilgrim nodded. "Two of 'em did."

King was on his feet now. "You just wait till the rest of the gang hears about this," he said, "especially that Cliff Cates. I can tell you right now what he'll say. He'll say, 'That's exactly what I told you would happen.' That is what he said would happen too, Eli. He says there ain't a man alive that can match your draw with a six-gun. I reckon bygod he oughtta know, too, considering how fast he is himself."

Pilgrim did not speak again until he had cleaned his plate. "That's the best meal I've had since the last time I ate in this building, Baldy," he said. "I don't know if I'll be ready again by suppertime or not."

"Well, I cooked two of them turkeys, so there'll be plenty of it left whenever you do get hungry."

Joe Garcia stepped through the doorway at that moment. "Saw the buckskin and the mule at the hitching rail, Eli," he said. "That sure took a load off my mind, and I'm mighty glad to have you back." He walked to the table and shook Eli's hand, then added. "I told Mr. Benson that your animals were down here at the cookshack, and he told me to tell you to come up to the main house, said he wants to talk with you a little while."

"Well," Pilgrim said, getting to his feet, "I don't guess it would be in my best interests to keep the gentleman waiting. I'll see you two men later." He dropped his empty platter and his coffee cup in the dishpan, then walked through the doorway.

Oliver Benson was sitting on the porch in a cane-bottom rocking chair, when Pilgrim reached the house. Moving like a much younger man, Benson got to his feet instantly. "Welcome back home, Mr. Pilgrim," he said. "Follow me into the house if you will, and let's have us a little talk."

Benson led the way to his living room, then took a seat behind a large desk in the corner. Pilgrim seated himself on the near side.

"I never took you for a man who would give up easily," the old man began, "so the very fact that you're back here must mean that you accomplished your mission."

"Yes, sir," Eli said. "I found all three men."

Benson bounced his fist off the table. "Found 'em and put their asses in the graveyard, did you?"

"Yes, sir. They won't be bushwhacking anybody else. Clem Horn was the man who shot Big Step. He was the last of the three to go down."

Benson bounced his fist three times. "Good, good, good," he said. He pulled one of his desk drawers open and extracted a few sheets of paper. "You know, I've been thinking about you quite a bit while you've been gone, son. Maybe part of it is because you came from my part of Ohio, but I reckon it's mostly 'cause you went after the man who killed my son. At any rate, I don't want to see you have to work for cowhand's wages all your life.

"The only way in the world to get ahead in life, my boy, is to get some property of your own. To tell you the truth, I've got more of that than I need, so I've decided to make it easy for you to get a piece of it for yourself. Now, you just listen to me for a while, then tell me what you think.

"There are three sections of land on the southwest corner of this ranch that I don't really need, and it would make a dandy little starter place for you. Three creeks and half a dozen springs on it, so you'd never run short of water. Some of the best grazing land in this part of the country, too.

"Now, I imagine you're sitting there thinking that you

can't afford to buy it, but I'm here to tell you that you can't afford not to. I'm gonna offer you all three sections for the unheard-of price of a thousand dollars, and you ain't gonna need to put one nickel up front. Pay me or my estate a hundred dollars a year for ten years and she's yours, lock, stock, and barrel. Now, do you know anyplace where you can beat a deal like that?"

"Lord, no." Pilgrim answered. "I never have even dreamed of finding a deal like that."

"Well, that's what I intend to do for you, and the quicker you get on down there and put up some kind of building on it, the better off you'll be."

"I've still got some of that money you gave me before the manhunt began, Mr. Benson. I didn't even spend half of it."

"Spend it now, then. Spend it to buy building materials and roofing for your new house down there on your own property. By the way, what're you gonna call the place?"

Eli sat biting his lower lip for a few moments. "I've always dreamed about having a ranch called the Lazy P. You know, P for Pilgrim."

"Of course I know," Benson said, "and that's as good a name as any. Now, I know that you're gonna need some help down there, so I'm gonna instruct Cliff Cates to help you get started. I've been told that you and him get along with each other just fine."

"Yes, sir," Pilgrim agreed, "sometimes Cliff seems like a brother to me."

"Well, you two brothers just get on down there and build something to live in. You'll need a barn, a crib, and a corral, too, so if you run out of money I reckon I can help you a little more. Cates knows the corners of the property well, and I'll see that Mr. Garcia gives him plenty of time off to help you. Now get on outta here. From now on you can consider yourself a property owner."

Eli got to his feet and put his hat back on his head. "Yes,

sir," he said. "I don't know how in the world I'll ever be able to show my appreciation for what you're doing, but I intend to try." He headed for the doorway.

Benson followed him to the porch and continued to talk. "You'd be smart to take a brood cow as part of your pay every month, son. My bulls'll make sure they all give you a calf every year. It won't be more'n a coupla years before you'll have as many cattle as your property'll support, then you can start sending a few head north to the rails along with my herds. Yes, sir, you can trail more'n enough cows to Kansas every year to pay the payment on your place. Do you understand what I'm saying?"

Pilgrim nodded. "Yes, sir. I understand exactly what you're saying, and like I said before, I certainly appreciate it."

"Well, I'll have a talk with Mr. Garcia and Cliff Cates both before the day's over, then you and your buddy can go on down there tomorrow and start figuring out what you're gonna build." He patted Pilgrim on the back, then turned and walked back into the house.

Eli untied the buckskin and the pack mule from the cookshack's hitching rail, then led them to the barn. He stored his packsaddle in the harness room and laid his saddle across a sawhorse, then fed and curried the animals. That done, he walked to the bunkhouse and stretched out on his cot.

He did not answer the supper bell when the cook rang it, for he had already eaten as much food as he wanted for this day. Half an hour later, the men began to drift into the bunkhouse. Each man came by and shook hands with him, but not a single one of them asked how his mission had turned out. It was just as if every man already knew the outcome. Hell, maybe they did, Eli was thinking.

It was more than an hour after dark when Cliff Cates finally walked into the bunkhouse. He came straight to Pilgrim's cot and offered a handshake that eventually turned into a bear hug. "Welcome home, old buddy," he said. "Mr. Benson's been talking to me for the past hour, and he told me how things turned out with the Horns. Hell, I coulda told him that, 'cause I already knew what was gonna happen when you left here." He was quiet for a few moments, then added, "The old man also told me about the property he was selling you. I'll tell you right now, friend, most folks spend a lifetime looking for a deal like he's giving you. Congratulations."

"Thank you, Cliff. I don't have any idea why he's treating me this way, but I'd be a fool not to accept it."

"Are you kidding me?" Cates asked loudly. "Are you kidding me when you say you don't know why he's doing it? Hell, there ain't no mystery there, Eli. You tracked down and killed the son of a bitch who bushwhacked his only son." He chuckled softly. "Thank you for giving me the chance to clear that up for you."

They sat on their bunks facing each other and talking for the next hour. Cates explained that he had been given his orders from Benson: he was to stick with Pilgrim like glue for the next month or so. They would camp out on Eli's property and put it in liveable condition, with both men remaining on the Oxbow payroll while they were doing so. They would take tools and tents along with a team and wagon, and stay down there as long as necessary.

"I guess we'll build the barn first," Eli said. "We can live in it till we get the cabin up. As soon as we get a roof over our heads we'll buy a cookstove and a table of some kind. I never did like having to eat off my lap."

Cates nodded. "It's your operation, old buddy, so you'll be calling the shots. I'm just going along for the ride. I do hope we get to stay down there long enough to get out of working the spring roundup, though. That's the only part of ranch work that I really hate."

They loaded a wagon with tools, food, and other necessities at sunup next morning, then headed south. Trailing two saddle horses, the vehicle was drawn by two large mules, and the wagon carried several sacks of shelled corn. A two-man tent and a large tarpaulin lay just inside the tailgate, and the men had even remembered to bring pillows along with their bedrolls. Since Cates knew the area best, he was elected to drive. "Do you know exactly where that southwestern corner is?" Pilgrim asked when they were well under way.

"Yep," Cates answered. "Joe Garcia showed it to me the first day I started riding line."

"I didn't know you ever did that," Eli said.

"First two months I was here I didn't do anything else." Cates said.

They had driven for about two hours when Cates brought the team to a halt. "I think we oughtta mount up and go the rest of the way on horseback," he said. "I want to show you one of your choices on location, before we start building anything. There's a good sandy-bottom spring about three miles from here that I want you to see. There's a nice, level place for a homestead there, too." He jumped to the ground and tied the team to a sapling.

They mounted their horses and rode on in the same direction. Little was said between them for the next hour, then Cates pulled up at the top of a small rise. "There it is," he said, pointing down the slope to an area that was almost as level as the water surface of a lake. "The spring is just this side of them two cedars. I figured you might want the trees in your front yard."

Pilgrim was impressed with the view. "You figured right, Cliff," he said. "I believe I can tell from here that you've already chosen the right place. We can put the barn and corral a little farther south, so the manure'll wash on down the slope."

Cates nodded. "That's what I had in mind," he said.

They rode on to the spring, then both men dismounted and drank a cup of the water. "Never tasted better," Pilgrim said, dipping himself a second cupful.

They walked around the area for about half an hour, by which time Pilgrim had decided that he had found his homestead. Then they remounted and headed back for the wagon. They would hang the tarpaulin and set up their tent, which would become their living quarters till they could build something permanent.

THE BUILDING of the corral went smoothly. They had decided early on to build it first, in order to avoid the aggravation of keeping their animals on picket ropes twenty-four hours a day. They used cedar posts, then cut the poles from whatever species of wood were handiest. The finished product required eight days of steady work.

With the corral done, it was time to go to work on the outbuildings. The men would use large cedar posts and hardwood poles to frame the barn and the shed, then build them out of tin. Both the barn and the cabin would have tin roofs, but Pilgrim intended to build the cabin out of heavy logs.

Pilgrim had no idea how much the material was going to cost, but he would know before the day was over. At daybreak, he and Cates were busy harnessing and hitching up the team for a trip to Cuero. He needed a few two-by-fours, but his main purpose in going to town was to bring back a wagonload of tin. He also intended to drive by Oxbow headquarters to pick up a few things they had forgotten to bring, and to inform Joe Garcia of the exact location he had chosen for his homestead.

The sun was just rising when they headed northeast toward Oxbow. "Too bad that we're gonna get to the cookshack too late to eat breakfast with Baldy," Cates said.

"We'll drink half a pot of his coffee, anyway," Eli said.

"If he's got a smoked ham lying around somewhere, I'll try to talk him out of it."

Cates chuckled. "You do that," he said. "I think I'll just stand around and listen."

They arrived at the cookshack two hours later and tied the team to the hitching rail. The cook had heard the rattling of the chains and opened the door to inspect his company. "I can tell by looking at you two that you ain't been eating too well," he said, "but all I can offer you is a cup of coffee. Come on in."

The men had barely filled their cups and seated themselves on the bench when Joe Garcia walked through the doorway. He poured himself a cup of coffee, then joined them on the bench. "I was in the corn crib when you two rolled in. I couldn't help but hear that squeaking wagon wheel."

"It started squeaking just a few minutes ago," Eli said. "It'll get about half a pound of grease before we leave here. I want to pick up some iron wedges and another post-hole digger, too." He jerked his thumb in a southwesterly direction. "I also thought you oughtta know where I decided to build my homestead. We've already built the corral, and we're gonna put the cabin right between Willow Branch and Pie Creek. You know where that sandy-bottom spring is beside the two big cedars?"

Garcia nodded. "Know it well," he said. "I've laid on my belly and drunk my fill outta that spring plenty of times. Fact is, that's what I always called it: Sandy Spring."

"Well, now you know where to find us if you need us," Eli said.

"I won't be needing you till roundup, so you've got another two weeks of lying around down there and being your own boss."

Cates set his cup down on the table noisily. "Hell, I thought maybe we were gonna get out of working that damned roundup."

"Not a chance," Garcia said. "Fact is, I couldn't let you

off even if I wanted to, 'cause there ain't nobody else around that I could get. Don't nobody in this part of the country want to work, especially during roundup time."

Eli was on his feet now. "Well, I guess we'll pick up a few more things, then grease that wagon wheel, Joe. You know where we are now, so if you need us, just get word to us." He walked through the doorway, followed closely by Cliff Cates.

Eli picked up the things he had come after, then drove the wagon to the shed to grease the wheel. They had just jacked up the wagon and slipped off the wheel when they saw Joe Garcia leave the cookshack and return to the corn crib. Cates chuckled. "Now's your chance to show me how good you are, Eli," he said, pointing to the cookshack. "I think I remember you saying something earlier about a smoked ham. I don't need any help greasing this wheel, so you just go on in there and do your stuff."

Without a word. Pilgrim headed for the cookshack. When he returned a few minutes later, he had a bundle wrapped in oilcloth under his arm. He put the bundle under the seat and hunted up an extra washpan and a water bucket, by which time Cates had the wheel greased and back on the wagon.

They arrived at Les Baker's hardware store in Cuero an hour before noon. "I'll tell you right now." Baker said when told of Eli's intentions, "if I was gonna build a barn nowadays, tin is exactly what I'd use. Hell, it don't leak, and it'll stand a lot longer'n wood. Nobody ain't convinced me yet that it costs any more to buy, either.

"It's a lot quicker to put up than wood, too. You just frame the walls with poles the same way you would deck the roof, then nail the tin on in sheets. Hell, you can build three tin barns while you're building one outta wood."

After discussing dimensions with Baker for a while, Eli decided that he would need at least three wagonloads of tin. He and Cates ate dinner in a nearby restaurant while the tin was being loaded, after which they picked up the two-by-fours and some extra lumber to build water and feed troughs, then headed for the Lazy P.

They off-loaded the material beside the corral an hour before sunset, then watered their animals and put on the nose bags. By the time they built a fire to make coffee and reheat their beans, darkness was closing in. "These beans taste a whole lot better'n they did yesterday," Cates said, washing a mouthful down with the strong coffee.

"They always do," Eli agreed. "Just about anything you cook in a pot tastes better after it sets up a day or two. I mean there ain't many things I can think of that taste better than warmed-over stew or chilli. My ma convinced me of that when I was growing up in Ohio."

Until now, they had been keeping the sacks of shelled corn in the tent in case it rained, which left them little room for moving around. "First thing I want us to do in the morning is get these damn feed sacks outta this tent and under some of that tin out there," Eli said. "After all, it's a sleeping tent, not a storeroom. When we get that damn corn outta here, we'll have room to turn around."

"Won't be nothing to that," Cates said. "We can stack the feed where that tin'll keep it dry easy." He cleared his throat a couple times, then added, "I can't really think of anything it would hurt even if the corn did get wet."

"Maybe not," Eli said, "but I know that corn swells when it gets wet, so there ain't no telling what else might happen to it."

Cates laughed. "Well, that's one way of putting it, and you may very well be right. We'll figure out a way to have some more room in the tent and keep the rain off the corn at the same time." Pilgrim kicked dirt over the fire, then both men crawled into the tent. They were sound asleep in a matter of minutes.

They had smoked ham and eggs for breakfast next morning. "I gotta hand it to you, Eli," Cates said around a mouthful of ham. "I reckon you know how to handle Baldy King.

You're probably the only man on the ranch who could have talked him outta this smoked ham. What the hell did you say to him?"

Pilgrim laughed loudly. "I told him he was the best-looking man I'd ever seen." Cates nodded as if he believed Eli's answer, and said nothing else on the matter.

After watering their animals from the spring and putting on their nose bags, the men began to hammer feed and water troughs together. The feed troughs would have a square bottom, while the water troughs would simply be two twelve-inch boards nailed in the shape of a V, with a short board nailed across each end so they would hold water. And unlike the feed troughs, the water troughs would have to be soaked in the spring's runoff for a couple days so the wood would swell enough to prevent leakage.

The troughs were built and the men were already driving stakes and stretching string to lay out the position of the barn and the shed by noon. Eli had no intention of building a hay loft, for if the ranch ever expanded to a larger operation he would need to build a new barn, anyway. For now, he could keep his animals' hay in the shed.

A WEEK later, the men moved their tent under a roof. They had framed the building and nailed down the last of the sheets of tin this afternoon. "We didn't get this roof on none too soon," Cates said as they dragged the tent inside. "I'd damn near bet a month's pay that it's gonna be raining cats and dogs before this night's over."

"You wouldn't get no bet outta me," Eli said. "I see the same clouds back yonder in the east that you do. I'll bet you one thing, though, I'll bet you that nothing we've got here gets wet. We did the right thing framing and roofing this barn first, and it looks like we got it done just in time."

"Don't say *we*," Cates said. "Hell, you're the one that

made that decision. If it had been left up to me, we'd probably be sleeping in the rain tonight."

"No, no, Cliff. You'd have made the same decision if it had been yours to make." He waved his arm around in a wide sweep. "Now we can take our own sweet time about building the walls."

A WEEK later, the barn and the shed were completed, and Pilgrim had a little tin left over for the roof of his cabin. There was no use to lay out the cabin yet, however, for this after-noon they had had a visitor. Hank Tuesday, one of the young Oxbow hands, had delivered the message that Joe Garcia was requesting their presence at ranch headquarters tomorrow. The spring roundup would begin three days from now, and there was much to do beforehand. Cates and Pilgrim sent the ranch manager their regards, along with their promise to be on hand before sunset tomorrow afternoon.

"Only good thing about a roundup," Cates said after the rider had gone, "is that they don't last very long. Garcia's got a well-experienced crew that can throw a calf, cut him, brand him, and turn him loose in less than two minutes. Now don't quote me on that, but that's damn sure what I've been told. The ropers are the main men, though, and that's why the good ones get paid a little more money. I never got all that good with a rope myself, or even tried to. I reckon after I got to the point where I could catch my own horse every morning, I didn't concentrate on getting any better at it. I've watched you, though, Eli. You're pretty good with that thing you've got hanging on your saddle. Garcia might put you to roping."

Pɪʟɢʀɪᴍ ᴀɴᴅ Cates arrived at ranch headquarters at mid-morning next day. It was immediately apparent that the fore-men had been out hiring extra help, for right away Eli saw half a dozen men that he had never seen before. As he and Cates put the wagon in the shed and unhitched the team, Joe Garcia showed up. "I don't want the roundup to take more'n two weeks," he said, "so I've hired a dozen extra men." He nodded to Cates. "I know how you feel about roundups, Cliff, so I tried to make sure you got an easy job. I've instructed Bo Walker to use you as a fireman, it'll be your job to keep the branding fires burning and the irons hot." He chuckled softly. "Actually, the two of you more or less made the trip up here for nothing, 'cause you're gonna be going right back down there where you came from.

"Walker and his crew will begin their part of the roundup down on the southwest boundary of the ranch, which includes the property you bought from Mr. Benson. In other words, you'll be bunching the cattle and branding 'em right there about where you're building your homestead. That plateau right about your corral is the best place for miles around for that purpose." He winked at Pilgrim, adding. "Since you haven't expressed a dislike for any particular part of cow hunting, I told Walker that you were a good man who was willing to work anywhere you were put. Did I tell him right?"

"Whatever he wants me to do is all right," Pilgrim answered. "It's all gonna be new to me anyway."

Garcia slapped him on the back. "That's the spirit, my boy," he said. "Put up your team, then let's go into the cookshack and get some coffee. We'll just sit around till dinnertime, then I reckon I'll be expected to make some kind of speech. At least that's the way it's always been before, so I'll wait till everybody gets here so I won't have to say anything twice."

Once they were in the cookshack, Pilgrim counted nine men that he had never seen before. Most of them were younger than himself, and several not yet out of their teens. "Don't let that peach fuzz on some of these young faces fool you, Eli," Cates said softly in Pilgrim's ear. "Some of 'em can rope a running calf at forty feet and it don't make no difference whether you want him horned or heeled. They grew up with a damn rope in their hands, and any boss who knows what he's doing will pay 'em top money."

Eli was looking at a particular boy who looked to be about fifteen years old. "You mean that little fellow over there is gonna be making more money than I am?" he asked.

Cates chuckled. "You can count on it," he said, then began to point to a few of the others, "and that one, and that one, and—"

"Hell, Cliff," Pilgrim interrupted. "I've got the picture. All I can say is more power to 'em. If they're good enough, let 'em give 'em the damned money."

"They will," Cates said, "and you'll see right away that the young fellows are good enough."

After dinner was over, Garcia made what he said was going to be a speech in the front yard. Announcing that, including the foremen, he had three crews of ten men each, he said that he expected the branding to be done in less than two weeks. "If it takes a little longer, then so be it," he added. "Bo Walker and his crew will start on the southern boundary and work north. Bill Iceman will work from ranch headquarters north, and Joe Bagwell's bunch will be still farther north. The northern part of the ranch is where most of the work will be.

"The cattle congregate up there for the simple reason that the grass is better. If either of the southern crews finishes ahead of time, you are to beat it north and offer Bagwell a hand. In other words, nobody is done, until everybody is done." He stood looking the crowd over for a moment longer, then added, "We'll put tents and bedrolls together and haul wagonloads of wood to the sites this afternoon, and spend the night there. Each crew will have its own cook and horse wrangler, and each wagon will carry a water barrel and six branding irons. You'll camp on-site tonight, and get to work shortly after daybreak." He hesitated for a few moments, then asked, "Are there any questions?"

When nobody spoke, Garcia dismissed the crowd with a wave of his arm. "Pay attention to your foremen. They know exactly what every one of you should be doing at any given moment, and they won't be bashful about telling you so. From now on, your business is with them, so don't expect me to solve any problems for you. To tell you the truth, I won't be there, and it's unlikely that I'll even see any of you again until the roundup's over." He turned his back and walked into the cookshack.

Pilgrim and Cates spent part of the afternoon loading their wagon with wood, being careful to load blocks that they could split into fuel for their cookstove if there was any left over from the branding fires. They had left their tent at the Lazy P, and Eli intended to offer his barn as a campsite for the other crewmen. He felt that they would be more than happy to spread their bedrolls under it if it began to look like rain. It would especially be handy for the cook; a cook always had things that a rainstorm would play hell with.

The men did use Pilgrim's barn for a campsite, and all of the calves they rounded up were branded on the plateau right above his homestead. Cates seemed happy enough with his job as the designated fireman and kept the irons red-hot at all times. Pilgrim did a little of everything, and throwing calves that weighed three hundred pounds or more took its toll on him. He was a tired man at quitting time every day and was usually asleep by the time his head hit the pillow at night. As Cates had suggested, Eli had also kept his eye on the ropers. It was absolutely amazing what some of the youngsters could do with a lariat, and sometimes at a distance comparable to a stone's throw.

Pilgrim had also been instructed by Bo Walker to wear his six-gun at all times. You never knew when a mad old cow would charge when a roper was dragging her calf off to burn a permanent mark on its hide. Every effort should be made to bluff the old mama cow, but in the event that she insisted on making a fight of it, she must be shot in her tracks. Eli had been named the designated shooter. Though several of the cows got slightly out of hand a few times, Pilgrim never had to shoot one during the duration of the roundup.

THE ROUNDUP lasted for fifteen days, and it was an education that Eli Pilgrim would not forget. He had not only looked after his own job but had paid close attention to everybody else's. When it was over, he felt that he could even oversee a roundup himself if he ever needed to. And he surely expected to need to one of these days. The Lazy P was eventually going to be a big outfit, and he intended to devote his life to seeing it happen.

With the roundup now over, there was one last meeting at the cookshack. Baldy King fed everybody after a fashion, or at least had a hot cup of sugared coffee for them. Men were all talking at once, but Pilgrim did glean one fact from all the information that was floating about: the Oxbow Ranch was running better than six thousand head of cattle. Six thousand head! Pilgrim repeated to himself. He had to chuckle when he realized that only three head of those cows were his own.

All of which reminded him that he must get Hank Fry to make up some branding irons for him. He had made a deal with Oliver Benson: he would touch one of the cows with his own iron the first week of every month, and ten dollars would be deducted from his pay. And Eli would do that religiously, for he knew that every big cattle operation in the world had started with a single cow.

When the crews were paid off, they began to clear out, and Pilgrim and Cates were no exceptions. They threw a few more odds and ends in the wagon and loaded it with baled hay, then headed for the Lazy P in plenty of time to get there by midafternoon. "I don't know about you, Eli," Cates said when they were almost home, "but I'm thirstier'n I've been in years. I think I'll ride in to Cuero and have a drink or two at the Elkhorn Saloon. Ain't seen Bob Strangelove in a coon's age, anyway."

"Sounds like a winner, old buddy," Eli said. "You mind if I go with you?"

"Hell, that's what I was getting at," Cates said. "Wouldn't be no fun drinking by myself."

Pilgrim nodded. "We'll feed and water the stock, then if you'll give me time to shave, I'll be right with you."

They did their chores, then headed for Cuero when the sun was still two hours high. There was a wagon road for most of the way that eventually ran into the Oxbow cutoff, which in turn ran into the main road close to the long wooden bridge and the campground. They reached the bridge at sunset, and Cates pointed to the campground. "Do you still have bad memories of that place and Johnny Hook?" he asked.

Eli shook his head. "Not especially," he said. "It's just a place where he tried to cut my throat and rob me, and it didn't work for him. He not only got himself killed, but he took four other people with him."

They rode on to the livery stable at a trot, for Eli wanted to say hello to his friend Hank Fry. Surprised to find the stable still open during the twilight hour, they rode through the open doorway. The big hostler was standing just outside his office lighting a lantern. He closed the globe and snuffed out the match. "Been a while since I've seen either one of you fellows," he said. "Come on into the office and tell me what's new." Both men dismounted and followed the liveryman up the steps. "I'd already be up at the Elkhorn getting a drink, if I hadn't promised old-man Jenkins that I'd stay open till he got here with his wagon. He wants me to put new rims on all four wheels, and I need the business."

"Wait him out, Hank," Eli said. "You yourself told me once that repeat business is the only way a man can stay in business."

"Well, I ain't changed my mind about that," Fry said. He punched Pilgrim in the belly playfully, then changed the subject. "No reason for me to ask what's been going on with you. Everybody in town knows that you've been on a manhunt, and the word's out around here that the Horn brothers are no longer with us. I reckon you accomplished your mission. Right?"

Pilgrim stood tight-lipped for a moment and did not answer the question. He jerked his thumb toward town. "Cliff and I were just talking about going up to the Elkhorn for a drink, so I guess we'll see you up there later if the old man brings his wagon on by."

Fry nodded. "You'll see me all right. Just as soon as Jenkins shows up, I'll be outta this place."

The men remounted and rode back through the doorway. When they reached the corner of Main Street and Esplanade, they tied their horses to the Elkhorn's hitching rail and stepped inside the building. Bob Strangelove himself was behind the bar. "Come in, strangers," he said. "Haven't seen either one of you in ages. The first drink's on the house, as usual."

"Does that include a quart of Jim Beam?" Cates asked.

Strangelove made a throat-cutting signal with his forefinger. "No," he said.

Pilgrim spoke to the bartender. "I'll have my regular pitcher of beer, Bob, and I guess you'd better give me a bottle, too. Hank Fry will be joining us as soon as he closes up his stable."

The bartender drew a pitcher of beer, then took a bottle off the shelf. "This is good whiskey, Eli, I even drank a glass of it myself. It's straight from Bourbon County, Kentucky, and the label claims it's seven years old. Do you believe that?"

"No," Pilgrim answered.

"Neither do I," Strangelove said, "but it really does go down easy."

Pilgrim paid for the beer and the whiskey, then led the way to a table. He poured himself a glass of beer while Cates opened the whiskey bottle. Neither man spoke till he had tasted his drink. "Slowest crowd I've ever seen in here, Eli," Cates said. "This place is usually at least half-full on any night of the week."

"I was thinking the same thing," Pilgrim said, "but I like it better this way. Not only can you see who's in here, you can see what they're doing."

"Yep," Cates said, refilling his shot glass.

They sat sipping and talking for more than an hour before Hank Fry showed up. "Finally got the old man's wagon and his money," the liveryman said, taking a seat and reaching for the bottle. "That's the main thing I like about doing business with Jenkins, he always insists on paying his bill up front. Don't ever recall him hiring me to do anything without his handing me the money right off."

"Sounds like the ideal customer," Cates said.

Fry sampled the whiskey, then commented: "Best-tasting stuff I've run across lately. A man usually has to hold his nose to get the bar whiskey down."

"This ain't bar whiskey." Cates said. "Bob took this off the back shelf."

"Oh," Fry said. He took another sip, then turned to Pilgrim. "What are you doing out at the Oxbow now, Eli?"

"We just finished the roundup, and Cliff and I have moved back down to my own property. We've got a barn and corral built, and now we've got to put up a liveable cabin."

"Your own property, you say?" Fry asked. "You bought some land of your own?"

Eli nodded, then told the hostler how he had come by the property that he had named the Lazy P. "Mr. Benson treated me more than right," he added. "He made buying the place so easy for me that I couldn't turn it down."

"Of course you couldn't," the hostler said, "and you'll damn sure never be sorry you bought it, either. Now, tell me exactly where it's located."

Pilgrim drew him a mental picture of his holdings and told him which road to take to get there. "It's right between Pie Creek and Willow Branch," he said. "You can't miss it."

Fry nodded. "I already know about where it is, and you can bet your butt that I'll be out there to look it over."

They sipped and talked for another hour, and Pilgrim finally became aware that a young man about his own age had been staring at him from the bar for quite some time. When Eli caught his eye, the young man slid off his stool and took a few steps in the direction of Pilgrim's table. Suddenly he stopped in his tracks and bent forward. "Get on your feet, Pilgrim!" he said loudly. When Eli failed to comply, the man repeated the order. "Get on your feet or take it right where you're sitting! You killed the Hook brothers and all three of the Horns, now let's see how you stack up against somebody like me!"

Even as Eli was rising from his chair, he was drawing his Peacemaker, and the antagonist took a shot between the eyes before he even cleared his holster. He dropped his Colt on his right boot, then fell to the floor sideways. He never moved again.

Bob Strangelove was there immediately. "I saw him sitting there staring at you several minutes ago, Eli," he said. "I had no way in the world of knowing what he was planning, but now it's obvious what was on his mind. I wonder what ever made him think he could take you. Hell, he was slow."

Pilgrim stood staring at the body for a long time. "Don't know," he said finally.

"Well, you've damn sure got all the witnesses you're gonna need. I guarantee you that I'll be the first to testify that you didn't kill him. Hell, that man committed suicide. His name was Guy Hill, and I damn sure don't know of anybody that's gonna miss him."

Pilgrim fished around in his pocket, then laid an eagle on the table. "Give this ten dollars to the undertaker, Bob. I reckon it should be enough to take care of the burial." He looked toward the front door, then motioned to Cates. "Let's go home, Cliff."

They were in bed before midnight and up again at dawn. They had smoked ham and scrambled eggs for breakfast, then began to drive stakes and stretch string to lay out the cabin. "I'm only gonna build three rooms," Eli said. "Unless I come up with a big family one of these days, it's all I'm ever gonna need. We'll make the floor the last thing we build, 'cause I'll probably have to count my money before we start on it. I'd like to use tongue-and-groove pine lumber if I can find it, and afford it."

"Finding it shouldn't be no problem." Cates said. "I'll bet Hess's lumberyard's got plenty of it. Now, how much money you'd have to cough up to get it, I wouldn't even try to guess."

They spent the morning laying out the homesite and leveling it with shovels, then harnessed up the team. They had already spotted the trees they were going to use for the foundation of the cabin: two large oaks more than a mile away. They would fell them with a crosscut saw, then snake them home with the mules. Once they were cut in the desired length, they could easily be pulled into place with the team.

Eli would build the cabin no taller than was necessary, for he had no desire to cut wood simply to heat unused space.

In his mind, he had already settled on an eight-foot ceiling. He would deck the building with oak poles, then nail on a tin roof, just as he had done with the barn. He would build no chimney but would use the same stove that he cooked on for heating. Heating should be no problem, for he would probably keep two of the rooms closed off most of the time, anyway.

They had snaked in the logs and laid the foundation, when they finally decided they had done enough for the day. The sun was two hours high when they turned the mules into their stables and poured shelled corn in their troughs. Eli filled the water trough with a dozen buckets of water, while Cates made a pot of coffee and reheated their beans. The men had just sat down to eat when they had a visitor. "Well, I'll be damned," Cates said as Hank Fry came riding out of the trees.

The liveryman dismounted and tied his horse to a corral post. "Rode straight to you, Eli," he said. "Just that one turn is all I had to worry about."

"Come on in the barn," Pilgrim said. "We were just sitting down to eat, and we've certainly got an extra plate."

"Don't mind if I do," Fry said. "although you might feel more like shooting me than feeding me when you hear what I've got to tell you."

"I doubt that," Eli said. "Grab a plate and a cup and make yourself at home."

All three men were soon sitting on a tarpaulin eating their supper. "How long do I have to wait before I hear what I came to tell me, Hank?" Pilgrim asked finally.

The hostler washed a mouthful of food down with a big swallow of coffee. "Well, I don't like being the one to tell you this, but you killing Guy Hill last night has brought Basil Allgood down on you. Now, I reckon I don't have to tell you that that ain't good news. He's killed a lot of men, Eli, and some people claim his draw is unmatched."

Pilgrim sat quietly digesting what he was hearing.

"Like I said," Fry continued, "I hate being the one to tell you all this, but I'm just doing what Allgood asked me to do.

This is exactly what he said: 'Tell Pilgrim that I said he's getting a little bit too big for his britches, and that I want him out of this county. Tell him if he shows up in Cuero again, that he'd better be ready to go for it all. Tell him he can find me at the Elkhorn almost any hour of the day.' "

Pilgrim remained quiet.

"Why, that son of a bitch!" Cates said loudly. "Who in the hell does he think he is?" He was quiet for a moment, then added, "I've seen both of 'em draw a six-gun, Hank, and Allgood can't hold a candle to Eli Pilgrim." He turned to Pilgrim. "That's the damn truth, too, Eli. What the son of a bitch is trying to do is scare you with his reputation."

Pilgrim said nothing and continued to stare at the bean pot.

Fry cleared his throat. "Anything you want me to tell Allgood, Eli?"

Eli nodded. "Tell him I'll be in the Elkhorn about noon tomorrow," he said.

THE TWO men discussed Allgood's threat very little during
the night, for it seemed that each of them had already resolved
for himself what was going to take place the next day. Both
men slept well considering the circumstances, and Pilgrim had
a fire going at dawn. He awoke Cates by toeing his leg with
his boot. "It's your turn to cook breakfast, Cliff," he said.
"There's still half a dozen eggs in that sack over there by the
water bucket; you can scramble them up with some of that
smoked ham. I'll feed the livestock while you're doing that.
Want me to fill the coffeepot with water for you?"

"Nope. You've already done the hard part; I don't even
know how you managed to get a fire started without some
pine kindling."

"Dead grass and hay," Eli said, "lots of dead grass and
hay." He headed for the stables to feed the animals.

Shortly after sunup, they sat by the fire eating ham and
eggs and drinking strong coffee. "There's something I want
to discuss with you when we finish eating," Cates said, "and
a coupla things I want to show you."

Eli nodded. "Let's discuss it now," he said, "then you
can show me later."

Cates took a swallow from his coffee cup, then wiped his
lips on his sleeve. "Well, it has to do with Basil Allgood's
draw. Now, he don't stand still while he's going for his gun.

I've been told that he always jumps to the side, so his op-
ponent has to shoot at a moving target. I remembered hearing
that the day I saw him shoot Ed Bates up at Hawks's livery
stable. He waved his left arm in the air, then jumped to his
right just as he went for his gun. The only reason I could
figure for him waving that arm was to try to throw Bates's
eye off. I believe bygod it worked, too, Eli, 'cause it looked
to me like Bates was following that left arm with his eyes."

"Are you saying you think he'll do the same thing
with me?"

"I don't know what he'll do," Cates said. "I'm just telling
you what he did with Bates. I've had several men tell me that
he always jumps, and that he always jumps to his right."

"I'll be remembering all of that," Pilgrim said. "Anything
to try to gain a split second."

Neither man spoke again until they had finished eating,
then Cates pointed through the barn door. "Let's get outside,"
he said. "I want to go over something with you."

A few moments later, the men stood facing each other at
a distance of thirty feet. "Unload your gun and put the shells
in your pocket," Cates said, "then try to outdraw me, and be
expecting me to jump."

Cates unloaded his own gun, then the men went into the
drill. A dozen times they drew their weapons, and each time
Pilgrim won the draw. Every time Cates went for his gun and
jumped to his right, Eli's gun barrel was there waiting for
him. "You've got it!" Cates said loudly, "you've got it! Let's
just hope Allgood tries that trick on you, because bygod
you're gonna nail him to the cross if he does." Cates reloaded
his Peacemaker and shoved it in his holster. "I don't want
you to get overconfident, old buddy," he added, "but Basil
Allgood's gonna come up a tad slow when he makes his play
against you."

They mounted their horses and headed for Cuero at nine
o'clock. Sticking to a walking gait, it was straight up noon
when they reached the Elkhorn Saloon. Seeing that there were

no vacant spaces at any of the saloon's three hitching rails, they tied their animals in front of a hardware store across the street. "Looks like the word's been spread far and wide," Cates said, once they had crossed the street and stepped up on the boardwalk. "Allgood likes a big audience, and I believe he's got it."

Pilgrim said nothing, just elbowed his way through the bat-wing doors and stepped inside the building. Obviously having been forewarned that Pilgrim was on the premises, Basil Allgood stood alone in the aisle beside the bar. A few men scrambled out of the way noisily after seeing Eli come to a halt with his body bent forward and his legs spread slightly apart.

"I see you've come to test me, Pilgrim," Allgood said. "I figured you'd be halfway to Fort Worth by now." He spat a stream of tobacco juice into a spittoon, then added with a smirk, "You ready to play?"

"You've got me a little bit scared, but you ain't got me bluffed, Allgood," Eli said quickly. "I got your message about getting outta the county, and I'm not quite ready to do that yet. I intend to live in DeWitt County for the rest of my life, and I'll ride into this town anytime I take a notion. Now, if you don't like the sound of that, make your play."

They drew at exactly the same time, and Pilgrim had the quicker hand. Basil Allgood indeed jumped to his right as he drew his gun, only to take a slug in the mouth the moment his feet touched the floor. He had managed to get his weapon out of its holster, but dropped it between his feet as the heavy caliber ripped through the back of his head. A second shot from Pilgrim's Peacemaker took him in the throat and knocked him into a nearby post. He slid down the post slowly, then fell on his side. He never moved again.

The room was eerily quiet for a few moments, then men began to talk in low tones. Still holding his Colt in his hand, Eli laid a double eagle on the bar in front of bartender Bob Strangelove. "Give this to the undertaker, Bob. If anybody thinks he oughtta have a grander burial, let them pay for it."

Strangelove handed the coin back to Pilgrim. "Put it in your pocket, fellow, the deceased has got plenty of money to pay for his own funeral." He waved his arm through the air to emphasize the size of the crowd. "You ain't gonna need no more witnesses, either. Allgood bought his ticket, and you punched it for him."

Pilgrim nodded, then turned and spoke to Cates: "Let's go home, Cliff, we've got a cabin to build."